HIGHWAY FATALITY

The man in the driver's seat of the Cadillac didn't turn his head as I approached him. His chin was propped on the steering wheel, and he was gazing out across the endless blue sea. I opened the door and looked into his face. It was paper white. The dark brown eyes were sightless. The body was unclothed except for a blood-stained bandage tied around his waist. Examining it more closely, I saw that it was a woman's slip. It was embroidered over the left breast with the name, "Fern," in slanting script.

I wondered who Fern was. . . .

THE NAME IS ARCHER

ROSS MACDONALD

BANTAM BOOKS
Toronto • New York • London • Sydney

THE NAME IS ARCHER
A Bantam Book / February 1955
2nd printing .... March 1955   3rd printing ...... May 1966
4th printing ... June 1966
New Bantam edition / July 1971
2nd printing ...... July 1971   7th printing . December 1974
3rd printing .... October 1971   8th printing ... October 1975
4th printing ...... June 1972   9th printing ..... June 1977
5th printing .. December 1972   10th printing ... October 1979
6th printing .... August 1974   11th printing . November 1983

ISBN 0-553-23650-4

Published simultaneously in the United States and Canada

Bantam Books are published by Bantam Books, Inc. Its trade-
mark, consisting of the words "Bantam Books" and the por-
trayal of a rooster, is Registered in U.S. Patent and Trademark
Office and in other countries. Marca Registrada. Bantam
Books, Inc., 666 Fifth Avenue, New York, New York 10103.

PRINTED IN THE UNITED STATES OF AMERICA

H   20 19 18 17 16 15 14 13 12 11

CONTENTS

Find the Woman

I SAT in my brand-new office with the odor of paint in my nostrils and waited for something to happen. I had been back on the Boulevard for one day. This was the beginning of the second day. Below the window, flashing in the morning sun, the traffic raced and roared with a noise like battle. It made me nervous. It made me want to move. I was all dressed up in civilian clothes with no place to go and nobody to go with.

Till Millicent Dreen came in.

I had seen her before, on the Strip with various escorts, and knew who she was: publicity director for Tele-Pictures. Mrs. Dreen was over forty and looked it, but there was electricity in her, plugged in to a secret source that time could never wear out. Look how high and tight I carry my body, her movements said. My hair is hennaed but comely, said her coiffure, inviting not to conviction but to suspension of disbelief. Her eyes were green and inconstant like the sea. They said what the hell.

She sat down by my desk and told me that her daughter had disappeared the day before, which was September the seventh.

"I was in Hollywood all day. We keep an apartment here, and there was some work I had to get out fast. Una isn't working, so I left her at the beach house by herself."

"Where is it?"

"A few miles above Santa Barbara."

"That's a long way to commute."

"It's worth it to me. When I can maneuver a week end away from this town, I like to get *really* away."

"Maybe your daughter feels the same, only more so. When did she leave?"

"Sometime yesterday. When I drove home to the beach house last night she was gone."

"Did you call the police?"

"Hardly. She's twenty-two and knows what she's doing. I hope. Anyway, apron strings don't become me." She smiled like a cat and moved her scarlet-taloned fingers in her narrow lap. "It was very late and I was—tired. I went to bed. But when I woke up this morning it occurred to me that she might have

1

drowned. I objected to it because she wasn't a strong swimmer, but she went in for solitary swimming. I think of the most dreadful things when I wake up in the morning."

"*Went* in for solitary swimming, Mrs. Dreen?"

"'Went' slipped out, didn't it? I told you I think of dreadful things when I wake up in the morning."

"If she drowned you should be talking to the police. They can arrange for dragging and such things. All I can give you is my sympathy."

As if to estimate the value of that commodity, her eyes flickered from my shoulders to my waist and up again to my face. "Frankly, I don't know about the police. I do know about you, Mr. Archer. You just got out of the army, didn't you?"

"Last week." I failed to add that she was my first postwar client.

"And you don't belong to anybody, I've heard. You've never been bought. Is that right?"

"Not outright. You can take an option on a piece of me, though. A hundred dollars would do for a starter."

She nodded briskly. From a bright black bag she gave me five twenties. "Naturally, I'm conscious of publicity angles. My daughter retired a year ago when she married—"

"Twenty-one is a good age to retire."

"From pictures, maybe you're right. But she could want to go back if her marriage breaks up. And I have to look out for myself. It isn't true that there's no such thing as bad publicity. *I* don't know why Una went away."

"Is your daughter Una Sand?"

"Of course. I assumed you knew." My ignorance of the details of her life seemed to cause her pain. She didn't have to tell me that she had a feeling for publicity angles.

Though Una Sand meant less to me than Hecuba, I remembered the name and with it a glazed blonde who had had a year or two in the sun, but who'd made a better pin-up than an actress.

"Wasn't her marriage happy? I mean, isn't it?"

"You see how easy it is to slip into the past tense?" Mrs. Dreen smiled another fierce and purring smile, and her fingers fluttered in glee before her immobile body. "I suppose her marriage is happy enough. Her Ensign's quite a personable young man—handsome in a masculine way, and passionate she tells me, and naive enough."

"Naive enough for what?"

"To marry Una. Jack Rossiter was quite a catch in this woman's town. He was runner-up at Forest Hills the last year he played tennis. And now of course he's a flier. Una did right well by herself, even if it doesn't last."

What do you expect of a war marriage? she seemed to be saying. Permanence? Fidelity? The works?

"As a matter of fact," she went on, "it was thinking about Jack, more than anything else, that brought me here to you. He's due back this week, and naturally" —like many unnatural people, she overused that adverb— "he'll expect her to be waiting for him. It'll be rather embarrassing for me if he comes home and I can't tell him where she's gone, or why, or with whom. You'd really think she'd leave a note."

"I can't keep up with you," I said. "A minute ago Una was in the clutches of the cruel crawling foam. Now she's taken off with a romantic stranger."

"I consider possibilities, is all. When I was Una's age, married to Dreen, I had quite a time settling down. I still do."

Our gazes, mine as impassive as hers I hoped, met, struck no spark, and disengaged. The female spider who eats her mate held no attraction for me.

"I'm getting to know you pretty well," I said with the necessary smile, "but not the missing girl. Who's she been knocking around with?"

"I don't think we need to go into that. She doesn't confide in me, in any case."

"Whatever you say. Shall we look at the scene of the crime?"

"There isn't any *crime*."

"The scene of the accident, then, or the departure. Maybe the beach house will give me something to go on."

She glanced at the wafer-thin watch on her brown wrist. Its diamonds glittered coldly. "Do I have to drive all the way back?"

"If you can spare the time, it might help. We'll take my car."

She rose decisively but gracefully, as though she had practiced the movement in front of a mirror. An expert bitch, I thought as I followed her high slim shoulders and tight-sheathed hips down the stairs to the bright street. I felt a little sorry for the army of men who had warmed themselves, or been burned, at that secret electricity. And I wondered if her daughter Una was like her.

When I did get to see Una, the current had been cut off; I learned about it only by the marks it left. It left marks.

We drove down Sunset to the sea and north on 101 Alternate. All the way to Santa Barbara, she read a typescript whose manila cover was marked: "Temporary—This script is not final and is given to you for advance information only." It occurred to me that the warning might apply to Mrs. Dreen's own story.

As we left the Santa Barbara city limits, she tossed the

script over her shoulder into the back seat. "It *really* smells. It's going to be a smash."

A few miles north of the city, a dirt road branched off to the left beside a filling station. It wound for a mile or more through broken country to her private beach. The beach house was set well back from the sea at the convergence of brown bluffs which huddled over it like scarred shoulders. To reach it we had to drive along the beach for a quarter of a mile, detouring to the very edge of the sea around the southern bluff.

The blue-white dazzle of sun, sand, and surf was like an arc-furnace. But I felt some breeze from the water when we got out of the car. A few languid clouds moved inland over our heads. A little high plane was gamboling among them like a terrier in a henyard.

"You have privacy," I said to Mrs. Dreen.

She stretched, and touched her varnished hair with her fingers. "One tires of the goldfish role. When I lie out there in the afternoons I—forget I have a name." She pointed to the middle of the cove beyond the breakers, where a white raft moved gently in the swells. "I simply take off my clothes and revert to protoplasm. *All* my clothes."

I looked up at the plane whose pilot was doodling in the sky. It dropped, turning like an early falling leaf, swooped like a hawk, climbed like an aspiration.

She said with a laugh: "If they come too low I cover my face, of course."

We had been moving away from the house towards the water. Nothing could have looked more innocent than the quiet cove held in the curve of the white beach like a benign blue eye in a tranquil brow. Then its colors shifted as a cloud passed over the sun. Cruel green and violent purple ran in the blue. I felt the old primitive terror and fascination. Mrs. Dreen shared the feeling and put it into words:

"It's got queer moods. I hate it sometimes as much as I love it." For an instant she looked old and uncertain. "I hope she isn't in there."

The tide had turned and was coming in, all the way from Hawaii and beyond, all the way from the shattered islands where bodies lay unburied in the burnt-out caves. The waves came up towards us, fumbling and gnawing at the beach like an immense soft mouth.

"Are there bad currents here, or anything like that?"

"No. It's deep, though. It must be twenty feet under the raft. I could never bottom it."

"I'd like to look at her room," I said. "It might tell us where she went, and even with whom. You'd know what clothes were missing?"

She laughed a little apologetically as she opened the door. "I used to dress my daughter, naturally. Not any more. Besides, more than half of her things must be in the Hollywood apartment. I'll try to help you, though."

It was good to step out of the vibrating brightness of the beach into shadowy stillness behind Venetian blinds. "I noticed that you unlocked the door," I said. "It's a big house with a lot of furniture in it. No servants?"

"I occasionally have to knuckle under to producers. But I won't to my employees. They'll be easier to get along with soon, now that the plane plants are shutting down."

We went to Una's room, which was light and airy in both atmosphere and furnishings. But it showed the lack of servants. Stockings, shoes, underwear, dresses, bathing suits, lipstick-smeared tissue littered the chairs and the floor. The bed was unmade. The framed photograph on the night table was obscured by two empty glasses which smelt of highball, and flanked by overflowing ash trays.

I moved the glasses and looked at the young man with the wings on his chest. Naive, handsome, passionate were words which suited the strong blunt nose, the full lips and square jaw, the wide proud eyes. For Mrs. Dreen he would have made a single healthy meal, and I wondered again if her daughter was a carnivore. At least the photograph of Jack Rossiter was the only sign of a man in her room. The two glasses could easily have been from separate nights. Or separate weeks, to judge by the condition of the room. Not that it wasn't an attractive room. It was like a pretty girl in disarray. But disarray.

We examined the room, the closets, the bathroom, and found nothing of importance, either positive or negative. When we had waded through the brilliant and muddled wardrobe which Una had shed, I turned to Mrs. Dreen.

"I guess I'll have to go back to Hollywood. It would help me if you'd come along. It would help me more if you'd tell me who your daughter knew. Or rather who she liked—I suppose she knew everybody. Remember you suggested yourself that there's a man in this."

"I take it you haven't found anything?"

"One thing I'm pretty sure of. She didn't intentionally go away for long. Her toilet articles and pills are still in her bathroom. She's got quite a collection of pills."

"Yes, Una's always been a hypochondriac. Also she left Jack's picture. She only had the one, because she liked it best."

"That isn't so conclusive," I said. "I don't suppose you'd know whether there's a bathing suit missing?"

"I really couldn't say, she had so many. She was at her best in them."

"Still *was?*"

"I guess so, as a working hypothesis. Unless you can find me evidence to the contrary."

"You didn't like your daughter much, did you?"

"No. I didn't like her father. And she was prettier than I."

"But not so intelligent?"

"Not as bitchy, you mean? She was bitchy enough. But I'm still worried about Jack. He loved her. Even if I didn't."

The telephone in the hall took the cue and began to ring. "This is Millicent Dreen," she said into it. "Yes, you may read it to me." A pause. " 'Kill the fatted calf, ice the champagne, turn down the sheets and break out the black silk nightie. Am coming home tomorrow.' Is that right?"

Then she said, "Hold it a minute. I wish to send an answer. To Ensign Jack Rossiter, USS *Guam*, CVE 173, Naval Air Station, Alameda—is that Ensign Rossiter's correct address? The text is: 'Dear Jack join me at the Hollywood apartment there is no one at the beach house. Millicent.' Repeat it, please. . . . Right. Thank you."

She turned from the phone and collapsed in the nearest chair, not forgetting to arrange her legs symmetrically.

"So Jack is coming home tomorrow?" I said. "All I had before was no evidence. Now I have no evidence and until tomorrow."

She leaned forward to look at me. "I've been wondering how far can I trust you."

"Not so far. But I'm not a blackmailer. I'm not a mindreader, either, and it's sort of hard to play tennis with the invisible man."

"The invisible man has nothing to do with this. I called him when Una didn't come home. Just before I came to your office."

"All right," I said. "You're the one that wants to find Una. You'll get around to telling me. In the meantime, who else did you call?"

"Hilda Karp, Una's best friend—her *only* female friend."

"Where can I get hold of her?"

"She married Gray Karp, the agent. They live in Beverly Hills."

Their house, set high on a plateau of rolling lawn, was huge and fashionably grotesque: Spanish Mission with a dash of Paranoia. The room where I waited for Mrs. Karp was as big as a small barn and full of blue furniture. The bar had a brass rail.

Hilda Karp was a Dresden blonde with an athletic body and brains. By appearing in it, she made the room seem more real. "Mr. Archer, I believe?" She had my card in her hand, the one with "Private Investigator" on it.

"Una Sand disappeared yesterday. Her mother said you were her best friend."

"Millicent—Mrs. Dreen—called me early this morning. But, as I said then, I haven't seen Una for several days."

"Why would she go away?"

Hilda Karp sat down on the arm of a chair, and looked thoughtful. "I can't understand why her mother should be worried. She can take care of herself, and she's gone away before. I don't know why this time. I know her well enough to know that she's unpredictable."

"Why did she go away before?"

"Why do girls leave home, Mr. Archer?"

"She picked a queer time to leave home. Her husband's coming home tomorrow."

"That's right, she told me he sent her a cable from Pearl. He's a nice boy."

"Did Una think so?"

She looked at me frigidly as only a pale blonde can look, and said nothing.

"Look," I said. "I'm trying to do a job for Mrs. Dreen. My job is laying skeletons to rest, not teaching them the choreography of the *Danse Macabre.*"

"Nicely put," she said. "Actually there's no skeleton. Una has played around, in a perfectly casual way I mean, with two or three men in the last year."

"Simultaneously, or one at a time?"

"One at a time. She's monandrous to that extent. The latest is Terry Neville."

"I thought he was married."

"In an interlocutory way only. For God's sake don't bring my name into it. My husband's in business in this town."

"He seems to be prosperous," I said, looking more at her than at the house. "Thank you very much, Mrs. Karp. Your name will never pass my lips."

"Hideous, isn't it? The name, I mean. But I couldn't help falling in love with the guy. I hope you find her. Jack will be terribly disappointed if you don't."

I had begun to turn towards the door, but turned back. "It couldn't be anything like this, could it? She heard he was coming home, she felt unworthy of him, unable to face him, so she decided to lam out?"

"Millicent said she didn't leave a letter. Women don't go

in for all such drama and pathos without leaving a letter. Or at least a marked copy of Tolstoi's *Resurrection*."

"I'll take your word for it." Her blue eyes were very bright in the great dim room. "How about this? She didn't like Jack at all. She went away for the sole purpose of letting him know that. A little sadism, maybe?"

"But she did like Jack. It's just that he was away for over a year. Whenever the subject came up in a mixed gathering, she always insisted that he was a wonderful lover."

"Like that, eh? Did Mrs. Dreen say you were Una's best friend?"

Her eyes were brighter and her thin, pretty mouth twisted in amusement. "Certainly. You should have heard her talk about me."

"Maybe I will. Thanks. Good-bye."

A telephone call to a screen writer I knew, the suit for which I had paid a hundred and fifty dollars of separation money in a moment of euphoria, and a false air of assurance got me past the studio guards and as far as the door of Terry Neville's dressing room. He had a bungalow to himself, which meant that he was as important as the publicity claimed. I didn't know what I was going to say to him, but I knocked on the door and, when someone said, "Who is it?" showed him.

Only the blind had not seen Terry Neville. He was over six feet, colorful, shapely, and fragrant like a distant garden of flowers. For a minute he went on reading and smoking in his brocaded armchair, carefully refraining from raising his eyes to look at me. He even turned a page of his book.

"Who are you?" he said finally. "I don't know you."

"Una Sand—"

"I don't know her, either." Grammatical solecisms had been weeded out of his speech, but nothing had been put in their place. His voice was impersonal and lifeless.

"Millicent Dreen's daughter," I said, humoring him. "Una Rossiter."

"Naturally I know Millicent Dreen. But you haven't said anything. Good day."

"Una disappeared yesterday. I thought you might be willing to help me find out why."

"You still haven't said anything." He got up and took a step towards me, very tall and wide. "What I said was *good day*."

But not tall and wide enough. I've always had an idea, probably incorrect, that I could handle any man who wears a scarlet silk bathrobe. He saw that idea on my face and changed his tune: "If you don't get out of here, my man, I'll call a guard."

"In the meantime I'd straighten out that marcel of yours. I might even be able to make a little trouble for you." I said that on the assumption that any man with his face and sexual opportunities would be on the brink of trouble most of the time.

It worked. "What do you mean by saying that?" he said. A sudden pallor made his carefully plucked black eyebrows stand out starkly. "You could get into a very great deal of hot water by standing there talking like that."

"What happened to Una?"

"I don't know. Get out of here."

"You're a liar."

Like one of the clean-cut young men in one of his own movies, he threw a punch at me. I let it go over my shoulder and while he was off balance placed the heel of my hand against his very flat solar plexus and pushed him down into his chair. Then I shut the door and walked fast to the front gate. I'd just as soon have gone on playing tennis with the invisible man.

"No luck, I take it?" Mrs. Dreen said when she opened the door of her apartment to me.

"I've got nothing to go on. If you really want to find your daughter you'd better go to Missing Persons. They've got the organization and the connections."

"I suppose Jack will be going to them. He's home already."

"I thought he was coming tomorrow."

"That telegram was sent yesterday. It was delayed somehow. His ship got in yesterday afternoon."

"Where is he now?"

"At the beach house by now, I guess. He flew down from Alameda in a Navy plane and called me from Santa Barbara."

"What did you tell him?"

"What could I tell him? That Una was gone. He's frantic. He thinks she may have drowned." It was late afternoon, and in spite of the whiskey which she was absorbing steadily, like an alcohol lamp, Mrs. Dreen's fires were burning low. Her hands and eyes were limp, and her voice was weary.

"Well," I said, "I might as well go back to Santa Barbara. I talked to Hilda Karp but she couldn't help me. Are you coming along?"

"Not again. I have to go to the studio tomorrow. Anyway, I don't want to see Jack just now. I'll stay here."

The sun was low over the sea, gold-leafing the water and bloodying the sky, when I got through Santa Barbara and back onto the coast highway. Not thinking it would do any good but by way of doing something or other to earn my keep,

I stopped at the filling station where the road turned off to Mrs. Dreen's beach house.

"Fill her up," I said to the woman attendant. I needed gas anyway.

"I've got some friends who live around here," I said when she held out her hand for her money. "Do you know where Mrs. Dreen lives?"

She looked at me from behind disapproving spectacles. "You should know. You were down there with her today, weren't you?"

I covered my confusion by handing her a five and telling her: "Keep the change."

"No, thank you."

"Don't misunderstand me. All I want you to do is tell me who was there yesterday. You see all. Tell a little."

"Who are you?"

I showed her my card.

"Oh." Her lips moved unconsciously, computing the size of the tip. "There was a guy in a green convert, I think it was a Chrysler. He went down around noon and drove out again around four, I guess it was, like a bat out of hell."

"That's what I wanted to hear. You're wonderful. What did he look like?"

"Sort of dark and pretty good-looking. It's kind of hard to describe. Like the guy that took the part of the pilot in that picture last week—*you* know—only not so good-looking."

"Terry Neville."

"That's right, only not so good-looking. I've seen him go down there plenty of times."

"I don't know who that would be," I said, "but thanks anyway. There wasn't anybody with him, was there?"

"Not that I could see."

I went down the road to the beach house like a bat into hell. The sun, huge and angry red, was horizontal now, half-eclipsed by the sea and almost perceptibly sinking. It spread a red glow over the shore like a soft and creeping fire. After a long time, I thought, the cliffs would crumble, the sea would dry up, the whole earth would burn out. There'd be nothing left but bone-white cratered ashes like the moon.

When I rounded the bluff and came within sight of the beach I saw a man coming out of the sea. In the creeping fire which the sun shed he, too, seemed to be burning. The diving mask over his face made him look strange and inhuman. He walked out of the water as if he had never set foot on land before.

I walked towards him. "Mr. Rossiter?"

"Yes." He raised the glass mask from his face and with it

the illusion of strangeness lifted. He was just a handsome young man, well-set-up, tanned, and worried-looking.

"My name is Archer."

He held out his hand, which was wet, after wiping it on his bathing trunks, which were also wet. "Oh, yes, Mr. Archer. My mother-in-law mentioned you over the phone."

"Are you enjoying your swim?"

"I am looking for the body of my wife." It sounded as if he meant it. I looked at him more closely. He was big and husky, but he was just a kid, twenty-two or -three at most. Out of school into the air, I thought. Probably met Una Sand at a party, fell hard for all that glamour, married her the week before he shipped out, and had dreamed bright dreams ever since. I remembered the brash telegram he had sent, as if life was like the people in slick magazine advertisements.

"What makes you think she drowned?"

"She wouldn't go away like this. She knew I was coming home this week. I cabled her from Pearl."

"Maybe she never got the cable."

After a pause he said: "Excuse me." He turned towards the waves which were breaking almost at his feet. The sun had disappeared, and the sea was turning gray and cold-looking, an anti-human element.

"Wait a minute. If she's in there, which I doubt, you should call the police. This is no way to look for her."

"If I don't find her before dark, I'll call them then," he said. "But if she's here, I want to find her myself." I could never have guessed his reason for that, but when I found it out it made sense. So far as anything in the situation made sense.

He walked a few steps into the surf, which was heavier now that the tide was coming in, plunged forward, and swam slowly towards the raft with his masked face under the water. His arms and legs beat the rhythm of the crawl as if his muscles took pleasure in it, but his face was downcast, searching the darkening sea floor. He swam in widening circles about the raft, raising his head about twice a minute for air.

He had completed several circles and I was beginning to feel that he wasn't really looking for anything, but expressing his sorrow, dancing a futile ritualistic water dance, when suddenly he took air and dived. For what seemed a long time but was probably about twenty seconds, the surface of the sea was empty except for the white raft. Then the masked head broke water, and Rossiter began to swim towards shore. He swam a laborious side stroke, with both arms submerged. It was twilight now, and I couldn't see him very well, but I could see that he was swimming very slowly. When he came nearer I saw a swirl of yellow hair.

He stood up, tore off his mask, and threw it away into the sea. He looked at me angrily, one arm holding the body of his wife against him. The white body half-floating in the shifting water was nude, a strange bright glistening catch from the sea floor.

"Go away," he said in a choked voice.

I went to get a blanket out of the car, and brought it to him where he laid her out on the beach. He huddled over her as if to protect her body from my gaze. He covered her and stroked her wet hair back from her face. Her face was not pretty. He covered that, too.

I said: "You'll have to call the police now."

After a time he answered: "I guess you're right. Will you help me carry her into the house?"

I helped him. Then I called the police in Santa Barbara, and told them that a woman had been drowned and where to find her. I left Jack Rossiter shivering in his wet trunks beside her blanketed body, and drove back to Hollywood for the second time.

Millicent Dreen was in her apartment in the Park-Wilshire. In the afternoon there had been a nearly full decanter of Scotch on her buffet. At ten o'clock it was on the coffee table beside her chair, and nearly empty. Her face and body had sagged. I wondered if every day she aged so many years, and every morning recreated herself through the power of her will.

She said: "I thought you were going back to Santa Barbara. I was just going to go to bed."

"I did go. Didn't Jack phone you?"

"No." She looked at me, and her green eyes were suddenly very much alive, almost fluorescent. "You found her," she said.

"Jack found her in the sea. She was drowned."

"I was afraid of that." But there was something like relief in her voice. As if worse things might have happened. As if at least she had lost no weapons and gained no foes in the daily battle to hold her position in the world's most competitive city.

"You hired me to find her," I said. "She's found, though I had nothing to do with finding her—and that's that. Unless you want me to find out who drowned her."

"What do you mean?"

"What I said. Perhaps it wasn't an accident. Or perhaps somebody stood by and watched her drown."

I had given her plenty of reason to be angry with me before, but for the first time that day she was angry. "I gave you a hundred dollars for doing nothing. Isn't that enough for you? Are you trying to drum up extra business?"

"I did one thing. I found out that Una wasn't by herself yesterday."

"Who was with her?" She stood up and walked quickly back and forth across the rug. As she walked her body was remolding itself into the forms of youth and vigor. She recreated herself before my eyes.

"The invisible man," I said. "My tennis partner."

Still she wouldn't speak the name. She was like the priestess of a cult whose tongue was forbidden to pronounce a secret word. But she said quickly and harshly: "If my daughter was killed I want to know who did it. I don't care who it was. But if you're giving me a line and if you make trouble for me and nothing comes of it, I'll have you kicked out of Southern California. I could do that."

Her eyes flashed, her breath came fast, and her sharp breast rose and fell with many of the appearances of genuine feeling. I liked her very much at that moment. So I went away, and instead of making trouble for her I made trouble for myself.

I found a booth in a drugstore on Wilshire and confirmed what I knew, that Terry Neville would have an unlisted number. I called a girl I knew who fed gossip to a movie columnist, and found out that Neville lived in Beverly Hills but spent most of his evenings around town. At this time of night he was usually at Ronald's or Chasen's, a little later at Ciro's. I went to Ronald's because it was nearer, and Terry Neville was there.

He was sitting in a booth for two in the long, low, smoke-filled room, eating smoked salmon and drinking stout. Across from him there was a sharp-faced terrier-like man who looked like his business manager and was drinking milk. Some Hollywood actors spend a lot of time with their managers, because they have a common interest.

I avoided the headwaiter and stepped up to Neville's table. He saw me and stood up, saying: "I warned you this afternoon. If you don't get out of here I'll call the police."

I said quietly: "I sort of am the police. Una is dead." He didn't answer and I went on: "This isn't a good place to talk. If you'll step outside for a minute I'd like to mention a couple of facts to you."

"You say you're a policeman," the sharp-faced man snapped, but quietly. "Where's your identification? Don't pay any attention to him, Terry."

Terry didn't say anything. I said: "I'm a private detective. I'm investigating the death of Una Rossiter. Shall we step outside, gentlemen?"

"We'll go out to the car," Terry Neville said tonelessly. "Come on, Ed," he added to the terrier-like man.

The car was not a green Chrysler convertible, but a black Packard limousine equipped with a uniformed chauffeur. When we entered the parking lot he got out of the car and opened the door. He was big and battered-looking.

I said: "I don't think I'll get in. I listen better standing up. I always stand up at concerts and confessions."

"You're not going to listen to anything," Ed said.

The parking lot was deserted and far back from the street, and I forgot to keep my eye on the chauffeur. He rabbit-punched me and a gush of pain surged into my head. He rabbit-punched me again and my eyes rattled in their sockets and my body became invertebrate. Two men moving in a maze of lights took hold of my upper arms and lifted me into the car. Unconsciousness was a big black limousine with a swiftly purring motor and the blinds down.

Though it leaves the neck sore for days, the effect of a rabbit punch on the centers of consciousness is sudden and brief. In two or three minutes I came out of it, to the sound of Ed's voice saying:

"We don't like hurting people and we aren't going to hurt you. But you've got to learn to understand, whatever your name is—"

"Sacher-Masoch," I said.

"A bright boy," said Ed. "But a bright boy can be too bright for his own good. You've got to learn to understand that you can't go around annoying people, especially very important people like Mr. Neville here."

Terry Neville was sitting in the far corner of the back seat, looking worried. Ed was between us. The car was in motion, and I could see lights moving beyond the chauffeur's shoulders hunched over the wheel. The blinds were down over the back windows.

"Mr. Neville should keep out of my cases," I said. "At the moment you'd better let me out of this car or I'll have you arrested for kidnaping."

Ed laughed, but not cheerfully. "You don't seem to realize what's happening to you. You're on your way to the police station, where Mr. Neville and I are going to charge you with attempted blackmail."

"Mr. Neville is a very brave little man," I said. "Inasmuch as he was seen leaving Una Sand's house shortly after she was killed. He was seen leaving in a great hurry and a green convertible."

"My God, Ed," Terry Neville said, "you're getting me in a frightful mess. You don't know what a frightful mess you're getting me in." His voice was high, with a ragged edge of hysteria.

"For God's sake, you're not afraid of this bum, are you?" Ed said in a terrier yap.

"You get out of here, Ed. This is a terrible thing, and you don't know how to handle it. I've got to talk to this man. Get out of this car."

He leaned forward to take the speaking tube, but Ed put a hand on his shoulder. "Play it your way, then, Terry. I still think I had the right play, but you spoiled it."

"Where are we going?" I said. I suspected that we were headed for Beverely Hills, where the police know who pays them their wages.

Neville said into the speaking tube: "Turn down a side street and park. Then take a walk around the block."

"That's better," I said when we had parked. Terry Neville looked frightened. Ed looked sulky and worried. For no good reason, I felt complacent.

"Spill it," I said to Terry Neville. "Did you kill the girl? Or did she accidentally drown—and you ran away so you wouldn't get mixed up in it? Or have you thought of a better one than that?"

"I'll tell you the truth," he said. "I didn't kill her. I didn't even know she was dead. But I was there yesterday afternoon. We were sunning ourselves on the raft, when a plane came over flying very low. I went away, because I didn't want to be seen there with her—"

"You mean you weren't exactly sunning yourselves?"

"Yes. That's right. This plane came over high at first, then he circled back and came down very low. I thought maybe he recognized me, and might be trying to take pictures or something."

"What kind of a plane was it?"

"I don't know. A military plane, I guess. A fighter plane. It was a single-seater painted blue. I don't know military planes."

"What did Una Sand do when you went away?"

"I don't know. I swam to shore, put on some clothes, and drove away. She stayed on the raft, I guess. But she was certainly all right when I left her. It would be a terrible thing for me if I was dragged into this thing, Mr.—"

"Archer."

"Mr. Archer. I'm terribly sorry if we hurt you. If I could make it right with you—" He pulled out a wallet.

His steady pallid whine bored me. Even his sheaf of bills bored me. The situation bored me.

I said: "I have no interest in messing up your brilliant career, Mr. Neville. I'd like to mess up your brilliant pan sometime, but that can wait. Until I have some reason to believe that you haven't told me the truth, I'll keep what you said under my hat. In the meantime, I want to hear what the coroner has to say."

They took me back to Ronald's, where my car was, and left me with many protestations of good fellowship. I said good night to them, rubbing the back of my neck with an exaggerated gesture. Certain other gestures occurred to me.

When I got back to Santa Barbara the coroner was working over Una. He said that there were no marks of violence on her body, and very little water in her lungs and stomach, but this condition was characteristic of about one drowning in ten.

I hadn't known that before, so I asked him to put it into sixty-four-dollar words. He was glad to.

"Sudden inhalation of water may result in a severe reflex spasm of the larynx, followed swiftly by asphyxia. Such a laryngeal spasm is more likely to occur if the victim's face is upward, allowing water to rush into the nostrils, and would be likely to be facilitated by emotional or nervous shock. It may have happened like that or it may not."

"Hell," I said, "she may not even be dead."

He gave me a sour look. "Thirty-six hours ago she wasn't."

I figured it out as I got in my car. Una couldn't have drowned much later than four o'clock in the afternoon on September the seventh.

It was three in the morning when I checked in at the Barbara Hotel. I got up at seven, had breakfast in a restaurant, and went to the beach house to talk to Jack Rossiter. It was only about eight o'clock when I got there, but Rossiter was sitting on the beach in a canvas chair watching the sea.

"You again?" he said when he saw me.

"I'd think you'd have had enough of the sea for a while. How long were you out?"

"A year." He seemed unwilling to talk.

"I hate bothering people," I said, "but my business is always making a nuisance out of me."

"Evidently. What exactly is your business?"

"I'm currently working for your mother-in-law. I'm still trying to find out what happened to her daughter."

"Are you trying to needle me?" He put his hands on the arms of the chair as if to get up. For a moment his knuckles were white. Then he relaxed. "You saw what happened, didn't you?"

"Yes. But do you mind my asking what time your ship got into San Francisco on September the seventh?"

"No. Four o'clock. Four o'clock in the afternoon."

"I suppose that could be checked?"

He didn't answer. There was a newspaper on the sand beside

his chair and he leaned over and handed it to me. It was the Late Night Final of a San Francisco newspaper for the seventh.

"Turn to page four," he said.

I turned to page four and found an article describing the arrival of the USS *Guam* at the Golden Gate, at four o'clock in the afternoon. A contingent of Waves had greeted the returning heroes, and a band had played "California, Here I Come."

"If you want to see Mrs. Dreen, she's in the house," Jack Rossiter said. "But it looks to me as if your job is finished."

"Thanks," I said.

"And if I don't see you again, good-bye."

"Are you leaving?"

"A friend is coming out from Santa Barbara to pick me up in a few minutes. I'm flying up to Alameda with him to see about getting leave. I just had a forty-eight, and I've got to be here for the inquest tomorrow. And the funeral." His voice was hard. His whole personality had hardened overnight. The evening before his nature had been wide open. Now it was closed and invulnerable.

"Good-bye," I said, and plodded through the soft sand to the house. On the way I thought of something, and walked faster.

When I knocked, Mrs. Dreen came to the door holding a cup of coffee, not very steadily. She was wearing a heavy wool dressing robe with a silk rope around the waist, and a silk cap on her head. Her eyes were bleary.

"Hello," she said. "I came back last night after all. I couldn't work today anyway. And I didn't think Jack should be by himself."

"He seems to be doing all right."

"I'm glad you think so. Will you come in?"

I stepped inside. "You said last night that you wanted to know who killed Una no matter who it was."

"Well?"

"Does that still go?"

"Yes. Why? Did you find out something?"

"Not exactly. I thought of something, that's all."

"The coroner believes it was an accident. I talked to him on the phone this morning." She sipped her black coffee. Her hand vibrated steadily, like a leaf in the wind.

"He may be right," I said. "He may be wrong."

There was the sound of a car outside, and I moved to the window and looked out. A station wagon stopped on the beach, and a Navy officer got out and walked towards Jack Rossiter. Rossiter got up and they shook hands.

"Will you call Jack, Mrs. Dreen, and tell him to come into the house for a minute?"

"If you wish." She went to the door and called him.

Rossiter came to the door and said a little impatiently: "What is it?"

"Come in," I said. "And tell me what time you left the ship the day before yesterday."

"Let's see. We got in at four—"

"No, you didn't. The ship did, but not you. Am I right?"

"I don't know what you mean."

"You know what I mean. It's so simple that it couldn't fool anybody for a minute, not if he knew anything about carriers. You flew your plane off the ship a couple of hours before she got into port. My guess is that you gave that telegram to a buddy to send for you before you left the ship. You flew down here, caught your wife being made love to by another man, landed on the beach—and drowned her."

"You're insane!" After a moment he said less violently: "I admit I flew off the ship. You could easily find that out anyway. I flew around for a couple of hours, getting in some flying time—"

"Where did you fly?"

"Along the coast. I don't get down this far. I landed at Alameda at five-thirty, and I can prove it."

"Who's your friend?" I pointed through the open door to the other officer, who was standing on the beach looking out to sea.

"Lieutenant Harris. I'm going to fly up to Alameda with him. I warn you, don't make any ridiculous accusations in his presence, or you'll suffer for it."

"I want to ask him a question," I said. "What sort of plane were you flying?"

"FM-3."

I went out of the house and down the slope to Lieutenant Harris. He turned towards me and I saw the wings on his blouse.

"Good morning, Lieutenant," I said. "You've done a good deal of flying, I suppose?"

"Thirty-two months. Why?"

"I want to settle a bet. Could a plane land on this beach and take off again?"

"I think maybe a Piper Cub could. I'd try it anyway. Does that settle the bet?"

"It was a fighter I had in mind. An FM-3."

"Not an FM-3," he said. "Not possibly. It might just conceivably be able to land but it'd never get off again. Not enough room, and very poor surface. Ask Jack, he'll tell you the same."

I went back to the house and said to Jack: "I was wrong. I'm sorry. As you said, I guess I'm all washed up with this case."

"Good-bye, Millicent," Jack said, and kissed her cheek. "If I'm not back tonight I'll be back first thing in the morning. Keep a stiff upper lip."

"You do, too, Jack."

He went away without looking at me again. So the case was ending as it had begun, with me and Mrs. Dreen alone in a room wondering what had happened to her daughter.

"You shouldn't have said what you did to him," she said. "He's had enough to bear."

My mind was working very fast. I wondered whether it was producing anything. "I suppose Lieutenant Harris knows what he's talking about. He says a fighter couldn't land and take off from this beach. There's no other place around here he could have landed without being seen. So he didn't land.

"But I still don't believe that he wasn't here. No young husband flying along the coast within range of the house where his wife was—well, he'd fly low and dip his wings to her, wouldn't he? Terry Neville saw the plane come down."

"Terry Neville?"

"I talked to him last night. He was with Una before she died. The two of them were out on the raft together when Jack's plane came down. Jack saw them, and saw what they were doing. They saw him. Terry Neville went away. Then what?"

"You're making this up," Mrs. Dreen said, but her green eyes were intent on my face.

"I'm making it up, of course. I wasn't here. After Terry Neville ran away, there was no one here but Una, and Jack in a plane circling over her head. I'm trying to figure out why Una died. I *have* to make it up. But I think she died of fright. I think Jack dived at her and forced her into the water. I think he kept on diving at her until she was gone. Then he flew back to Alameda and chalked up his flying time."

"Fantasy," she said. "And very ugly. I don't believe it."

"You should. You've got that cable, haven't you?"

"I don't know what you're talking about."

"Jack sent Una a cable from Pearl, telling her what day he was arriving. Una mentioned it to Hilda Karp. Hilda Karp mentioned it to me. It's funny you didn't say anything about it."

"I didn't know about it," Millicent Dreen said. Her eyes were blank.

I went on, paying no attention to her denial: "My guess is that the cable said not only that Jack's ship was coming in on the seventh, but that he'd fly over the beach house that afternoon. Fortunately, I don't have to depend on guesswork. The cable will be on file at Western Union, and the police will be able to look at it. I'm going into town now."

"Wait," she said. "Don't go to the police about it. You'll only get Jack in trouble. I destroyed the cable to protect him, but I'll tell you what was in it. Your guess was right. He said he'd fly over on the seventh."

"When did you destroy it?"

"Yesterday, before I came to you. I was afraid it would implicate Jack."

"Why did you come to me at all, if you wanted to protect Jack? It seems that you knew what happened."

"I wasn't sure. I didn't know what had happened to her, and until I found out I didn't know what to do."

"You're still not sure," I said. "But I'm beginning to be. For one thing, it's certain that Una never got her cable, at least not as it was sent. Otherwise she wouldn't have been doing what she was doing on the afternoon that her husband was going to fly over and say hello. You changed the date on it, perhaps? So that Una expected Jack a day later? Then you arranged to be in Hollywood on the seventh, so that Una could spend a final afternoon with Terry Neville."

"Perhaps." Her face was completely alive, controlled but full of dangerous energy, like a cobra listening to music.

"Perhaps you wanted Jack for yourself," I said. "Perhaps you had another reason, I don't know. I think even a psycho-analyst would have a hard time working through your motivations, Mrs. Dreen, and I'm not one. All I know is that you precipitated a murder. Your plan worked even better than you expected."

"It was accidental death," she said hoarsely. "If you go to the police you'll only make a fool of yourself, and cause trouble for Jack."

"You care about Jack, don't you?"

"Why shouldn't I?" she said. "He was mine before he ever saw Una. She took him away from me."

"And now you think you've got him back." I got up to go. "I hope for your sake he doesn't figure out for himself what I've just figured out."

"Do you think he will?" Sudden terror had jerked her face apart.

I didn't answer her.

Gone Girl

IT WAS A Friday night. I was tooling home from the Mexican border in a light blue convertible and a dark blue mood. I had followed a man from Fresno to San Diego and lost him in the maze of streets in Old Town. When I picked up his trail again, it was cold. He had crossed the border, and my instructions went no further than the United States.

Halfway home, just above Emerald Bay, I overtook the worst driver in the world. He was driving a black fishtail Cadillac as if he were tacking a sailboat. The heavy car wove back and forth across the freeway, using two of its four lanes, and sometimes three. It was late, and I was in a hurry to get some sleep. I started to pass it on the right, at a time when it was riding the double line. The Cadillac drifted towards me like an unguided missile, and forced me off the road in a screeching skid.

I speeded up to pass on the left. Simultaneously, the driver of the Cadillac accelerated. My acceleration couldn't match his. We raced neck and neck down the middle of the road. I wondered if he was drunk or crazy or afraid of me. Then the freeway ended. I was doing eighty on the wrong side of a two-lane highway, and a truck came over a rise ahead like a blazing double comet. I floorboarded the gas pedal and cut over sharply to the right, threatening the Cadillac's fenders and its driver's life. In the approaching headlights, his face was as blank and white as a piece of paper, with charred black holes for eyes. His shoulders were naked.

At the last possible second he slowed enough to let me get by. The truck went off onto the shoulder, honking angrily. I braked gradually, hoping to force the Cadillac to stop. It looped past me in an insane arc, tires skittering, and was sucked away into darkness.

When I finally came to a full stop, I had to pry my fingers off the wheel. My knees were remote and watery. After smoking part of a cigarette, I U-turned and drove very cautiously back to Emerald Bay. I was long past the hot-rod age, and I needed rest.

The first motel I came to, the Siesta, was decorated with a vacancy sign and a neon Mexican sleeping luminously under a sombrero. Envying him, I parked on the gravel apron in front of the motel office. There was a light inside. The glass-paned door was standing open, and I went in. The little room was pleasantly furnished with rattan and chintz. I jangled the bell on the desk a few times. No one appeared, so I sat down to wait and lit a cigarette. An electric clock on the wall said a quarter to one.

I must have dozed for a few minutes. A dream rushed by the threshold of my consciousness, making a gentle noise. Death was in the dream. He drove a black Cadillac loaded with flowers. When I woke up, the cigarette was starting to burn my fingers. A thin man in a gray flannel shirt was standing over me with a doubtful look on his face.

He was big-nosed and small-chinned, and he wasn't as young as he gave the impression of being. His teeth were bad, the sandy hair was thinning and receding. He was the typical old youth who scrounged and wheedled his living around motor courts and restaurants and hotels, and hung on desperately to the frayed edge of other people's lives.

"What do you want?" he said. "Who are you? What do you want?" His voice was reedy and changeable like an adolescent's.

"A room."

"Is that all you want?"

From where I sat, it sounded like an accusation. I let it pass. "What else is there? Circassian dancing girls? Free popcorn?"

He tried to smile without showing his bad teeth. The smile was a dismal failure, like my joke. "I'm sorry, sir," he said. "You woke me up. I never make much sense right after I just wake up."

"Have a nightmare?"

His vague eyes expanded like blue bubblegum bubbles. "Why did you ask me that?"

"Because I just had one. But skip it. Do you have a vacancy or don't you?"

"Yessir. Sorry, sir." He swallowed whatever bitter taste he had in his mouth, and assumed an impersonal obsequious manner. "You got any luggage, sir?"

"No luggage."

Moving silently in tennis sneakers like a frail ghost of the boy he once had been, he went behind the counter, and took my name, address, license number, and five dollars. In return, he gave me a key numbered fourteen and told me where to use it. Apparently he despaired of a tip.

Room fourteen was like any other middle-class motel room
touched with the California-Spanish mania. Artificially rough-
ened plaster painted adobe color, poinsettia-red curtains, imitation parchment lampshade on a twisted black iron stand.
A Rivera reproduction of a sleeping Mexican hung on the
wall over the bed. I succumbed to its suggestion right away,
and dreamed about Circassian dancing girls.

Along towards morning one of them got frightened, through
no fault of mine, and began to scream her little Circassian
lungs out. I sat up in bed, making soothing noises, and woke
up. It was nearly nine by my wristwatch. The screaming
ceased and began again, spoiling the morning like a fire siren
outside the window. I pulled on my trousers over the underwear I'd been sleeping in, and went outside.

A young woman was standing on the walk outside the next
room. She had a key in one hand and a handful of blood
in the other. She wore a wide multi-colored skirt and a low-
cut gypsy sort of blouse. The blouse was distended and her
mouth was open, and she was yelling her head off. It was a fine
dark head, but I hated her for spoiling my morning sleep.

I took her by the shoulders and said, "Stop it."

The screaming stopped. She looked down sleepily at the
blood on her hand. It was as thick as axle grease, and almost
as dark in color.

"Where did you get that?"

"I slipped and fell in it. I didn't see it."

Dropping the key on the walk, she pulled her skirt to one
side with her clean hand. Her legs were bare and brown. Her
skirt was stained at the back with the same thick fluid.

"Where? In this room?"

She faltered, "Yes."

Doors were opening up and down the drive. Half a dozen
people began to converge on us. A dark-faced man about four
and a half feet high came scampering from the direction of
the office, his little pointed shoes dancing in the gravel.

"Come inside and show me," I said to the girl.

"I can't. I won't." Her eyes were very heavy, and surrounded by the bluish pallor of shock.

The little man slid to a stop between us, reached up and
gripped the upper part of her arm. "What is the matter, Ella?
Are you crazy, disturbing the guests?"

She said, "Blood," and leaned against me with her eyes
closed.

His sharp glance probed the situation. He turned to the
other guests, who had formed a murmuring semicircle around
us.

"It is perfectly hokay. Do not be concerned, ladies and

gentlemen. My daughter cut herself a little bit. It is perfectly all right."

Circling her waist with one long arm, he hustled her through the open door and slammed it behind him. I caught it on my foot and followed them in.

The room was a duplicate of mine, including the reproduction over the unmade bed, but everything was reversed as in a mirror image. The girl took a few weak steps by herself and sat on the edge of the bed. Then she noticed the blood spots on the sheets. She stood up quickly. Her mouth opened, rimmed with white teeth.

"Don't do it," I said. "We know you have a very fine pair of lungs."

The little man turned on me. "Who do you think you are?"

"The name is Archer. I have the next room."

"Get out of this one, please."

"I don't think I will."

He lowered his greased black head as if he were going to butt me. Under his sharkskin jacket, a hunch protruded from his back like a displaced elbow. He seemed to reconsider the butting gambit, and decided in favor of diplomacy.

"You are jumping to conclusions, mister. It is not so serious as it looks. We had a little accident here last night."

"Sure, your daughter cut herself. She heals remarkably fast."

"Nothing like that." He fluttered one long hand. "I said to the people outside the first thing that came to my mind. Actually, it was a little scuffle. One of the guests suffered a nosebleed."

The girl moved like a sleepwalker to the bathroom door and switched on the light. There was a pool of blood coagulating on the black and white checkerboard linoleum, streaked where she had slipped and fallen in it.

"Some nosebleed," I said to the little man. "Do you run this joint?"

"I am the proprietor of the Siesta motor hotel, yes. My name is Salanda. The gentleman is susceptible to nosebleed. He told me so himself."

"Where is he now?"

"He checked out early this morning."

"In good health?"

"Certainly in good health."

I looked around the room. Apart from the unmade bed with the brown spots on the sheets, it contained no signs of occupancy. Someone had spilled a pint of blood and vanished.

The little man opened the door wide and invited me with a sweep of his arm to leave. "If you will excuse me, sir, I wish to have this cleaned up as quickly as possible. Ella, will you tell Lorraine to get to work on it right away pronto? Then maybe you better lie down for a little while, eh?"

"I'm all right now, father. Don't worry about me."

When I checked out a few minutes later, she was sitting behind the desk in the front office, looking pale but composed. I dropped my key on the desk in front of her.

"Feeling better, Ella?"

"Oh. I didn't recognize you with all your clothes on."

"That's a good line. May I use it?"

She lowered her eyes and blushed. "You're making fun of me. I know I acted foolishly this morning."

"I'm not so sure. What do *you* think happened in thirteen last night?"

"My father told you, didn't he?"

"He gave me a version, two of them in fact. I doubt that they're the final shooting script."

Her hand went to the central hollow in her blouse. Her arms and shoulders were slender and brown, the tips of her fingers carmine. "Shooting?"

"A cinema term," I said. "But there might have been a real shooting at that. Don't you think so?"

Her front teeth pinched her lower lip. She looked like somebody's pet rabbit. I restrained an impulse to pat her sleek brown head.

"That's ridiculous. This is respectable motel. Anyway, father asked me not to discuss it with anybody."

"Why would he do that?"

"He loves this place, that's why. He doesn't want any scandal made out of nothing. If we lost our good reputation here, it would break my father's heart."

"He doesn't strike me as the sentimental type."

She stood up, smoothing her skirt. I saw that she'd changed it. "You leave him alone. He's a dear little man. I don't know what you think you're doing, trying to stir up trouble where there isn't any."

I backed away from her righteous indignation—female indignation is always righteous—and went out to my car. The early spring sun was dazzling. Beyond the freeway and the drifted sugary dunes, the bay was Prussian blue. The road cut inland across the base of the peninsula and returned to the sea a few miles north of the town. Here a wide blacktop parking space shelved off to the left of the highway, overlooking the white beach and whiter breakers. Signs at each end of the turnout stated that this was a County Park, No Beach Fires.

The beach and the blacktop expanse above it were deserted

except for a single car, which looked very lonely. It was a long black Cadillac nosed into the cable fence at the edge of the beach. I braked and turned off the highway and got out. The man in the driver's seat of the Cadillac didn't turn his head as I approached him. His chin was propped on the steering wheel, and he was gazing out across the endless blue sea.

I opened the door and looked into his face. It was paper white. The dark brown eyes were sightless. The body was unclothed except for the thick hair matted on the chest, and a clumsy bandage tied around the waist. The bandage was composed of several blood-stained towels, held in place by a knotted piece of nylon fabric whose nature I didn't recognize immediately. Examining it more closely, I saw that it was a woman's slip. The left breast of the garment was embroidered in purple with a heart, containing the name, "Fern," in slanting script. I wondered who Fern was.

The man who was wearing her purple heart had dark curly hair, heavy black eyebrows, a heavy chin sprouting black beard. He was rough-looking in spite of his anemia and the lipstick smudged on his mouth.

There was no registration on the steeringpost, and nothing in the glove compartment but a half-empty box of shells for a .38 automatic. The ignition was still turned on. So were the dash and headlights, but they were dim. The gas gauge registered empty. Curlyhead must have pulled off the highway soon after he passed me, and driven all the rest of the night in one place.

I untied the slip, which didn't look as if it would take fingerprints, and went over it for a label. It had one: Gretchen, Palm Springs. It occurred to me that it was Saturday morning and that I'd gone all winter without a week end in the desert. I retied the slip the way I'd found it, and drove back to the Siesta Motel.

Ella's welcome was a few degrees colder than absolute zero. "Well!" She glared down her pretty rabbit nose at me. "I thought we were rid of you."

"So did I. But I just couldn't tear myself away."

She gave me a peculiar look, neither hard nor soft, but mixed. Her hand went to her hair, then reached for a registration card. "I suppose if you want to rent a room, I can't stop you. Only please don't imagine you're making an impression on me. You're not. You leave me cold, mister."

"Archer," I said. "Lew Archer. Don't bother with the card. I came back to use your phone."

"Aren't there any other phones?" She pushed the telephone across the desk. "I guess it's all right, long as it isn't a toll call."

"I'm calling the Highway Patrol. Do you know their local number?"

"I don't remember." She handed me the telephone directory.

"There's been an accident," I said as I dialed.

"A highway accident? Where did it happen?"

"Right here, sister. Right here in room thirteen."

But I didn't tell that to the Highway Patrol. I told them I had found a dead man in a car on the parking lot above the county beach. The girl listened with widening eyes and nostrils. Before I finished she rose in a flurry and left the office by the rear door.

She came back with the proprietor. His eyes were black and bright like nailheads in leather, and the scampering dance of his feet was almost frenzied. "What is this?"

"I came across a dead man up the road a piece."

"So why do you come back here to telephone?" His head was in butting position, his hands outspread and gripping the corners of the desk. "Has it got anything to do with us?"

"He's wearing a couple of your towels."

"What?"

"And he was bleeding heavily before he died. I think somebody shot him in the stomach. Maybe you did."

"You're loco," he said, but not very emphatically. "Crazy accusations like that, they will get you into trouble. What is your business?"

"I'm a private detective."

"You followed him here, is that it? You were going to arrest him, so he shot himself?"

"Wrong on both accounts," I said. "I came here to sleep. And they don't shoot themselves in the stomach. It's too uncertain, and slow. No suicide wants to die of peritonitis."

"So what are you doing now, trying to make scandal for my business?"

"If your business includes trying to cover for murder."

"He shot himself," the little man insisted.

"How do you know?"

"Donny. I spoke to him just now."

"And how does Donny know?"

"The man told him."

"Is Donny your night keyboy?"

"He was. I think I will fire him, for stupidity. He didn't even tell me about this mess. I had to find it out for myself. The hard way."

"Donny means well," the girl said at his shoulder. "I'm sure he didn't realize what happened."

"Who does?" I said. "I want to talk to Donny. But first let's have a look at the register."

He took a pile of cards from a drawer and riffled through
them. His large hands, hairy-backed, were calm and expert,
like animals that lived a serene life of their own, independent
of their emotional owner. They dealt me one of the cards
across the desk. It was inscribed in block capitals: Richard
Rowe, Detroit, Mich.

I said: "There was a woman with him."

"Impossible."

"Or he was a transvestite."

He surveyed me blankly, thinking of something else. "The
HP, did you tell them to come here? They know it happened
here?"

"Not yet. But they'll find your towels. He used them for
bandage."

"I see. Yes. Of course." He struck himself with a clenched
fist on the temple. It made a noise like someone maltreating
a pumpkin. "You are a private detective, you say. Now if you
informed the police that you were on the trail of a fugitive, a
fugitive from justice. . . . He shot himself rather than face
arrest. . . . For five hundred dollars?"

"I'm not that private," I said. "I have some public responsibility. Besides, the cops would do a little checking and catch
me out."

"Not necessarily. He *was* a fugitive from justice, you know."

"I hear you telling me."

"Give me a little time, and I can even present you with
his record."

The girl was leaning back away from her father, her eyes
starred with broken illusions. "Daddy," she said weakly.

He didn't hear her. All of his bright black attention was
fixed on me. "Seven hundred dollars?"

"No sale. The higher you raise it, the guiltier you look.
Were you here last night?"

"You are being absurd," he said. "I spent the entire evening
with my wife. We drove up to Los Angeles to attend the
ballet." By way of supporting evidence, he hummed a couple
of bars from Tchaikovsky. "We didn't arrive back here in
Emerald Bay until nearly two o'clock."

"Alibis can be fixed."

"By criminals, yes," he said. "I am not a criminal."

The girl put a hand on his shoulder. He cringed away, his
face creased by monkey fury, but his face was hidden from her.

"Daddy," she said. "Was he murdered, do you think?"

"How do I know?" His voice was wild and high, as if she
had touched the spring of his emotion. "I wasn't here. I only
know what Donny told me."

The girl was examining me with narrowed eyes, as if I

were a new kind of animal she had discovered and was trying
to think of a use for.

"This gentleman is a detective," she said, "or claims to be."

I pulled out my photostat and slapped it down on the desk.
The little man picked it up and looked from it to my face.
"Will you go to work for me?"

"Doing what, telling little white lies?"

The girl answered for him: "See what you can find out
about this—this death. On my word of honor, Father had
nothing to do with it."

I made a snap decision, the kind you live to regret. "All
right. I'll take a fifty-dollar advance. Which is a good deal
less than five hundred. My first advice to you is to tell the
police everything you know. Provided that you're innocent."

"You insult me," he said.

But he flicked a fifty-dollar bill from the cash drawer and
pressed it into my hand fervently, like a love token. I had a
queasy feeling that I had been conned into taking his money,
not much of it but enough. The feeling deepened when he still
refused to talk. I had to use all the arts of persuasion even to
get Donny's address out of him.

The keyboy lived in a shack on the edge of a desolate stretch
of dunes. I guessed that it had once been somebody's beach
house, before sand had drifted like unthawing snow in the
angles of the walls and winter storms had broken the tiles and
cracked the concrete foundations. Huge chunks of concrete
were piled haphazardly on what had been a terrace overlooking the sea.

On one of the tilted slabs, Donny was stretched like a long
albino lizard in the sun. The onshore wind carried the sound
of my motor to his ears. He sat up blinking, recognized me
when I stopped the car, and ran into the house.

I descended flagstone steps and knocked on the warped door.
"Open up, Donny."

"Go away," he answered huskily. His eye gleamed like a
snail through a crack in the wood.

"I'm working for Mr. Salanda. He wants us to have a talk."

"You can go and take a running jump at yourself, you and
Mr. Salanda both."

"Open it or I'll break it down."

I waited for a while. He shot back the bolt. The door creaked
reluctantly open. He leaned against the doorpost, searching
my face with his eyes, his hairless body shivering from an
internal chill. I pushed past him, through a kitchenette that
was indescribably filthy, littered with the remnants of old
meals, and gaseous with their odors. He followed me silently
on bare soles into a larger room whose sprung floorboards un-

dulated under my feet. The picture window had been broken
and patched with cardboard. The stone fireplace was choked
with garbage. The only furniture was an army cot in one corner
where Donny apparently slept.

"Nice homey place you have here. It has that lived-in
quality."

He seemed to take it as a compliment, and I wondered if I
was dealing with a moron. "It suits me. I never was much of a
one for fancy quarters. I like it here, where I can hear the
ocean at night."

"What else do you hear at night, Donny?"

He missed the point of the question, or pretended to. "All
different things. Big trucks going past on the highway. I like
to hear those night sounds. Now I guess I can't go on living
here. Mr. Salanda owns it, he lets me live here for nothing.
Now he'll be kicking me out of here, I guess."

"On account of what happened last night?"

"Uh-huh." He subsided onto the cot, his doleful head supported by his hands.

I stood over him. "Just what did happen last night, Donny?"

"A bad thing," he said. "This fella checked in about ten
o'clock—"

"The man with the dark curly hair?"

"That's the one. He checked in about ten, and I gave him
room thirteen. Around about midnight I thought I heard a
gun go off from there. It took me a little while to get my nerve
up, then I went back to see what was going on. This fella came
out of the room, without no clothes on. Just some kind of a
bandage around his waist. He looked like some kind of a crazy
Indian or something. He had a gun in his hand, and he was
staggering, and I could see that he was bleeding some. He
come right up to me and pushed the gun in my gut and told
me to keep my trap shut. He said I wasn't to tell anybody I
saw him, now or later. He said if I opened my mouth about
it to anybody, that he would come back and kill me. But now
he's dead, isn't he?"

"He's dead."

I could smell the fear on Donny: there's an unexplained
trace of canine in my chromosomes. The hairs were prickling
on the back of my neck, and I wondered if Donny's fear was
of the past or for the future. The pimples stood out in bas-
relief against his pale lugubrious face.

"I think he was murdered, Donny. You're lying, aren't you?"

"Me lying?" But his reaction was slow and feeble.

"The dead man didn't check in alone. He had a woman
with him."

"What woman?" he said in elaborate surprise.

"You tell me. Her name was Fern. I think she did the shooting, and you caught her red-handed. The wounded man got out of the room and into his car and away. The woman stayed behind to talk to you. She probably paid you to dispose of his clothes and fake a new registration card for the room. But you both overlooked the blood on the floor of the bathroom. Am I right?"

"You couldn't be wronger, mister. Are you a cop?"

"A private detective. You're in deep trouble, Donny. You'd better talk yourself out of it if you can, before the cops start on you."

"I didn't do anything." His voice broke like a boy's. It went strangely with the glints of gray in his hair.

"Faking the register is a serious rap, even if they don't hang accessory to murder on you."

He began to expostulate in formless sentences that ran together. At the same time his hand was moving across the dirty gray blanket. It burrowed under the pillow and came out holding a crumpled card. He tried to stuff it into his mouth and chew it. I tore it away from between his discolored teeth.

It was a registration card from the motel, signed in a boyish scrawl: Mr. and Mrs. Richard Rowe, Detroit, Mich.

Donny was trembling violently. Below his cheap cotton shorts, his bony knees vibrated like tuning forks. "It wasn't my fault," he cried. "She held a gun on me."

"What did you do with the man's clothes?"

"Nothing. She didn't even let me into the room. She bundled them up and took them away herself."

"Where did she go?"

"Down the highway towards town. She walked away on the shoulder of the road and that was the last I saw of her."

"How much did she pay you, Donny?"

"Nothing, not a cent. I already told you, she held a gun on me."

"And you were so scared you kept quiet until this morning?"

"That's right. I was scared. Who wouldn't be scared?"

"She's gone now," I said. "You can give me a description of her."

"Yeah." He made a visible effort to pull his vague thoughts together. One of his eyes was a little off center, lending his face a stunned, amorphous appearance. "She was a big tall dame with blondey hair."

"Dyed?"

"I guess so, I dunno. She wore it in a braid like, on top of her head. She was kind of fat, built like a lady wrestler, great big watermelons on her. Big legs."

"How was she dressed?"

"I didn't hardly notice, I was so scared. I think she had some kind of a purple coat on, with black fur around the neck. Plenty of rings on her fingers and stuff."

"How old?"

"Pretty old, I'd say. Older than me, and I'm going on thirty-nine."

"And she did the shooting?"

"I guess so. She told me to say if anybody asked me, I was to say that Mr. Rowe shot himself."

"You're very suggestible, aren't you, Donny? It's a dangerous way to be, with people pushing each other around the way they do."

"I didn't get that, mister. Come again." He batted his pale blue eyes at me, smiling expectantly.

"Skip it," I said and left him.

A few hundred yards up the highway I passed an HP car with two uniformed men in the front seat looking grim. Donny was in for it now. I pushed him out of my mind and drove across country to Palm Springs.

Palm Springs is still a one-horse town, but the horse is a Palomino with silver trappings. Most of the girls were Palomino, too. The main street was a cross-section of Hollywood and Vine transported across the desert by some unnatural force and disguised in western costumes which fooled nobody. Not even me.

I found Gretchen's lingerie shop in an expensive-looking arcade built around an imitation flagstone patio. In the patio's center a little fountain gurgled pleasantly, flinging small lariats of spray against the heat. It was late in March, and the season was ending. Most of the shops, including the one I entered, were deserted except for the hired help.

It was a small shop, faintly perfumed by a legion of vanished dolls. Stocking and robes and other garments were coiled on the glass counters or hung like brilliant treesnakes on display stands along the narrow walls. A henna-headed woman emerged from rustling recesses at the rear and came tripping towards me on her toes.

"You are looking for a gift, sir?" she cried with a wilted kind of gaiety. Behind her painted mask, she was tired and aging and it was Saturday afternoon and the lucky ones were dunking themselves in kidney-shaped swimming pools behind walls she couldn't climb.

"Not exactly. In fact, not at all. A peculiar thing happened to me last night. I'd like to tell you about it, but it's kind of a complicated story."

She looked me over quizzically and decided that I worked

for a living, too. The phony smile faded away. Another smile took its place, which I liked better. "You look as if you'd had a fairly rough night. And you could do with a shave."

"I met a girl," I said. "Actually she was a mature woman, a statuesque blonde to be exact. I picked her up on the beach at Laguna, if you want me to be brutally frank."

"I couldn't bear it if you weren't. What kind of a pitch is this, brother?"

"Wait. You're spoiling my story. Something clicked when we met, in that sunset light, on the edge of the warm summer sea."

"It's always bloody cold when I go in."

"It wasn't last night. We swam in the moonlight and had a gay time and all. Then she went away. I didn't realize until she was gone that I didn't know her telephone number, or even her last name."

"Married woman, eh? What do you think I am, a lonely hearts club?" Still, she was interested, though she probably didn't believe me. "She mentioned me, is that it? What was her first name?"

"Fern."

"Unusual name. You say she was a big blonde?"

"Magnificently proportioned," I said. "If I had a classical education I'd call her Junoesque."

"You're kidding me, aren't you?"

"A little."

"I thought so. Personally I don't mind a little kidding. What did she say about me?"

"Nothing but good. As a matter of fact, I was complimenting her on her—er—garments."

"I see." She was long past blushing. "We had a customer last fall some time, by the name of Fern. Fern Dee. She had some kind of a job at the Joshua Club, I think. But she doesn't fit the description at all. This one was a brunette, a middle-sized brunette, quite young. I remember the name Fern because she wanted it embroidered on all the things she bought. A corny idea if you ask me, but that was her girlish desire and who am I to argue with girlish desires."

"Is she still in town?"

"I haven't see her lately, not for months. But it couldn't be the woman you're looking for. Or could it?"

"How long ago was she in here?"

She pondered. "Early last fall, around the start of the season. She only came in that once, and made a big purchase, stockings and nightwear and underthings. The works. I remember thinking at the time, here was a girlie who suddenly hit the chips but heavily."

"She might have put on weight since then, and dyed her hair. Strange things can happen to the female form."

"You're telling me," she said. "How old was—your friend?"

"About forty, I'd say, give or take a little."

"It couldn't be the same one then. The girl I'm talking about was twenty-five at the outside, and I don't make mistakes about women's ages. I've seen too many of them in all stages, from Quentin quail to hags, and I certainly do mean hags."

"I bet you have."

She studied me with eyes shadowed by mascara and experience. "You a policeman?"

"I have been."

"You want to tell mother what it's all about?"

"Another time. Where's the Joshua Club?"

"It won't be open yet."

"I'll try it anyway."

She shrugged her thin shoulders and gave me directions. I thanked her.

It occupied a plain-faced one-story building half a block off the main street. The padded leather door swung inward when I pushed it. I passed through a lobby with a retractable roof, which contained a jungle growth of banana trees. The big main room was decorated with tinted desert photomurals. Behind a rattan bar with a fishnet canopy, a white-coated Caribbean type was drying shot-glasses with a dirty towel. His face looked uncommunicative.

On the orchestra dais beyond the piled chairs in the dining area, a young man in shirt sleeves was playing bop piano. His fingers shadowed the tune, ran circles around it, played leap-frog with it, and managed never to hit it on the nose. I stood beside him for a while and listened to him work. He looked up finally, still strumming with his left hand in the bass. He had soft-centered eyes and frozen-looking nostrils and a whistling mouth.

"Nice piano," I said.

"I think so."

"Fifty-second Street?"

"It's the street with the beat and I'm not effete." His left hand struck the same chord three times and dropped away from the keys. "Looking for somebody, friend?"

"Fern Dee. She asked me to drop by some time."

"Too bad. Another wasted trip. She left here end of last year, the dear. She wasn't a bad little nightingale but she was no pro, Joe, you know? She had it but she couldn't project it. When she warbled the evening died, no matter how hard she tried, I don't wanna be snide."

"Where did she lam, Sam, or don't you give a damn?"

He smiled like a corpse in a deft mortician's hands. "I heard the boss retired her to private life. Took her home to live with him. That is what I heard. But I don't mix with the big boy socially, so I couldn't say for sure that she's impure. Is it anything to you?"

"Something, but she's over twenty-one."

"Not more than a couple of years over twenty-one." His eyes darkened, and his thin mouth twisted sideways angrily. "I hate to see it happen to a pretty little twist like Fern. Not that I yearn—"

I broke in on his nonsense rhymes: "Who's the big boss you mentioned, the one Fern went to live with?"

"Angel. Who else?"

"What heaven does he inhabit?"

"You must be new in these parts—" His eyes swiveled and focused on something over my shoulder. His mouth opened and closed.

A grating tenor said behind me: "Got a question you want answered, bud?"

The pianist went back to the piano as if the ugly tenor had wiped me out, annulled my very existence. I turned to its source. He was standing in a narrow doorway behind the drums, a man in his thirties with thick black curly hair and a heavy jaw blue-shadowed by closely shaven beard. He was almost the living image of the dead man in the Cadillac. The likeness gave me a jolt. The heavy black gun in his hand gave me another.

He came around the drums and approached me, bull-shoul-dered in a fuzzy tweed jacket, holding the gun in front of him like a dangerous gift. The pianist was doing wry things in quickened tempo with the dead march from *Saul*. A wit.

The dead man's almost-double waved his cruel chin and the crueler gun in unison. "Come inside, unless you're a government man. If you are, I'll have a look at your credentials."

"I'm a freelance."

"Inside then."

The muzzle of the automatic came into my solar plexus like a pointing iron finger. Obeying its injunction, I made my way between empty music stands and through the narrow door behind the drums. The iron finger, probing my back, directed me down a lightless corridor to a small square office containing a metal desk, a safe, a filing cabinet. It was windowless, lit by fluorescent tubes in the ceiling. Under their pitiless glare, the face above the gun looked more than ever like the dead man's face. I wondered if I had been mistaken about his deadness, or if the desert heat had addled my brain.

"I'm the manager here," he said, standing so close that I

could smell the piney stuff he used on his crisp dark hair.
"You got anything to ask about the members of the staff, you
ask me."

"Will I get an answer?"

"Try me, bud."

"The name is Archer," I said. "I'm a private detective."

"Working for who?"

"You wouldn't be interested."

"I am, though, very much interested." The gun hopped
forward like a toad into my stomach again, with the weight
of his shoulder behind it. "Working for who did you say?"

I swallowed anger and nausea, estimating my chances of
knocking the gun to one side and taking him bare-handed.
The chances seemed pretty slim. He was heavier than I was,
and he held the automatic as if it had grown out of the
end of his arm. You've seen too many movies, I told myself. I
told him: "A motel owner on the coast. A man was shot in
one of his rooms last night. I happened to check in there a
few minutes later. The old boy hired me to look into the
shooting."

"Who was it got himself ventilated?"

"He could be your brother," I said. "Do you have a
brother?"

He lost his color. The center of his attention shifted from
the gun to my face. The gun nodded. I knocked it up and
sideways with a hard left uppercut. Its discharge burned the
side of my face and drilled a hole in the wall. My right sank
into his neck. The gun thumped the cork floor.

He went down but not out, his spread hand scrabbling for
the gun, then closing on it. I kicked his wrist. He grunted but
wouldn't let go of it. I threw a punch at the short hairs on the
back of his neck. He took it and came up under it with the
gun, shaking his head from side to side.

"Up with the hands now," he murmured. He was one of
those men whose voices go soft and mild when they are in
killing mood. He had the glassy impervious eyes of a killer.
"Is Bart dead? My brother?"

"Very dead. He was shot in the belly."

"Who shot him?"

"That's the question."

"Who shot him?" he said in a quite white-faced rage. The
single eye of the gun stared emptily at my midriff. "It could
happen to you, bud, here and now."

"A woman was with him. She took a quick powder after it
happened."

"I heard you say a name to Alfie, the piano-player. Was it
Fern?"

"It could have been."

"What do you mean, it could have been?"

"She was there in the room, apparently. If you can give me a description of her?"

His hard brown eyes looked past me. "I can do better than that. There's a picture of her on the wall behind you. Take a look at it. Keep those hands up high."

I shifted my feet and turned uneasily. The wall was blank. I heard him draw a breath and move, and tried to evade his blow. No use. It caught the back of my head. I pitched forward against the blank wall and slid down it into three dimensions of blankness.

The blankness coagulated into colored shapes. The shapes were half human and half beast and they dissolved and reformed. A dead man with a hairy breast climbed out of a hole and doubled and quadrupled. I ran away from them through a twisting tunnel which led to an echo chamber. Under the roaring surge of the nightmare music, a rasping tenor was saying:

"I figure it like this. Vario's tip was good. Bart found her in Acapulco, and he was bringing her back from there. She conned him into stopping off at this motel for the night. Bart always went for her."

"I didn't know that," a dry old voice put in. "This is very interesting news about Bart and Fern. You should have told me before about this. Then I would not have sent him for her and this would not have happened. Would it, Gino?"

My mind was still partly absent, wandering underground in the echoing caves. I couldn't recall the voices, or who they were talking about. I had barely sense enough to keep my eyes closed and go on listening. I was lying on my back on a hard surface. The voices were above me.

The tenor said: "You can't blame Bartolomeo. She's the one, the dirty treacherous lying little bitch."

"Calm yourself, Gino. I blame nobody. But more than ever now, we want her back, isn't that right?"

"I'll kill her," he said softly, almost wistfully.

"Perhaps. It may not be necessary now. I dislike promiscuous killing—"

"Since when, Angel?"

"Don't interrupt, it's not polite. I learned to put first things first. Now what is the most important thing? Why did we want her back in the first place? I will tell you: to shut her mouth. The government heard she left me, they wanted her to testify about my income. We wanted to find her first and shut her mouth, isn't that right?"

"I know how to shut her mouth," the younger man said very quietly.

"First we try a better way, my way. You learn when you're as old as I am there is a use for everything, and not to be wasteful. Not even wasteful with somebody else's blood. She shot your brother, right? So now we have something on her, strong enough to keep her mouth shut for good. She'd get off with second degree, with what she's got, but even that is five to ten in Tehachapi. I think all I need to do is tell her that. First we have to find her, eh?"

"I'll find her. Bart didn't have any trouble finding her."

"With Vario's tip to help him, no. But I think I'll keep you here with me, Gino. You're too hot-blooded, you and your brother both. I want her alive. Then I can talk to her, and then we'll see."

"You're going soft in your old age, Angel."

"Am I?" There was a light slapping sound, of a blow on flesh. "I have killed many men, for good reasons. So I think you will take that back."

"I take it back."

"And call me Mr. Funk. If I am so old, you will treat my gray hairs with respect. Call me Mr. Funk."

"Mr. Funk."

"All right, your friend here, does he know where Fern is?"

"I don't think so."

"Mr. Funk."

"Mr. Funk." Gino's voice was a whining snarl.

"I think he's coming to. His eyelids fluttered."

The toe of a shoe prodded my side. Somebody slapped my face a number of times. I opened my eyes and sat up. The back of my head was throbbing like an engine fueled by pain. Gino rose from a squatting position and stood over me.

"Stand up."

I rose shakily to my feet. I was in a stone-walled room with a high beamed ceiling, sparsely furnished with stiff old black oak chairs and tables. The room and the furniture seemed to have been built for a race of giants.

The man behind Gino was small and old and weary. He might have been an unsuccessful grocer or a superannuated barkeep who had come to California for his health. Clearly his health was poor. Even in the stifling heat he looked pale and chilly, as if he had caught chronic death from one of his victims. He moved closer to me, his legs shuffling feebly in wrinkled blue trousers that bagged at the knees. His shrunken torso was swathed in a heavy blue turtleneck sweater. He had two days' beard on his chin, like moth-eaten gray plush.

"Gino informs me that you are investigating a shooting."
His accent was Middle-European and very faint, as if he had
forgotten his origins. "Where did this happen, exactly?"

"I don't think I'll tell you that. You can read it in the
papers tomorrow night if you are interested."

"I am not prepared to wait. I am impatient. Do you know
where Fern is?"

"I wouldn't be here if I did."

"But you know where she was last night."

"I couldn't be sure."

"Tell me anyway to the best of your knowledge."

"I don't think I will."

"He doesn't think he will," the old man said to Gino.

"I think you better let me out of here. Kidnaping is a
tough rap. You don't want to die in the pen."

He smiled at me, with a tolerance more terrible than anger.
His eyes were like thin stab-wounds filled with watery blood.
Shuffling unhurriedly to the head of the mahogany table
behind him, he pressed a spot in the rug with the toe of one
felt slipper. Two men in blue serge suits entered the room and
stepped towards me briskly. They belonged to the race of
giants it had been built for.

Gino moved behind me and reached to pin my arms. I
pivoted, landed one short punch, and took a very hard counter
below the belt. Something behind me slammed my kidneys with
the heft of a trailer truck bumper. I turned on weakening legs
and caught a chin with my elbow. Gino's fist, or one of the
beams from the ceiling, landed on my neck. My head rang
like a gong. Under its clangor, Angel was saying pleasantly:

"Where was Fern last night?"

I didn't say.

The men in blue serge held me upright by the arms while
Gino used my head as a punching bag. I rolled with his lefts
and rights as well as I could, but his timing improved and mine
deteriorated. His face wavered and receded. At intervals
Angel inquired politely if I was willing to assist him now. I
asked myself confusedly in the hail of fists what I was holding
out for or who I was protecting. Probably I was holding out
for myself. If seemed important to me not to give in to violence. But my identity was dissolving and receding like the
face in front of me.

I concentrated on hating Gino's face. That kept it clear and
steady for a while: a stupid square-jawed face barred by a
single black brow, two close-set brown eyes staring glassily.
His fists continued to rock me like an air-hammer.

Finally Angel placed a clawed hand on his shoulder, and
nodded to my handlers. They deposited me in a chair. It swung

on an invisible wire from the ceiling in great circles. It swung out wide over the desert, across a bleak horizon, into darkness.

I came to, cursing. Gino was standing over me again. There was an empty water-glass in his hand, and my face was dripping. Angel spoke up beside him, with a trace of irritation in his voice:

"You stand up good under punishment. Why go to all the trouble, though? I want a little information, that is all. My friend, my little girl-friend, ran away. I'm impatient to get her back."

"You're going about it the wrong way."

Gino leaned close, and laughed harshly. He shattered the glass on the arm of my chair, held the jagged base up to my eyes. Fear ran through me, cold and light in my veins. My eyes were my connection with everything. Blindness would be the end of me. I closed my eyes, shutting out the cruel edges of the broken thing in his hand.

"Nix, Gino," the old man said. "I have a better idea, as usual. There is heat on, remember."

They retreated to the far side of the table and conferred there in low voices. The young man left the room. The old man came back to me. His storm troopers stood one on each side of me, looking down at him in ignorant awe.

"What is your name, young fellow?"

I told him. My mouth was puffed and lisping, tongue tangled in ropes of blood.

"I like a young fellow who can take it, Mr. Archer. You say that you're a detective. You find people for a living, is that right?"

"I have a client," I said.

"Now you have another. Whoever he is, I can buy and sell him, believe me. Fifty times over." His thin blue hands scoured each other. They made a sound like two dry sticks rubbing together on a dead tree.

"Narcotics?" I said. "Are you the wheel in the heroin racket? I've heard of you."

His watery eyes veiled themselves like a bird's. "Now don't ask foolish questions, or I will lose my respect for you entirely."

"That would break my heart."

"Then comfort yourself with this." He brought an old-fashioned purse out of his hip pocket, abstracted a crumpled bill and smoothed it out on my knee. It was a five-hundred-dollar bill.

"This girl of mine you are going to find for me, she is young and foolish. I am old and foolish, to have trusted her. No matter. Find her for me and bring her back and I will give you another bill like this one. Take it."

"Take it," one of my guards repeated. "Mr. Funk said for you to take it."

I took it. "You're wasting your money. I don't even know what she looks like. I don't know anything about her."

"Gino is bringing a picture. He came across her last fall at a recording studio in Hollywood where Alfie had a date. He gave her an audition and took her on at the club, more for her looks than for the talent she had. As a singer she flopped. But she is a pretty little thing, about five foot four, nice figure, dark brown hair, big hazel eyes. I found a use for her." Lechery flickered briefly in his eyes and went out.

"You find a use for everything."

"That is good economics. I often think if I wasn't what I am, I would make a good economist. Nothing would go to waste." He paused and dragged his dying old mind back to the subject: "She was here for a couple of months, then she ran out on me, silly girl. I heard last week that she was in Acapulco, and the federal Grand Jury was going to subpoena her. I have tax troubles, Mr. Archer, all my life I have tax troubles. Unfortunately I let Fern help with my books a little bit. She could do me great harm. So I sent Bart to Mexico to bring her back. But I meant no harm to her. I still intend her no harm, even now. A little talk, a little realistic discussion with Fern, that is all that will be necessary. So even the shooting of my good friend Bart serves its purpose. Where did it happen, by the way?"

The question flicked out like a hook on the end of a long line.

"In San Diego," I said, "at a place near the airport: the Mission Motel."

He smiled paternally. "Now you are showing good sense."

Gino came back with a silver-framed photograph in his hand. He handed it to Angel, who passed it on to me. It was a studio portrait, of the kind intended for publicity cheesecake. On a black velvet divan, against an artificial night sky, a young woman reclined in a gossamer robe that was split to show one bent leg. Shadows accentuated the lines of her body and the fine bones in her face. Under the heavy makeup which widened the mouth and darkened the half-closed eyes, I recognized Ella Salanda. The picture was signed in white, in the lower righthanded corner: "To my Angel, with all my love, Fern."

A sickness assailed me, worse than the sickness induced by Gino's fists. Angel breathed into my face: "Fern Dee is a stage name. Her real name I never learned. She told me one time that if her family knew where she was they would die of shame." He chuckled drily. "She will not want them to know that she killed a man."

I drew away from his charnel-house breath. My guards escorted me out. Gino started to follow, but Angel called him back.

"Don't wait to hear from me," the old man said after me. "I expect to hear from you."

The building stood on a rise in the open desert. It was huge and turreted, like somebody's idea of a castle in Spain. The last rays of the sun washed its walls in purple light and cast long shadows across its barren acreage. It was surrounded by a ten-foot hurricane fence topped with three strands of barbed wire.

Palm Springs was a clutter of white stones in the distance, diamonded by an occasional light. The dull red sun was balanced like a glowing cigar-butt on the rim of the hills above the town. A man with a bulky shoulder harness under his brown suede windbreaker drove me towards it. The sun fell out of sight, and darkness gathered like an impalpable ash on the desert, like a column of blue-gray smoke towering into the sky.

The sky was blue-black and swarming with stars when I got back to Emerald Bay. A black Cadillac followed me out of Palm Springs. I lost it in the winding streets of Pasadena. So far as I could see, I had lost it for good.

The neon Mexican lay peaceful under the stars. A smaller sign at his feet asserted that there was No Vacancy. The lights in the long low stucco buildings behind him shone brightly. The office door was open behind a screen, throwing a barred rectangle of light on the gravel. I stepped into it, and froze.

Behind the registration desk in the office, a woman was avidly reading a magazine. Her shoulders and bosom were massive. Her hair was blond, piled on her head in coroneted braids. There were rings on her fingers, a triple strand of cultured pearls around her thick white throat. She was the woman Donny had described to me.

I pulled the screen door open and said rudely: "Who are you?"

She glanced up, twisting her mouth in a sour grimace. "Well! I'll thank you to keep a civil tongue in your head."

"Sorry. I thought I'd seen you before somewhere."

"Well, you haven't." She looked me over coldly. "What happened to your face, anyway?"

"I had a little plastic surgery done. By an amateur surgeon."

She clucked disapprovingly. "If you're looking for a room,

we're full up for the night. I don't believe I'd rent you a room even if we weren't. Look at your clothes."

"Uh-huh. Where's Mr. Salanda?"

"Is it any business of yours?"

"He wants to see me. I'm doing a job for him."

"What kind of a job?"

I mimicked her: "Is it any business of yours?" I was irritated. Under her mounds of flesh she had a personality as thin and hard and abrasive as a rasp.

"Watch who you're getting flip with, sonny boy." She rose, and her shadow loomed immense across the back door of the room. The magazine fell closed on the desk: it was *Teen-age Confessions*. "I am Mrs. Salanda. Are you a handyman?"

"A sort of one," I said. "I'm a garbage collector in the moral field. You look as if you could use me."

The crack went over her head. "Well, you're wrong. And I don't think my husband hired you, either. This is a respectable motel."

"Uh-huh. Are you Ella's mother?"

"I should say not. That little snip is no daughter of mine."

"Her stepmother?"

"Mind your own business. You better get out of here. The police are keeping a close watch on this place tonight, if you're planning any tricks."

"Where's Ella now?"

"I don't know and I don't care. She's probably gallivanting off around the countryside. It's all she's good for. One day at home in the last six months, that's a fine record for a young unmarried girl." Her face was thick and bloated with anger against her stepdaughter. She went on talking blindly, as if she had forgotten me entirely: "I told her father he was an old fool to take her back. How does he know what she's been up to? I say let the ungrateful filly go and fend for herself."

"Is that what you say, Mabel?" Salanda had softly opened the door behind her. He came forward into the room, doubly dwarfed by her blond magnitude. "I say if it wasn't for you, my dear, Ella wouldn't have been driven away from home in the first place."

She turned on him in a blubbering rage. He drew himself up tall and reached to snap his fingers under her nose. "Go back into the house. You are a disgrace to women, a disgrace to motherhood."

"I'm not *her* mother, thank God."

"Thank God," he echoed, shaking his fist at her. She retreated like a schooner under full sail, menaced by a gunboat. The door closed on her. Salanda turned to me:

"I'm sorry, Mr. Archer. I have difficulties with my wife, I

am ashamed to say it. I was an imbecile to marry again. I gained a senseless hulk of flesh, and lost my daughter. Old imbecile!" he denounced himself, wagging his great head sadly. "I married in hot blood. Sexual passion has always been my downfall. It runs in my family, this insane hunger for blonde-ness and stupidity and size." He spread his arms in a wide and futile embrace on emptiness.

"Forget it."

"If I could." He came closer to examine my face. "You are injured, Mr. Archer. Your mouth is damaged. There is blood on your chin."

"I was in a slight brawl."

"On my account?"

"On my own. But I think it's time you leveled with me."

"Leveled with you?"

"Told me the truth. You knew who was shot last night, and who shot him, and why."

He touched my arm, with a quick, tentative grace. "I have only one daughter, Mr. Archer, only the one child. It was my duty to defend her, as best as I could."

"Defend her from what?"

"From shame, from the police, from prison." He flung one arm out, indicating the whole range of human disaster. "I am a man of honor, Mr. Archer. But private honor stands higher with me than public honor. The man was abducting my daughter. She brought him here in the hope of being rescued. Her last hope."

"I think that's true. You should have told me this before."

"I was alarmed, upset. I feared your intentions. Any minute the police were due to arrive."

"But you had a right to shoot him. It wasn't even a crime. The crime was his."

"I didn't know that then. The truth came out to me gradual-ly. I feared that Ella was involved with him." His flat black gaze sought my face and rested on it. "However, I did not shoot him, Mr. Archer. I was not even here at the time. I told you that this morning, and you may take my word for it."

"Was Mrs. Salanda here?"

"No sir, she was not. Why should you ask me that?"

"Donny described the woman who checked in with the dead man. The description fits your wife."

"Donny was lying. I told him to give a false description of the woman. Apparently he was unequal to the task of in-venting one."

"Can you prove that she was with you?"

"Certainly I can. We had reserved seats at the theatre. Those who sat around us can testify that the seats were not empty. Mrs. Salanda and I, we are not an inconspicuous couple." He smiled wryly.

"Ella killed him then."

He neither assented, nor denied it. "I was hoping that you were on my side, my side and Ella's. Am I wrong?"

"I'll have to talk to her, before I know myself. Where is she?"

"I do not know, Mr. Archer, sincerely I do not know. She went away this afternoon, after the policemen questioned her. They were suspicious, but we managed to soothe their suspicions. They did not know that she had just come home, from another life, and I did not tell them. Mabel wanted to tell them. I silenced her." His white teeth clicked together.

"What about Donny?"

"They took him down to the station for questioning. He told them nothing damaging. Donny can appear very stupid when he wishes. He has the reputation of an idiot, but he is not so dumb. Donny has been with me for many years. He has a deep devotion for my daughter. I got him released tonight."

"You should have taken my advice," I said, "taken the police into your confidence. Nothing would have happened to you. The dead man was a mobster, and what he was doing amounts to kidnaping. Your daughter was a witness against his boss."

"She told me that. I am glad that it is true. Ella has not always told me the truth. She has been a hard girl to bring up, without a good mother to set her an example. Where has she been these last six months, Mr. Archer?"

"Singing in a night club in Palm Springs. Her boss was a racketeer."

"A racketeer?" His mouth and nose screwed up, as if he sniffed the odor of corruption.

"Where she was isn't important, compared with where she is now. The boss is still after her. He hired me to look for her."

Salanda regarded me with fear and dislike, as if the odor originated in me. "You let him hire you?"

"It was my best chance of getting out of his place alive. I'm not his boy, if that's what you mean."

"You ask me to believe you?"

"I'm telling you. Ella is in danger. As a matter of fact, we all are." I didn't tell him about the second black Cadillac. Gino would be driving it, wandering the night roads with a ready gun in his armpit and revenge corroding his heart.

"My daughter is aware of the danger," he said. "She warned me of it."

"She must have told you where she was going."

"No. But she may be at the beach house. The house where Donny lives. I will come with you."

"You stay here. Keep your doors locked. If any strangers show and start prowling the place, call the police."

He bolted the door behind me as I went out. Yellow traffic lights cast wan reflections on the asphalt. Streams of cars went by to the north, to the south. To the west, where the sea lay, a great black emptiness opened under the stars. The beach house sat on its white margin, a little over a mile from the motel.

For the second time that day, I knocked on the warped kitchen door. There was light behind it, shining through the cracks. A shadow obscured the light.

"Who is it?" Donny said. Fear or some other emotion had filled his mouth with pebbles.

"You know me, Donny."

The door groaned on its hinges. He gestured dumbly to me to come in, his face a white blur. When he turned his head, and the light from the living room caught his face, I saw that grief was the emotion that marked it. His eyes were swollen as if he had been crying. More than ever he resembled a dilapidated boy whose growing pains had never paid off in manhood.

"Anybody with you?"

Sounds of movement in the living room answered my question. I brushed him aside and went in. Ella Salanda was bent over an open suitcase on the camp cot. She straightened, her mouth thin, eyes wide and dark. The .38 automatic in her hand gleamed dully under the naked bulb suspended from the ceiling.

"I'm getting out of here," she said, "and you're not going to stop me."

"I'm not sure I want to try. Where are you going, Fern?"

Donny spoke behind me, in his grief-thickened voice: "She's going away from me. She promised to stay here if I did what she told me. She promised to be my girl—"

"Shut up, stupid." Her voice cut like a lash, and Donny gasped as if the lash had been laid across his back.

"What did she tell you to do, Donny? Tell me just what you did."

"When she checked in last night with the fella from Detroit, she made a sign I wasn't to let on I knew her. Later on she left me a note. She wrote it with a lipstick on a piece of paper towel. I still got it hidden, in the kitchen."

"What did she write in the note?"

He lingered behind me, fearful of the gun in the girl's hand, more fearful of her anger.

She said: "Don't be crazy, Donny. He doesn't know a thing, not a thing. He can't do anything to either of us."

"I don't care what happens, to me or anybody else," the anguished voice said behind me. "You're running out on me, breaking your promise to me. I always knew it was too good to be true. Now I just don't care any more."

"I care," she said. "I care what happens to me." Her eyes shifted to me, above the unwavering gun. "I won't stay here. I'll shoot you if I have to."

"It shouldn't be necessary. Put it down, Fern. It's Bartolomeo's gun, isn't it? I found the shells to fit it in his glove compartment."

"How do you know so much?"

"I talked to Angel."

"Is he here?" Panic whined in her voice.

"No. I came alone."

"You better leave the same way then, while you can go under your own power."

"I'm staying. You need protection, whether you know it or not. And I need information. Donny, go in the kitchen and bring me that note."

"Don't do it, Donny. I'm warning you."

His sneakered feet made soft indecisive sounds. I advanced on the girl, talking quietly and steadily: "You conspired to kill a man, but you don't have to be afraid. He had it coming. Tell the whole story to the cops, and my guess is they won't even book you. Hell, you can even become famous. The government wants you as a witness in a tax case."

"What kind of a case?"

"A tax case against Angel. It's probably the only kind of rap they can pin on him. You can send him up for the rest of his life like Capone. You'll be a heroine, Fern."

"Don't call me Fern. I hate that name." There were sudden tears in her eyes. "I hate everything connected with that name. I hate myself."

"You'll hate yourself more if you don't put down that gun. Shoot me and it all starts over again. The cops will be on your trail, Angel's troopers will be gunning for you."

Now only the cot was between us, the cot and the unsteady gun facing me above it.

"This is the turning point," I said. "You've made a lot of bum decisions and almost ruined yourself, playing footsie with the evilest men there are. You can go on the way you have been, getting in deeper until you end up in a refrigerated drawer, or you can come back out of it now, into a decent life."

"A decent life? Here? With my father married to Mabel?"

"I don't think Mabel will last much longer. Anyway, I'm not Mabel. I'm on your side."

I waited. She dropped the gun on the blanket. I scooped it up and turned to Donny:

"Let me see that note."

He disappeared through the kitchen door, head and shoulders drooping on the long stalk of his body.

"What could I do?" the girl said. "I was caught. It was Bart or me. All the way up from Acapulco I planned how I could get away. He held a gun in my side when we crossed the border; the same way when we stopped for gas or to eat at the drive-ins. I realized he had to be killed. My father's motel looked like my only chance. So I talked Bart into staying there with me overnight. He had no idea who the place belonged to. I didn't know what I was going to do. I only knew it had to be something drastic. Once I was back with Angel in the desert, that was the end of me. Even if he didn't kill me, it meant I'd have to go on living with him. Anything was better than that. So I wrote a note to Donny in the bathroom, and dropped it out the window. He was always crazy about me."

Her mouth had grown softer. She looked remarkably young and virginal. The faint blue hollows under her eyes were dewy. "Donny shot Bart with Bart's own gun. He had more nerve than I had. I lost my nerve when I went back into the room this morning. I didn't know about the blood in the bathroom. It was the last straw."

She was wrong. Something crashed in the kitchen. A cool draft swept the living room. A gun spoke twice, out of sight. Donny fell backwards through the doorway, a piece of brownish paper clutched in his hand. Blood gleamed on his shoulder like a red badge.

I stepped behind the cot and pulled the girl down to the floor with me. Gino came through the door, his two-colored sports shoe stepping on Donny's laboring chest. I shot the gun out of his hand. He floundered back against the wall, clutching at his wrist.

I sighted carefully for my second shot, until the black bar of his eyebrows was steady in the sights of the .38. The hole it made was invisible. Gino fell loosely forward, prone on the floor beside the man he had killed.

Ella Salanda ran across the room. She knelt, and cradled Donny's head in her lap. Incredible, he spoke, in a loud sighing voice:

"You won't go away again, Ella? I did what you told me. You promised."

"Sure I promised. I won't leave you, Donny. Crazy man. Crazy fool."

"You like me better than you used to? Now?"

"I like you, Donny. You're the most man there is."

She held the poor insignificant head in her hands. He sighed, and his life came out bright-colored at the mouth. It was Donny who went away.

His hand relaxed, and I read the lipstick note she had written him on a piece of porous tissue:

"Donny: This man will kill me unless you kill him first. His gun will be in his clothes on the chair beside the bed. Come in and get it at midnight and shoot to kill. Good luck. I'll stay and be your girl if you do this, just like you always wished. Love. Ella."

I looked at the pair on the floor. She was rocking his lifeless head against her breast. Beside them, Gino looked very small and lonely, a dummy leaking darkness from his brow.

Donny had his wish and I had mine. I wondered what Ella's was.

"Will you call Mrs. Dreen, and tell him to come into
the house for a minute?"

The Bearded Lady

THE UNLATCHED DOOR swung inward when I knocked. I walked
into the studio, which was high and dim as a hayloft. The big
north window in the opposite wall was hung with monkscloth
draperies that shut out the morning light. I found the switch
beside the door and snapped it on. Several fluorescent tubes
suspended from the naked rafters flickered and burnt blue-
white.

A strange woman faced me under the cruel light. She was
only a charcoal sketch on an easel, but she gave me a chill.
Her nude body, posed casually on a chair, was slim and round
and pleasant to look at. Her face wasn't pleasant at all. Bushy
black eyebrows almost hid her eyes. A walrus moustache
bracketed her mouth, and a thick beard fanned down over her
torso.

The door creaked behind me. The girl who appeared in the
doorway wore a starched white uniform. Her face had a little
starch in it, too, though not enough to spoil her good looks
entirely. Her black hair was drawn back severely from her
forehead.

"May I ask what you're doing here?"

"You may ask. I'm looking for Mr. Western."

"Really? Have you tried looking behind the pictures?"

"Does he spend much time there?"

"No, and another thing he doesn't do—he doesn't receive
visitors in his studio when he isn't here himself."

"Sorry. The door was open. I walked in."

"You can reverse the process."

"Just a minute. Hugh isn't sick?"

She glanced down at her white uniform and shook her head.

"Are you a friend of his?" I said.

"I try to be." She smiled slightly. "It isn't always easy, with
a sib. I'm his sister."

"Not the one he was always talking about?"

"I'm the only one he has."

I reached back into my mental grab bag of war souvenirs.
"Mary. The name was Mary."

"It still is Mary. Are *you* a friend of Hugh's?"

"I guess I qualify. I used to be."

"When?" The question was brusque. I got the impression she didn't approve of Hugh's friends, or some of them.

"In the Philippines. He was attached to my group as a combat artist. The name is Archer, by the way. Lew Archer."

"Oh. Of course."

Her disapproval didn't extend to me, at least not yet. She gave me her hand. It was cool and firm, and went with her steady gaze. I said:

"Hugh gave me the wrong impression of you. I thought you were still a kid in school."

"That was four years ago, remember. People grow up in four years. Anyway, some of them do."

She was a very serious girl for her age. I changed the subject.

"I saw the announcement of his show in the L.A. papers. I'm driving through to San Francisco, and I thought I'd look him up."

"I know he'll be glad to see you. I'll go and wake him. He keeps the most dreadful hours. Sit down, won't you, Mr. Archer?"

I had been standing with my back to the bearded nude, more or less consciously shielding her from it. When I moved aside and she saw it, she didn't turn a hair.

"What next?" was all she said.

But I couldn't help wondering what had happened to Hugh Western's sense of humor. I looked around the room for something that might explain the ugly sketch.

It was a typical working artist's studio. The tables and benches were cluttered with things that are used to make pictures: palettes and daubed sheets of glass, sketch pads, scratchboards, bleeding tubes of paint. Pictures in half a dozen mediums and half a dozen stages of completion hung or leaned against the burlap-covered walls. Some of them looked wild and queer to me, but none so wild and queer as the sketch on the easel.

There was one puzzling thing in the room, besides the pictures. The wooden doorframe was scarred with a row of deep round indentations, four of them. They were new, and about on a level with my eyes. They looked as if an incredible fist had struck the wood a superhuman blow.

"He isn't in his room," the girl said from the doorway. Her voice was very carefully controlled.

"Maybe he got up early."

"His bed hasn't been slept in. He's been out all night."

"I wouldn't worry. He's an adult after all."

"Yes, but he doesn't always act like one." Some feeling buzzed under her calm tone. I couldn't tell if it was fear or anger. "He's twelve years older than I am, and still a boy at heart. A middle-aging boy."

"I know what you mean. I was his unofficial keeper for a while. I guess he's a genius, or pretty close to it, but he needs somebody to tell him to come in out of the rain."

"Thank you for informing me. I didn't know."

"Now don't get mad at me."

"I'm sorry. I suppose I'm a little upset."

"Has he been giving you a bad time?"

"Not really. Not lately, that is. He's come down to earth since he got engaged to Alice. But he still makes the weirdest friends. He can tell a fake Van Gogh with his eyes shut, literally, but he's got no discrimination about people at all."

"You wouldn't be talking about me? Or am I having ideas of reference?"

"No." She smiled again. I liked her smile. "I guess I acted terribly suspicious when I walked in on you. Some pretty dubious characters come to see him."

"Anyone in particular?" I said it lightly. Just above her head I could see the giant fist-mark on the doorframe.

Before she could answer, a siren bayed in the distance. She cocked her head. "Ten to one it's for me."

"Police?"

"Ambulance. The police sirens have a different tone. I'm an X-ray technician at the hospital, so I've learned to listen for the ambulance. And I'm on call this morning."

I followed her into the hall. "Hugh's show opens tonight. He's bound to come back for that."

She turned at the opposite door, her face brightening. "You know, he may have spent the night working in the gallery. He's awfully fussy about how his pictures are hung."

"Why don't I phone the gallery?"

"There's never anybody in the office till nine." She looked at her unfeminine steel wristwatch. "It's twenty to."

"When did you last see him?"

"At dinner last night. We ate early. He went back to the gallery after dinner. He said he was only going to work a couple of hours."

"And you stayed here?"

"Until about eight, when I was called to the hospital. I didn't get home until quite late, and I thought he was in bed." She looked at me uncertainly, with a little wrinkle of doubt between her straight eyebrows. "Could you be cross-questioning me?"

"Sorry. It's my occupational disease."

"What do you do in real life?"

"Isn't this real?"

"I mean now you're out of the army. Are you a lawyer?"

"A private detective."

"Oh. I see." The wrinkle between her eyebrows deepened. I wondered what she'd been reading.

"But I'm on vacation." I hoped.

A phone burred behind her apartment door. She went to answer it, and came back wearing a coat. "It *was* for me. Somebody fell out of a loquat tree and broke a leg. You'll have to excuse me, Mr. Archer."

"Wait a second. If you'll tell me where the art gallery is, I'll see if Hugh's there now."

"Of course, you don't know San Marcos."

She led me to the French windows at the rear end of the hall. They opened on a blacktop parking space which was over-shadowed on the far side by a large stucco building, the shape of a flattened cube. Outside the windows was a balcony from which a concrete staircase slanted down to the parking lot. She stepped outside and pointed to the stucco cube:

"That's the gallery. It's no problem to find, is it? You can take a shortcut down the alley to the front."

A tall young man in a black leotard was polishing a red convertible in the parking lot. He struck a pose, in the fifth position, and waved his hand:

"Bonjour, Marie."

"Bonjour, my phony Frenchman." There was an edge of contempt on her good humor. "Have you seen Hugh this morning?"

"Not I. Is the prodigal missing again?"

"I wouldn't say missing—"

"I was wondering where your car was. It's not in the garage." His voice was much too musical.

"Who's he?" I asked her in an undertone.

"Hilary Todd. He runs the art shop downstairs. If the car's gone, Hugh can't be at the gallery. I'll have to take a taxi to the hospital."

"I'll drive you."

"I wouldn't think of it. There's a cabstand across the street." She added over her shoulder: "Call me at the hospital if you see Hugh."

I went down the stairs to the parking lot. Hilary Todd was still polishing the hood of his convertible, though it shone like a mirror. His shoulders were broad and packed with shifting muscle. Some of the ballet boys were strong and could be dangerous. Not that he was a boy, exactly. He had a little round bald spot that gleamed like a silver dollar among his hair.

"Bonjour," I said to his back.

"Yes?"

My French appeared to offend his ears. He turned and

straightened. I saw how tall he was, tall enough to make me feel squat, though I was over six feet. He had compensated for the bald spot by growing sideburns. In combination with his liquid eyes, they gave him a Latin look. Pig Latin.

"Do you know Hugh Western pretty well?"

"If it's any concern of yours."

"It is."

"Now why would that be?"

"I asked the question, sonny. Answer it."

He blushed and lowered his eyes, as if I had been reading his evil thoughts. He stuttered a little. "I—I—well, I've lived below him for a couple of years. I've sold a few of his pictures. Why?"

"I thought you might know where he is, even if his sister doesn't."

"How should I know where he is? Are you a policeman?"

"Not exactly."

"Not at all, you mean?" He regained his poise. "Then you have no right to take this overbearing attitude. I know absolutely nothing about Hugh. And I'm very busy."

He turned abruptly and continued his polishing job, his fine useless muscles writhing under the leotard.

I walked down the narrow alley which led to the street. Through the cypress hedge on the left, I caught a glimpse of umbrella tables growing like giant multicolored mushrooms in a restaurant patio. On the other side was the wall of the gallery, its white blankness broken by a single iron-barred window above the level of my head.

The front of the gallery was Greek-masked by a high-pillared porch. A broad flight of concrete steps rose to it from the street. A girl was standing at the head of the steps, half leaning on one of the pillars.

She turned towards me, and the slanting sunlight aureoled her bare head. She had a startling kind of beauty: yellow hair, light hazel eyes, brown skin. She filled her tailored suit like sand in a sack.

"Good morning."

She pretended not to hear me. Her right foot was tapping the pavement impatiently. I crossed the porch to the high bronze door and pushed. It didn't give.

"There's nobody here yet," she said. "The gallery doesn't open until ten."

"Then what are you doing here?"

"I happen to work here."

"Why don't you open up?"

"I have no key. In any case," she added primly, "we don't allow visitors before ten."

"I'm not a tourist, at least at the moment. I came to see Mr. Western."

"Hugh?" She looked at me directly for the first time. "Hugh's not here. He lives around the corner on Rubio Street."

"I just came from there."

"Well, he isn't here." She gave the words a curious emphasis. "There's nobody here but me. And I won't be here much longer if Dr. Silliman doesn't come."

"Silliman?"

"Dr. Silliman is our curator." She made it sound as if she owned the gallery. After a while she said in a softer voice: "Why are you looking for Hugh? Do you have some business with him?"

"Western's an old friend of mine."

"Really?"

She lost interest in the conversation. We stood together in silence for several minutes. She was tapping her foot again. I watched the Saturday-morning crowd on the street: women in slacks, women in shorts and dirndls, a few men in ten-gallon hats, a few in berets. A large minority of the people had Spanish or Indian faces. Nearly half the cars in the road carried out-of-state licenses. San Marcos was a unique blend of western border town, ocean resort, and artists' colony.

A small man in a purple corduroy jacket detached himself from the crowd and bounded up the steps. His movements were quick as a monkey's. His lined face had a simian look, too. A brush of frizzled gray hair added about three inches to his height.

"I'm sorry if I kept you waiting, Alice."

She made a *nada* gesture. "It's perfectly all right. This gentleman is a friend of Hugh's."

He turned to me. His smile went on and off. "Good morning, sir. What was the name?"

I told him. He shook my hand. His fingers were like thin steel hooks.

"Western ought to be here at any minute. Have you tried his flat?"

"Yes. His sister thought he might have spent the night in the gallery."

"Oh, but that's impossible. You mean he didn't come home last night?"

"Apparently not."

"You didn't tell me that," the blond girl said.

"I didn't know you were interested."

"Alice has every right to be interested." Silliman's eyes glowed with a gossip's second-hand pleasure. "She and Hugh are going to be married. Next month, isn't it, Alice? Do you know Miss Turner, by the way, Mr. Archer?"

"Hello, Mr. Archer." Her voice was shallow and hostile. I gathered that Silliman had embarrassed her.

"I'm sure he'll be along shortly," he said reassuringly. "We still have some work to do on the program for the private showing tonight. Will you come in and wait?"

I said I would.

He took a heavy key ring out of his jacket pocket and unlocked the bronze door, relocking it behind us. Alice Turner touched a switch which lit up the high-ceilinged lobby and the Greek statues standing like frozen sentinels along the walls. There were several nymphs and Venuses in marble, but I was more interested in Alice. She had everything the Venuses had, and the added advantage of being alive. She also had Hugh Western, it seemed, and that surprised me. He was a little old for her, and a little used. She didn't look like one of those girls who'd have to settle for an aging bachelor. But then Hugh Western had talent.

She removed a bundle of letters from the mail box and took them into the office which opened off the lobby. Silliman turned to me with a monkey grin.

"She's quite a girl, is she not? Trust Hugh to draw a circle around the prettiest girl in town. And she comes from a very good family, an excellent family. Her father, the Admiral, is one of our trustees, you know, and Alice has inherited his interest in the arts. Of course she has a more personal interest now. Had you known of their engagement?"

"I haven't seen Hugh for years, not since the war."

"Then I should have held my tongue and let him tell you himself."

As we were talking, he led me through the central gallery, which ran the length of the building like the nave of a church. To the left and right, in what would have been the aisles, the walls of smaller exhibition rooms rose halfway to the ceiling. Above them was a mezzanine reached by an open iron staircase.

He started up it, still talking: "If you haven't seen Hugh since the war, you'll be interested in the work he's been doing lately."

I was interested, though not for artistic reasons. The wall of of the mezzanine was hung with twenty-odd paintings: landscapes, portraits, groups of semi-abstract figures, and more abstract still lifes. I recognized some of the scenes he had sketched in the Philippine jungle, transposed into the permanence of oil. In the central position there was a portrait of a bearded man whom I'd hardly have known without the label, "Self-Portrait."

Hugh had changed. He had put on weight and lost his youth entirely. There were vertical lines in the forehead, gray flecks in the hair and beard. The light eyes seemed to be smiling sardonically. But when I looked at them from another angle, they were bleak and somber. It was a face a man might see in his bathroom mirror on a cold gray hangover morning.

I turned to the curator hovering at my elbow. "When did he raise the beard?"

"A couple of years ago, I believe, shortly after he joined us as resident painter."

"Is he obsessed with beards?"

"I don't quite know what you mean."

"Neither do I. But I came across a funny thing in his studio this morning. A sketch of a woman, a nude, with a heavy black beard. Does that make sense to you?"

The old man smiled. "I've long since given up trying to make sense of Hugh. He has his own esthetic logic, I suppose. But I'd have to see this sketch before I could form an opinion. He may have simply been doodling."

"I doubt it. It was big, and carefully done." I brought out the question that had been nagging at the back of my mind. "Is there something the matter with him, emotionally? He hasn't gone off the deep end?"

His answer was sharp. "Certainly not. He's simply wrapped up in his work, and he lives by impulse. He's never on time for appointments." He looked at his watch. "He promised last night to meet me here this morning at nine, and it's almost nine-thirty."

"When did you see him last night?"

"I left the key of the gallery with him when I went home for dinner. He wanted to rehang some of these paintings. About eight or a little after he walked over to my house to return the key. We have only the one key, since we can't afford a watchman."

"Did he say where he was going after that?"

"He had an appointment, he didn't say with whom. It seemed to be urgent, since he wouldn't stop for a drink. Well." He glanced at his watch again. "I suppose I'd better be getting down to work, Western or no Western."

Alice was waiting for us at the foot of the stairs. Both of her hands gripped the wrought-iron bannister. Her voice was no more than a whisper, but it seemed to fill the great room with leaden echoes:

"Dr. Silliman, the Chardin's gone."

He stopped so suddenly I nearly ran into him. "That's impossible."

"I know. But it's gone, frame and all."

He bounded down the remaining steps and disappeared into one of the smaller rooms under the mezzanine. Alice followed him more slowly. I caught up with her:

"There's a picture missing?"

"Father's best picture, one of the best Chardins in the country. He loaned it to the gallery for a month."

"Is it worth a lot of money?"

"Yes, it's very valuable. But it means a lot more to Father than the money—" She turned in the doorway and gave me a closed look, as if she'd realized she was telling her family secrets to a stranger.

Silliman was standing with his back to us, staring at a blank space on the opposite wall. He looked badly shaken when he turned around.

"I *told* the board that we should install a burglar alarm— the insurance people recommended it. But Admiral Turner was the only one who supported me. Now of course they'll be blaming me." His nervous eyes roved around and paused on Alice. "And what is your father going to say?"

"He'll be sick." She looked sick herself.

They were getting nowhere, and I cut in: "When did you see it last?"

Silliman answered me. "Yesterday afternoon, about five-thirty. I showed it to a visitor just before we closed. We check the visitors very closely from the office, since we have no guards."

"Who was the visitor?"

"A lady—an elderly lady from Pasadena. She's above suspicion, of course. I escorted her out myself, and she was the last one in, I know for a fact."

"Aren't you forgetting Hugh?"

"By George, I was. He was here until eight last night. But you surely don't suggest that Western took it? He's our resident painter, he's devoted to the gallery."

"He might have been careless. If he was working on the mezzanine and left the door unlocked—"

"He always kept it locked," Alice said coldly. "Hugh isn't careless about the things that matter."

"Is there another entrance?"

"No," Silliman said. "The building was planned for security. There's only the one window in my office, and it's heavily barred. We do have an air-conditioning system, but the inlets are much too small for anyone to get through."

"Let's have a look at the window."

The old man was too upset to question my authority. He led me through a storeroom stacked with old gilt-framed pictures whose painters deserved to be hung, if the pictures didn't. The single casement in the office was shut and bolted behind a Venetian blind. I pulled the cord and peered out through the dusty glass. The vertical bars outside the window were no more than three inches apart. None of them looked as if it had been tampered with. Across the alley, I could see a few tourists obliviously eating breakfast behind the restaurant hedge.

Silliman was leaning on the desk, one hand on the cradle phone. Indecision was twisting his face out of shape. "I do hate to call the police in a matter like this. I suppose I must, though, mustn't I?"

Alice covered his hand with hers, the line of her back a taut curve across the desk. "Hadn't you better talk to Father first? He was here with Hugh last night—I should have remembered before. It's barely possible he took the Chardin home with him."

"Really? You really think so?" Silliman let go of the telephone and clasped his hands hopefully under his chin.

"It wouldn't be like Father to do that without letting you know. But the month is nearly up, isn't it?"

"Three more days." His hand returned to the phone. "Is the Admiral at home?"

"He'll be down at the club by now. Do you have your car?"

"Not this morning."

I made one of my famous quick decisions, the kind you wake up in the middle of the night reconsidering five years later. San Francisco could wait. My curiosity was touched, and something deeper than curiosity. Something of the responsibility I'd felt for Hugh in the Philippines, when I was the practical one and he was the evergreen adolescent who thought the jungle was as safe as a scene by Le Douanier Rousseau. Though we were nearly the same age, I'd felt like his elder brother. I still did.

"My car's around the corner," I said. "I'll be glad to drive you."

The San Marcos Beach Club was a long low building painted an unobtrusive green and standing well back from the road. Everything about it was unobtrusive, including the private policeman who stood inside the plate-glass doors and watched us come up the walk.

"Looking for the Admiral, Miss Turner? I think he's up on the north deck."

We crossed a tiled lanai shaded with potted palms, and climbed a flight of stairs to a sun deck lined with cabanas. I

could see the mountains that walled the city off from the
desert in the northeast, and the sea below with its waves
glinting like blue fish scales. The swimming pool on the lee
side of the deck was still and clear.

Admiral Turner was taking the sun in a canvas chair. He
stood up when he saw us, a big old man in shorts and a sleeve-
less shirt. Sun and wind had reddened his face and crinkled the
flesh around his eyes. Age had slackened his body, but there
was nothing aged or infirm about his voice. It still held the
brazen echo of command.

"What's this, Alice? I thought you were at work."

"We came to ask you a question, Admiral." Silliman hesitated, coughing behind his hand. He looked at Alice.

"Speak out, man. Why is everybody looking so green
around the gills?"

Silliman forced the words out: "Did you take the Chardin
home with you last night?"

"I did not. Is it gone?"

"It's missing from the gallery," Alice said. She held herself uncertainly, as though the old man frightened her a little.
"We thought you might have taken it."

"Me take it? That's absurd! Absolutely absurd and prepos-
terous!" The short white hair bristled on his head. "When
was it taken?"

"We don't know. It was gone when we opened the gallery.
We discovered it just now."

"God damn it, what goes on?" He glared at her and then
he glared at me, from eyes like round blue gun muzzles. "And
who the hell are you?"

He was only a retired admiral, and I'd been out of uniform
for years, but he gave me a qualm. Alice put in:

"A friend of Hugh's, Father. Mr. Archer."

He didn't offer his hand. I looked away. A woman in a
white bathing suit was poised on the ten-foot board at the end
of the pool. She took three quick steps and a bounce. Her
body hung jack-knifed in the air, straightened and dropped,
cut the water with hardly a splash.

"Where is Hugh?" the Admiral said petulantly. "If this
is some of his carelessness, I'll ream the bastard."

"Father!"

"Don't father me. Where is he, Allie? You ought to know
if anyone does."

"But I don't." She added in a small voice: "He's been gone
all night."

"He has?" The old man sat down suddenly, as if his legs
were too weak to bear the weight of his feelings. "He didn't
say anything to me about going away."

The woman in the white bathing suit came up the steps behind him. "Who's gone away?" she said.

The Admiral craned his wattled neck to look at her. She was worth the effort from anyone, though she wouldn't see thirty again. Her dripping body was tanned and disciplined, full in the right places and narrow in the others. I didn't remember her face, but her shape seemed familiar. Silliman introduced her as Admiral Turner's wife. When she pulled off her rubber cap, her red hair flared like a minor conflagration.

"You won't believe what they've been telling me, Sarah. My Chardin's been stolen."

"Which one?"

"I've only the one. The 'Apple on a Table'."

She turned on Silliman like a pouncing cat. "Is it insured?"

"For twenty-five thousand dollars. But I'm afraid it's irreplaceable."

"And who's gone away?"

"Hugh has," Alice said. "Of course it's nothing to do with the picture."

"You're sure?" She turned to her husband with an intensity that made her almost ungainly. "Hugh was at the gallery when you dropped in there last night. You told me so yourself. And hasn't he been trying to buy the Chardin?"

"I don't believe it," Alice said flatly. "He didn't have the money."

"I know that perfectly well. He was acting as agent for someone. Wasn't he, Johnston?"

"Yes," the old man admitted. "He wouldn't tell me who his principal was, which is one of the reasons I wouldn't listen to the offer. Still, it's foolish to jump to conclusions about Hugh. I was with him when he left the gallery, and I know for a fact he didn't have the Chardin. It was the last thing I looked at."

"What time did he leave you?"

"Some time around eight—I don't remember exactly." He seemed to be growing older and smaller under her questioning. "He walked with me as far as my car."

"There was nothing to prevent him from walking right back."

"I don't know what you're trying to prove," Alice said.

The older woman smiled poisonously. "I'm simply trying to bring out the facts, so we'll know what to do. I notice that no one has suggested calling in the police." She looked at each of the others in turn. "Well? Do we call them? Or do we assume as a working hypothesis that dear Hugh took the picture?"

Nobody answered her for a while. The Admiral finally

broke the ugly silence. "We can't bring in the authorities if
Hugh's involved. He's virtually a member of the family."

Alice put a grateful hand on his shoulder, but Silliman said
uneasily, "We'll have to take some steps. If we don't make
an effort to recover it, we may not be able to collect the insurance."

"I realize that," the Admiral said. "We'll have to take that
chance."

Sarah Turner smiled with tight-lipped complacency. She'd
won her point, though I still wasn't sure what her point was.
During the family argument I'd moved a few feet away, leaning on the railing at the head of the stairs and pretending not
to listen.

She moved towards me now, her narrow eyes appraising me
as if maleness was a commodity she prized.

"And who are you?" she said, her sharp smile widening.

I identified myself. I didn't smile back. But she came up
very close to me. I could smell the chlorine on her, and under
it the not so very subtle odor of sex.

"You look uncomfortable," she said. "Why don't you come
swimming with me?"

"My hydrophobia won't let me. Sorry."

"What a pity. I hate to do things alone."

Silliman nudged me gently. He said in an undertone: "I
really must be getting back to the gallery. I can call a cab if
you prefer."

"No, I'll drive you." I wanted a chance to talk to him in
private.

There were quick footsteps in the patio below. I looked
down and saw the naked crown of Hilary Todd's head. At
almost the same instant he glanced up at us. He turned abruptly and started to walk away, then changed his mind when
Silliman called down.

"Hello there. Are you looking for the Turners?"

"As a matter of fact, I am."

From the corner of my eye, I noticed Sarah Turner's reaction to the sound of his voice. She stiffened, and her hand
went up to her flaming hair.

"They're up here," Silliman said.

Todd climbed the stairs with obvious reluctance. We passed
him going down. In a pastel shirt and a matching tie under a
bright tweed jacket he looked very elegant, and very self-
conscious and tense. Sarah Turner met him at the head of
the stairs. I wanted to linger a bit, for eavesdropping purposes,
but Silliman hustled me out.

"Mrs. Turner seems very much aware of Todd," I said to
him in the car. "Do they have things in common?"

He answered tartly: "I've never considered the question. They're no more than casual acquaintances, so far as I know."

"What about Hugh? Is he just a casual acquaintance of hers, too?"

He studied me for a minute as the convertible picked up speed. "You notice things, don't you?"

"Noticing things is my business."

"Just what is your business? You're not an artist?"

"Hardly. I'm a private detective."

"A detective?" He jumped in the seat, as if I had offered to bite him. "You're not a friend of Western's then? Are you from the insurance company?"

"Not me. I'm a friend of Hugh's, and that's my only interest in this case. I more or less stumbled into it."

"I see." But he sounded a little dubious.

"Getting back to Mrs. Turner—she didn't make that scene with her husband for fun. She must have had some reason. Love or hate."

Silliman held his tongue for a minute, but he couldn't resist a chance to gossip. "I expect that it's a mixture of love and hate. She's been interested in Hugh ever since the Admiral brought her here. She's not a San Marcos girl, you know." He seemed to take comfort from that. "She was a Wave officer in Washington during the war. The Admiral noticed her —Sarah knows how to make herself conspicuous—and added her to his personal staff. When he retired he married her and came here to live in his family home. Alice's mother has been dead for many years. Well, Sarah hadn't been here two months before she was making eyes at Hugh." He pressed his lips together in spinsterly disapproval. "The rest is local history."

"They had an affair?"

"A rather one-sided affair, so far as I could judge. She was quite insane about him. I don't believe he responded, except in the physical sense. Your friend is quite a demon with the ladies." There was a whisper of envy in Silliman's disapproval.

"But I understood he was going to marry Alice."

"Oh, he is, he is. At least he certainly was until this dreadful business came up. His—ah—involvement with Sarah occurred before he knew Alice. She was away at art school until a few months ago."

"Does Alice know about his affair with her stepmother?"

"I daresay she does. I hear the two women don't get along at all well, though there may be other reasons for that. Alice refuses to live in the same house; she's moved into the gardener's cottage behind the Turner house. I think her trouble with Sarah is one reason why she came to work for me. Of course, there's the money consideration, too. The family isn't well off."

"I thought they were rolling in it," I said, "from the way he brushed off the matter of the insurance. Twenty-five thousand dollars, did you say?"

"Yes. He's quite fond of Hugh."

"If he's not well heeled, how does he happen to have such a valuable painting?"

"It was a gift, when he married his first wife. Her father was in the French Embassy in Washington, and he gave them the Chardin as a wedding present. You can understand the Admiral's attachment to it."

"Better than I can his decision not to call in the police. How do you feel about that, doctor?"

He didn't answer for a while. We were nearing the center of the city and I had to watch the traffic. I couldn't keep track of what went on in his face.

"After all it *is* his picture," he said carefully. "And his prospective son-in-law."

"You don't think Hugh's responsible, though?"

"I don't know what to think. I'm thoroughly rattled. And I won't know what to think until I have a chance to talk to Western." He gave me a sharp look. "Are you going to make a search for him?"

"Somebody has to. I seem to be elected."

When I let him out in front of the gallery, I asked him where Mary Western worked.

"The City Hospital." He told me how to find it. "But you will be discreet, Mr. Archer? You won't do or say anything rash? I'm in a very delicate position."

"I'll be very suave and bland." But I slammed the door hard in his face.

There were several patients in the X-ray waiting room, in various stages of dilapidation and disrepair. The plump blonde at the reception desk told me that Miss Western was in the dark room. Would I wait? I sat down and admired the way her sunburned shoulders glowed through her nylon uniform. In a few minutes Mary came into the room, starched and controlled and efficient-looking. She blinked in the strong light from the window. I got a quick impression that there was a lost child hidden behind her façade.

"Have you seen Hugh?"

"No. Come out for a minute." I took her elbow and drew her into the corridor.

"What is it?" Her voice was quiet, but it had risen in pitch. "Has something happened to him?"

"Not to *him*. Admiral Turner's picture's been stolen from the gallery. The Chardin."

"But how does Hugh come into this?"

"Somebody seems to think he took it."

"Somebody?"

"Mrs. Turner, to be specific."

"*Sarah!* She'd say anything to get back at him for ditching her."

I filed that one away. "Maybe so. The fact is, the Admiral seems to suspect him, too. So much so that he's keeping the police out of it."

"Admiral Turner is a senile fool. If Hugh were here to defend himself—"

"But that's the point. He isn't."

"I've got to find him." She turned towards the door.

"It may not be so easy."

She looked back in quick anger, her round chin prominent. "You suspect him, too."

"I do not. But a crime's been committed, remember. Crimes often come in pairs."

She turned, her eyes large and very dark. "You do think something has happened to my brother."

"I don't think anything. But if I were certain that he's all right, I'd be on my way to San Francisco now."

"You believe it's as bad as that," she said in a whisper. "I've got to go to the police."

"It's up to you. You'll want to keep them out of it, though, if there's the slightest chance—" I left the sentence unfinished.

She finished it: "That Hugh is a thief? There isn't. But I'll tell you what we'll do. He may be up at his shack in the mountains. He's gone off there before without telling anyone. Will you drive up with me?" She laid a light hand on my arm. "I can go myself if you have to get away."

"I'm sticking around," I said. "Can you get time off?"

"I'm taking it. All they can do is fire me, and there aren't enough good technicians to go around. Anyway, I put in three hours' overtime last night. Be with you in two minutes."

And she was.

I put the top of the convertible down. As we drove out of the city the wind blew away her smooth glaze of efficiency, colored her cheeks and loosened her sleek hair.

"You should do this oftener," I said.

"Do what?"

"Get out in the country and relax."

"I'm not exactly relaxed, with my brother accused of theft, and missing into the bargain."

"Anyway, you're not working. Has it ever occurred to you that perhaps you work too hard?"

"Has it ever occurred to you that somebody has to work or nothing will get done? You and Hugh are more alike than I thought."

"In some ways that's a compliment. You make it sound like an insult."

"I didn't mean it that way, exactly. But Hugh and I are so different. I admit he works hard at his painting, but he's never tried to make a steady living. Since I left school, I've had to look after the bread and butter for both of us. His salary as resident painter keeps him in artist's supplies, and that's about all."

"I thought he was doing well. His show's had a big advance buildup in the L.A. papers."

"Critics don't buy pictures," she said bluntly. "He's having the show to try to sell some paintings, so he can afford to get married. Hugh has suddenly realized that money is one of the essentials." She added with some bitterness, "The realization came a little late."

"He's been doing some outside work, though, hasn't he? Isn't he a part-time agent or something?"

"For Hendryx, yes." She made the name sound like a dirty word. "I'd just as soon he didn't take any of that man's money."

"Who's Hendryx?"

"A man."

"I gathered that. What's the matter with his money?"

"I really don't know. I have no idea where it comes from. But he has it."

"You don't like him?"

"No. I don't like him, and I don't like the men who work for him. They look like a gang of thugs to me. But Hugh wouldn't notice that. He's horribly dense where people are concerned. I don't mean that Hugh's done anything wrong," she added quickly. "He's bought a few paintings for Hendryx on commission."

"I see." I didn't like what I saw, but I named it. "The Admiral said something about Hugh trying to buy the Chardin for an unnamed purchaser. Would that be Hendryx?"

"It could be," she said.

"Tell me more about Hendryx."

"I don't know any more. I only met him once. That was enough. I know that he's an evil old man, and he has a body-guard who carries him upstairs."

"Carries him upstairs?"

"Yes. He's crippled. As a matter of fact, he offered me a job."

"Carrying him upstairs?"

"He didn't specify my duties. He didn't get that far." Her voice was so chilly it quick-froze the conversation. "Now could we drop the subject, Mr. Archer?"

The road had begun to rise towards the mountains. Yellow and black Slide Area signs sprang up along the shoulders. By holding the gas pedal nearly to the floor, I kept our speed around fifty.

"You've had quite a busy morning," Mary said after a while, "meeting the Turners and all."

"Social mobility is my stock in trade."

"Did you meet Alice, too?"

I said I had.

"And what did you think of her?"

"I shouldn't say it to another girl, but she's a lovely one."

"Vanity isn't one of my vices," Mary said. "She's beautiful. And she's really devoted to Hugh."

"I gathered that."

"I don't think Alice has ever been in love before. And painting means almost as much to her as it does to him."

"He's a lucky man." I remembered the disillusioned eyes of the self-portrait, and hoped that his luck was holding.

The road twisted and climbed through red clay cutbanks and fields of dry chaparral.

"How long does this go on?" I asked.

"It's about another two miles."

We zigzagged up the mountainside for ten or twelve minutes more. Finally the road began to level out. I was watching its edge so closely that I didn't see the cabin until we were almost on top of it. It was a one-story frame building standing in a little hollow at the edge of the high mesa. Attached to one side was an open tarpaulin shelter from which the rear end of a gray coupe protruded. I looked at Mary.

She nodded. "It's our car." Her voice was bright with relief.

I stopped the convertible in the lane in front of the cabin. As soon as the engine died, the silence began. A single hawk high over our heads swung round and round on his invisible wire. Apart from that, the entire world seemed empty. As we walked down the ill-kept gravel drive, I was startled by the sound of my own footsteps.

The door was unlocked. The cabin had only one room. It was a bachelor hodgepodge, untouched by the human hand for months at a time. Cooking utensils, paint-stained dungarees and painter's tools and bedding were scattered on the floor and furniture. There was an open bottle of whiskey, half empty, on the kitchen table in the center of the room. It would have been just another mountain shack if it hadn't been for the watercolors on the walls, like brilliant little windows, and the one big window which opened on the sky.

Mary had crossed to the window and was looking out. I moved up to her shoulder. Blue space fell away in front of us all the way down to the sea, and beyond to the curved horizon. San Marcos and its suburbs were spread out like an air map between the sea and the mountains.

"I wonder where he can be," she said. "Perhaps he's gone for a hike. After all, he doesn't know we're looking for him."

I looked down the mountainside, which fell almost sheer from the window.

"No," I said. "He doesn't."

The red clay slope was sown with boulders. Nothing grew there except a few dust-colored mountain bushes. And a foot, wearing a man's shoe, which projected from a cleft between two rocks.

I went out without a word. A path led round the cabin to the edge of the slope. Hugh Western was there, attached to the solitary foot. He was lying, or hanging, head down with his face in the clay, about twenty feet below the edge. One of his legs was doubled under him. The other was caught between the boulders. I climbed around the rocks and bent down to look at his head.

The right temple was smashed. The face was smashed; I raised the rigid body to look at it. He had been dead for hours, but the sharp strong odor of whiskey still hung around him.

A tiny gravel avalanche rattled past me. Mary was at the top of the slope.

"Don't come down here."

She paid no attention to the warning. I stayed where I was, crouched over the body, trying to hide the ruined head from her. She leaned over the boulder and looked down, her eyes bright black in her drained face. I moved to one side. She took her brother's head in her hands.

"If you pass out," I said, "I don't know whether I can carry you up."

"I won't pass out."

She lifted the body by the shoulders to look at the face. It was a little unsettling to see how strong she was. Her fingers moved gently over the wounded temple. "This is what killed him. It looks like a blow from a fist."

I kneeled down beside her and saw the row of rounded indentations in the skull.

"He must have fallen," she said, "and struck his head on the rocks. Nobody could have hit him that hard."

"I'm afraid somebody did, though." Somebody whose fist was hard enough to leave its mark in wood.

Two long hours later I parked my car in front of the art shop on Rubio Street. Its windows were jammed with Impressionist and Post-Impressionist reproductions, and one very bad original oil of surf as stiff and static as whipped cream. The sign above the windows was lettered in flowing script: *Chez Hilary*. The cardboard sign on the door was simpler and to the point; it said: *Closed*.

The stairs and hallway seemed dark, but it was good to get out of the sun. The sun reminded me of what I had found at high noon on the mesa. It wasn't the middle of the afternoon yet, but my nerves felt stretched and scratchy, as though it was late at night. My eyes were aching.

Mary unlocked the door of her apartment, stepped aside to let me pass. She paused at the door of her room to tell me there was whiskey on the sideboard. I offered to make her a drink. No, thanks, she never drank. The door shut behind her. I mixed a whiskey and water and tried to relax in an easy chair. I couldn't relax. My mind kept playing back the questions and the answers, and the questions that had no answers.

We had called the sheriff from the nearest firewarden's post, and led him and his deputies back up the mountain to the body. Photographs were taken, the cabin and its surroundings searched, many questions asked. Mary didn't mention the lost Chardin. Neither did I.

Some of the questions were answered after the county coroner arrived. Hugh Western had been dead since sometime between eight and ten o'clock the previous night; the coroner couldn't place the time more definitely before analyzing the stomach contents. The blow on the temple had killed him. The injuries to his face, which had failed to bleed, had probably been inflicted after death. Which meant that he was dead when his body fell or was thrown down the mountainside.

His clothes had been soaked with whiskey to make it look like a drunken accident. But the murderer had gone too far in covering, and outwitted himself. The whiskey bottle in the cabin showed no fingerprints, not even Western's. And there were no fingerprints on the steering wheel of his coupe. Bottle and wheel had been wiped clean.

I stood up when Mary came back into the room. She had brushed her black hair gleaming, and changed to a dress of soft black jersey which fitted her like skin. A thought raced through my mind like a nasty little rodent. I wondered what she would look like with a beard.

"Can I have another look at the studio? I'm interested in that sketch."

She looked at me for a moment, frowning a little dazedly. "Sketch?"

"The one of the lady with the beard."

She crossed the hall ahead of me, walking slowly and carefully as if the floor were unsafe and a rapid movement might plunge her into black chaos. The door of the studio was still unlocked. She held it open for me and pressed the light switch.

When the fluorescent lights blinked on, I saw that the bearded nude was gone. There was nothing left of her but the four torn corners of the drawing paper thumbtacked to the empty easel. I turned to Mary.

"Did you take it down?"

"No. I haven't been in the studio since this morning."

"Somebody's stolen it then. Is there anything else missing?"

"I can't be sure, it's such a mess in here." She moved around the room looking at the pictures on the walls and pausing finally by a table in the corner. "There was a bronze cast on this table. It isn't here now."

"What sort of a cast?"

"The cast of a fist. Hugh made it from the fist of that man —that dreadful man I told you about."

"What dreadful man?"

"I think his name is Devlin. He's Hendryx' bodyguard. Hugh's always been interested in hands, and the man has enormous hands."

Her eyes unfocused suddenly. I guessed she was thinking of the same thing I was: the marks on the side of Hugh's head, which might have been made by a giant fist.

"Look." I pointed to the scars on the doorframe. "Could the cast of Devlin's fist have made these marks?"

She felt the indentations with trembling fingers. "I think so —I don't know." She turned to me with a dark question in her eyes.

"If that's what they are," I said, "it probably means that he was killed in this studio. You should tell the police about it. And I think it's time they knew about the Chardin."

She gave me a look of passive resistance. Then she gave in. "Yes, I'll have to tell them. They'll find out soon enough, anyway. But I'm surer now than ever that Hugh didn't take it."

"What does the picture look like? If we could find it, we might find the killer attached to it."

"You think so? Well, it's a picture of a little boy looking at an apple. Wait a minute: Hilary has a copy. It was painted by one of the students at the college, and it isn't very expert. It'll give you an idea, though, if you want to go down to his shop and look at it."

"The shop is closed."

"He may be there anyway. He has a little apartment at the back."

I started for the hall, but turned before I got there. "Just who is Hilary Todd?"

"I don't know where he's from originally. He was stationed here during the war, and simply stayed on. His parents had money at one time, and he studied painting and ballet in Paris, or so he claims."

"Art seems to be the main industry in San Marcos."

"You've just been meeting the wrong people."

I went down the outside stairs to the parking lot, wondering what that implied about her brother. Todd's convertible stood near the mouth of the alley. I knocked on the back door of the art shop. There was no answer, but behind the Venetian-blinded door I heard a murmur of voices, a growling and a twittering. Todd had a woman with him. I knocked again.

After more delay the door was partly opened. Todd looked out through the crack. He was wiping his mouth with a red-stained handkerchief. The stains were too bright to be blood. Above the handkerchief his eyes were very bright and narrow, like slivers of polished agate.

"Good afternoon."

I moved forward as though I fully expected to be let in. He opened the door reluctantly under the nudging pressure of my shoulder, and backed into a narrow passage between two wall-board partitions.

"What can I do for you, Mr.——? I don't believe I know your name."

Before I could answer, a woman's voice said clearly, "It's Mr. Archer, isn't it?"

Sarah Turner appeared in the doorway behind him, carrying a highball glass and looking freshly groomed. Her red hair was unruffled, her red mouth gleaming as if she had just finished painting it.

"Good afternoon, Mrs. Turner."

"Good afternoon, Mr. Archer." She leaned in the doorway, almost too much at ease. "Do you know Hilary, Mr. Archer? You should. Everybody should. Hilary's simply loaded and dripping with charm, aren't you, dear?" Her mouth curled in a thin smile.

Todd looked at her with hatred, then turned to me without changing his look. "Did you wish to speak to me?"

"I did. You have a copy of Admiral Turner's Chardin."

"A copy, yes."

"Can I have a look at it?"

"What on earth for?"

"I want to be able to identify the original. It's probably connected with the murder."

I watched them both as I said the word. Neither showed surprise.

"We heard about it on the radio," the woman said. "It must have been dreadful for you."

"Dreadful," Todd echoed her, injecting synthetic sympathy into his dark eyes.

"Worse for Western," I said, "and for whoever did it. Do you still think he stole the picture, Mrs. Turner?"

Todd glanced at her sharply. She was embarrassed, as I'd intended her to be. She dunked her embarrassment in her highball glass, swallowing deeply from it and leaving a red half-moon on its rim.

"I never thought he stole it," her wet mouth lied. "I merely suggested the possibility."

"I see. Didn't you say something about Western trying to buy the picture from your husband? That he was acting as agent for somebody else?"

"I wasn't the one who said that. I didn't know it."

"The Admiral said it then. It would be interesting to know who the other man was. He wanted the Chardin, and it looks to me as if Hugh Western died because somebody wanted the Chardin."

Todd had been listening hard and saying nothing. "I don't see any necessary connection," he said now. "But if you'll come in and sit down I'll show you my copy."

"You wouldn't know who it was that Western was acting for?"

He spread his palms outward in a Continental gesture. "How would I know?"

"You're in the picture business."

"I *was* in the picture business." He turned abruptly and left the room.

Sarah Turner had crossed to a portable bar in the corner. She was splintering ice with a silver-handled ice pick. "May I make you one, Mr. Archer?"

"No, thanks." I sat down in a cubistic chair designed for people with square corners, and watched her take half of her new highball in a single gulp. "What did Todd mean when he said he *was* in the picture business? Doesn't he run this place?"

"He's having to give it up. The *boutique's* gone broke, and he's going around testing shoulders to weep on."

"Yours?" A queer kind of hostile intimacy had risen between us, and I tried to make the most of it.

"Where did you get that notion?"

"I thought he was a friend of yours."

"Did you?" Her laugh was too loud to be pleasant. "You ask a great many questions, Mr. Archer."

"They seem to be indicated. The cops in a town like this are pretty backward about stepping on people's toes."

"You're not."

"No. I'm just passing through. I can follow my hunches."

"What do you hope to gain?"

"Nothing for myself. I'd like to see justice done."

She sat down facing me, her knees almost touching mine. They were pretty knees, and uncovered. I felt crowded. Her voice, full of facile emotion, crowded me more:

"Were you terribly fond of Hugh?"

"I liked him." My answer was automatic. I was thinking of something else: the way she sat in her chair with her knees together, her body sloping backward, sure of its firm lines. I'd seen the same pose in charcoal that morning.

"I liked him, too," she was saying. "Very much. And I've been thinking—I've remembered something. Something that Hilary mentioned a couple of weeks ago, about Walter Hendryx wanting to buy the Chardin. It seems Hugh and Walter Hendryx were talking in the shop—"

She broke off suddenly. She had looked up and seen Todd leaning through the doorway, his face alive with anger. His shoulders moved slightly in her direction. She recoiled, clutching her glass. If I hadn't been there, I guessed he would have hit her. As it was, he said in a monotone:

"How cozy. Haven't you had quite a bit to drink, Sarah darling?"

She was afraid of him, but unwilling to admit it. "I have to do something to make present company bearable."

"You should be thoroughly anesthetized by now."

"If you say so, darling."

She hurled her half-empty glass at the wall beside the door. It shattered, denting the wallboard and splashing a photograph of Nijinsky as the Faun. Some of the liquid splattered on Todd's blue suede shoes.

"Very nice," he said. "I love your girlish antics, Sarah. I also love the way you run at the mouth." He turned to me: "This is the copy, Mr. Archer. Don't mind her, she's just a weensy bit drunky."

He held it up for me to see, an oil painting about a yard square showing a small boy in a blue waistcoat sitting at a table. In the center of the linen tablecloth there was a blue dish containing a red apple. The boy was looking at the apple as if he intended to eat it. The copyist had included the signature and date: Chardin, 1744.

"It's not very satisfactory," Todd said, "if you've ever seen the original. But of course you haven't?"

"No."

"That's too bad. You probably never will now, and it's really perfect. Perfect. It's the finest Chardin west of Chicago."

"I haven't given up hope of seeing it."

"You might as well, old boy. It'll be well on its way by now, to Europe, or South America. Picture thieves move fast, before the news of the theft catches up with them and spoils the market. They'll sell the Chardin to a private buyer in Paris or Buenos Aires, and that'll be the end of it."

"Why 'they'?"

"Oh, they operate in gangs. One man can't handle the theft and the disposal of a picture by himself. Division of labor is necessary, and specialization."

"You sound like a specialist yourself."

"I am, in a way." He smiled obliquely. "Not in the way you mean. I was in museum work before the war."

He stooped and propped the picture against the wall. I glanced at Sarah Turner. She was hunched forward in her chair, still and silent, her hands spread over her face.

"And now," he said to me, "I suppose you'd better go. I've done what I can for you. And I'll give you a tip if you like. Picture thieves don't do murder, they're simply not the type. So I'm afraid your precious hypothesis is based on bad information."

"Thanks very much," I said. "I certainly appreciate that. Also your hospitality."

"Don't mention it."

He raised an ironic brow, and turned to the door. I followed him out through the deserted shop. Most of the stock seemed to be in the window. Its atmosphere was sad and broken-down, the atmosphere of an empty-hearted, unprosperous, second-hand Bohemia. Todd didn't look around like a proprietor. He had already abandoned the place in his mind, it seemed.

He unlocked the front door. The last thing he said before he shut it behind me was:

"I wouldn't go bothering Walter Hendryx about that story of Sarah's. She's not a very trustworthy reporter, and Hendryx isn't as tolerant of intruders as I am."

So it was true.

I left my car where it was and crossed to a taxi stand on the opposite corner. There was a yellow cab at the stand, with a brown-faced driver reading a comic book behind the wheel.

The comic book had dead women on the cover. The driver detached his hot eyes from its interior, leaned wearily over the back of the seat and opened the door for me. "Where to?"

"A man called Walter Hendryx—know where he lives?"

"Off of Foothill Drive. I been up there before. It's a two-fifty run, outside the city limits." His Jersey accent didn't quite go with his Sicilian features.

"Newark?"

"Trenton." He showed bad teeth in a good smile. "You want to make something out of it?"

"Nope. Let's go."

He spoke to me over his shoulder when we were out of the heavy downtown traffic. "You got your passport?"

"What kind of a place are you taking me to?"

"They don't like visitors. You got to have a visa to get in, and a writ of habeas corpus to get out. The old man's scared of burglars or something."

"Why?"

"He's got about ten million reasons, the way I hear it. Ten millions bucks." He smacked his lips.

"Where did he get it?"

"You tell me. I'll drop everything and take off for the same place."

"You and me both."

"I heard he's a big contractor in L.A.," the driver said. "I drove a reporter up here a couple of months ago, from one of the L.A. papers. He was after an interview with the old guy, something about a tax case."

"What about a tax case?"

"I wouldn't know. It's way over my head, friend, all that tax business. I have enough trouble with my own forms."

"What happened to the reporter?"

"I drove him right back down. The old man wouldn't see him. He likes his privacy."

"I'm beginning to get the idea."

"You a reporter, too, by any chance?"

"No."

He was too polite to ask me any more questions.

We left the city limits. The mountains rose ahead, violet and unshadowed in the sun's lengthening rays. Foothill Drive wound through a canyon, across a high-level bridge, up the side of a hill from which the sea was visible like a low blue cloud on the horizon. We turned off the road through an open gate on which a sign was posted: *Trespassers Will Be Prosecuted.*

A second gate closed the road at the top of the hill. It was a double gate of wrought iron hung between a stone gatepost and a stone gatehouse. A heavy wire fence stretched out from it on both sides, following the contours of the hills as far as I could see. Hendryx' estate was about the size of a small European country.

The driver honked his horn. A thick-waisted man in a Panama hat came out of the stone cottage. He squeezed through a narrow postern and waddled up to the cab. "Well?"

"I came to see Mr. Hendryx about a picture."

He opened the cab door and looked me over, from eyes that were heavily shuttered with old scar tissue. "You ain't the one that was here this morning."

I had my first good idea of the day. "You mean the tall fellow with the sideburns?"

"Yeah."

"I just came from him."

He rubbed his heavy chin with his knuckles, making a rasping noise. The knuckles were jammed.

"I guess it's all right," he said finally. "Give me your name and I'll phone it down to the house. You can drive down."

He opened the gate and let us through into a shallow valley. Below, in a maze of shrubbery, a long, low house was flanked by tennis courts and stables. Sunk in the terraced lawn behind the house was an oval pool like a wide green eye staring at the sky. A short man in bathing trunks was sitting in a Thinker pose on the diving board at one end.

He and the pool dropped out of sight as the cab slid down the eucalyptus-lined road. It stopped under a portico at the side of the house. A uniformed maid was waiting at the door.

"This is further than that reporter got," the driver said in an undertone. "Maybe you got connections?"

"The best people in town."

"Mr. Archer?" the maid said. "Mr. Hendryx is having his bath. I'll show you the way."

I told the driver to wait, and followed her through the house. I saw when I stepped outside that the man on the diving board wasn't short at all. He only seemed to be short because he was so wide. Muscle bulged out his neck, clustered on his shoulders and chest, encased his arms and legs. He looked like a graduate of Muscle Beach, a subman trying hard to be a superman.

There was another man floating in the water, the blotched brown swell of his stomach breaking the surface like the shellback of a Galapagos tortoise. Thinker stood up, accompanied by his parasitic muscles, and called to him:

"Mr. Hendryx!"

The man in the water rolled over lazily and paddled to the side of the pool. Even his head was tortoise-like, seamed and bald and impervious-looking. He stood up in the waist-deep water and raised his thin brown arms. The other man bent over him. He drew him out of the water and steadied him on his feet, rubbing him with a towel.

"Thank you, Devlin."

"Yessir."

Leaning far forward with his arms dangling like those of a withered, hairless ape, Hendryx shuffled towards me. The joints of his knees and ankles were knobbed and stiffened by what looked like arthritis. He peered up at me from his permanent crouch:

"You want to see me?" The voice that came out of his crippled body was surprisingly rich and deep. He wasn't as old as he looked. "What is it?"

"A painting was stolen last night from the San Marcos gallery: Chardin's 'Apple on a Table'. I've heard that you were interested in it."

"You've been misinformed. Good afternoon." His face closed like a fist.

"You haven't heard the rest of it."

Disregarding me, he called to the maid who was waiting at a distance: "Show this man out."

Devlin came up beside me, strutting like a wrestler, his great curved hands conspicuous.

"The rest of it," I said, "is that Hugh Western was murdered at the same time. I think you knew him?"

"I knew him, yes. His death is unfortunate. Regrettable. But so far as I know, it has nothing to do with the Chardin and nothing to do with me. Will you go now, or do I have to have you removed?"

He raised his cold eyes to mine. I stared him down, but there wasn't much satisfaction in that.

"You take murder pretty lightly, Hendryx."

"Mr. Hendryx to you," Devlin said in my ear. "Come on now, bud. You heard what Mr. Hendryx said."

"I don't take orders from him."

"I do," he said with a lopsided grin like a heat-split in a melon. "I take orders from him." His light small eyes shifted to Hendryx. "You want for me to throw him out?"

Hendryx nodded, backing away. His eyes were heating up, as if the prospect of violence excited him. Devlin's hand took my wrist. His fingers closed around it and overlapped.

"What is this, Devlin?" I said. "I thought Hugh Western was a pal of yours."

"Sure thing."

"I'm trying to find out who killed him. Aren't you interested? Or did you slap him down yourself?"

"The hell." Devlin blinked stupidly, trying to hold two questions in his mind at the same time.

Hendryx said from a safe distance: "Don't talk. Just give him a going-over and toss him out."

Devlin looked at Hendryx. His grip was like a thick handcuff on my wrist. I jerked his arm up and ducked under it, breaking the hold, and chopped at his nape. The bulging back of his neck was hard as a redwood bole.

He wheeled, and reached for me again. The muscles in his arm moved like drugged serpents. He was slow. My right fist found his chin and snapped it back on his neck. He recovered, and swung at me. I stepped inside of the roundhouse and hammered his ridged stomach, twice, four times. It was like knocking my fists against the side of a corrugated iron building. His great arms closed on me. I slipped down and away.

When he came after me, I shifted my attack to his head, jabbing with the left until he was off balance on his heels. Then I pivoted and threw a long right hook which changed to an uppercut. An electric shock surged up my arm. Devlin lay down on the green tiles, chilled like a side of beef.

I looked across him at Hendryx. There was no fear in his eyes, only calculation. He backed into a canvas chair and sat down clumsily.

"You're fairly tough, it seems. Perhaps you used to be a fighter? I've owned a few fighters in my time. You might have a future at it, if you were younger."

"It's a sucker's game. So is larceny."

"Larceny-farceny," he said surprisingly. "What did you say you do?"

"I'm a private detective."

"Private, eh?" His mouth curved in a lipless tortoise grin. "You interest me, Mr. Archer. I could find a use for you— a place in my organization."

"What kind of an organization?"

"I'm a builder, a mass-producer of houses. Like most successful entrepreneurs, I make enemies: cranks and bleeding hearts and psychopathic veterans who think the world owes them something. Devlin here isn't quite the man I thought he was. But you—"

"Forget it. I'm pretty choosy about the people I work for."

"An idealist, eh? A clean-cut young American idealist." The smile was still on his mouth; it was saturnine. "Well, Mr. Idealist, you're wasting your time. I know nothing about this picture or anything connected with it. You're also wasting *my* time."

"It seems to be expendable. I think you're lying, incidentally."

Hendryx didn't answer me directly. He called to the maid: "Telephone the gate. Tell Shaw we're having a little trouble with a guest. Then you can come back and look after this." He jerked a thumb at Muscle-Boy, who was showing signs of life."

I said to the maid: "Don't bother telephoning. I wouldn't stick around here if I was paid to."

She shrugged and looked at Hendryx. He nodded. I followed her out.

"You didn't stay long," the cab driver said.

"No. Do you know where Admiral Turner lives?"

"Curiously enough, I do. I should charge extra for the directory service."

I didn't encourage him to continue the conversation. "Take me there."

He let me out in a street of big old houses set far back from the sidewalk behind sandstone walls and high eugenia hedges. I paid him off and climbed the sloping walk to the Turner house. It was a weathered frame building, gabled and turreted in the style of the nineties. A gray-haired housekeeper who had survived from the same period answered my knock.

"The Admiral's in the garden," she said. "Will you come out?"

The garden was massed with many-colored begonias, and surrounded by a vine-covered wall. The Admiral, in stained and faded suntans, was chopping weeds in a flowerbed with furious concentration. When he saw me he leaned on his hoe and wiped his wet forehead with the back of his hand.

"You should come in out of the sun," the housekeeper said in a nagging way. "A man of your age—"

"Nonsense! Go away, Mrs. Harris." She went. "What can I do for you, Mr.—?"

"Archer. I guess you've heard that we found Hugh Western's body."

"Sarah came home and told me half an hour ago. It's a foul thing, and completely mystifying. He was to have married—"

His voice broke off. He glanced towards the stone cottage, at the rear of the garden. Alice Turner was there at an open window. She wasn't looking in our direction. She had a tiny paintbrush in her hand, and she was working at an easel.

"It's not as mystifying as it was. I'm starting to put the pieces together, Admiral."

He turned back to me quickly. His eyes became hard and empty again, like gun muzzles.

"Just who are you? What's your interest in this case?"

"I'm a friend of Hugh Western's, from Los Angeles. I

stopped off here to see him, and found him dead. I hardly think my interest is out of place."

"No, of course not," he grumbled. "On the other hand, I don't believe in amateur detectives running around like chickens with their heads cut off, fouling up the authorities."

"I'm not exactly an amateur. I used to be a cop. And any fouling up there's been has been done by other people."

"Are you accusing me?"

"If the shoe fits."

He met my eyes for a time, trying to master me and the situation. But he was old and bewildered. Slowly the aggressive ego faded from his gaze. He became almost querulous.

"You'll excuse me. I don't know what it's all about. I've been rather upset by everything that's happened."

"What about your daughter?" Alice was still at the window, working at her picture and paying no attention to our voices. "Doesn't she know Hugh is dead?"

"Yes. She knows. You mustn't misunderstand what Alice is doing. There are many ways of enduring grief, and we have a custom in the Turner family of working it out of our system. Hard work is the cure for a great many evils." He changed the subject, and his tone, abruptly. "And what is your idea of what's happened?"

"It's no more than a suspicion, a pretty foggy one. I'm not sure who stole your picture, but I think I know where it is."

"Well?"

"There's a man named Walter Hendryx who lives in the foothills outside the city. You know him?"

"Slightly."

"He probably has the Chardin. I'm morally certain he has it, as a matter of fact, though I don't know how he got it."

The Admiral tried to smile, and made a dismal failure of it. "You're not suggesting that Hendryx took it? He's not exactly mobile, you know."

"Hilary Todd is very mobile," I said. "Todd visited Hendryx this morning. I'd be willing to bet even money he had the Chardin with him."

"You didn't see it, however?"

"I don't have to. I've seen Todd."

A woman's voice said from the shadow of the back porch: "The man is right, Johnston."

Sarah Turner came down the path towards us, her high heels spiking the flagstones angrily.

"Hilary did it!" she cried. "He stole the picture and murdered Hugh. I saw him last night at midnight. He had red mountain clay on his clothes."

"It's strange you didn't mention it before," the Admiral said dryly.

I looked into her face. Her eyes were bloodshot, and the eyelids were swollen with weeping. Her mouth was swollen, too. When she opened it to reply, I could see that the lower lip was split.

"I just remembered."

I wondered if the blow that split her lip had reminded her.

"And where did you see Hilary Todd last night at midnight?"

"Where?"

In the instant of silence that followed, I heard footsteps behind me. Alice had come out of her cottage. She walked like a sleepwalker dreaming a bad dream, and stopped beside her father without a word to any of us.

Sarah's face had been twisting in search of an answer, and found it. "I met him at the Presidio. I dropped in there for a cup of coffee after the show."

"You are a liar, Sarah," the Admiral said. "The Presidio closes at ten o'clock."

"It wasn't the Presidio," she said rapidly. "It was the bar across the street, the Club Fourteen. I had dinner at the Presidio, and I confused them—"

The Admiral brushed past her without waiting to hear more, and started for the house. Alice went with him. The old man walked unsteadily, leaning on her arm.

"Did you really see Hilary last night?" I asked her.

She stood there for a minute, looking at me. Her face was disorganized, raddled with passion. "Yes, I saw him. I had a date with him at ten o'clock. I waited in his flat for over two hours. He didn't show up until after midnight. I couldn't tell *him* that." She jerked one shoulder contemptuously toward the house.

"And he had red clay on his clothes?"

"Yes. It took me a while to connect it with Hugh."

"Are you going to tell the police?"

She smiled a secret and unpleasant smile. "How can I? I've got a marriage to go on with, such as it is."

"You told me."

"I like you." Without moving, she gave the impression of leaning towards me. "I'm fed up with all the little stinkers that populate this town."

I kept it cool and clean, and very nasty: "Were you fed up with Hugh Western, Mrs. Turner?"

"What do you mean?"

"I heard that he dropped you hard a couple of months ago. Somebody dropped *him* hard last night in his studio."

"I haven't been near his studio for weeks."

"Never did any posing for him?"

Her face seemed to grow smaller and sharper. She laid one narrow taloned hand on my arm. "Can I trust you, Mr. Archer?"

"Not if you murdered Hugh."

"I didn't; I swear I didn't. Hilary did."

"But you were there last night."

"No."

"I think you were. There was a charcoal sketch on the easel, and you posed for it, didn't you?"

Her nerves were badly strained, but she tried to be coquettish. "How would you know?"

"The way you carry your body. It reminds me of the picture."

"Do you approve?"

"Listen, Mrs. Turner. You don't seem to realize that that sketch is evidence, and destroying it is a crime."

"I didn't destroy it."

"Then where did you put it?"

"I haven't said I took it."

"But you did."

"Yes, I did," she admitted finally. "But it isn't evidence in this case. I posed for it six months ago, and Hugh had it in his studio. When I heard he was dead this afternoon, I went to get it, just to be sure it wouldn't turn up in the papers. He had it on the easel for some reason, and had ruined it with a beard. I don't know why."

"The beard would make sense if your story was changed a little. If you quarreled while Hugh was sketching you last night, and you hit him over the head with a metal fist. You might had drawn the beard yourself, to cover up."

"Don't be ridiculous. If I had anything to cover up I would have destroyed the sketch. Anyway, I can't draw."

"Hilary can."

"Go to hell," she said between her teeth. "You're just a little stinker like the rest of them."

She walked emphatically to the house. I followed her into the long, dim hallway. Halfway up the stairs to the second floor she turned and flung down to me: "I hadn't destroyed it, but I'm going to now."

There was nothing I could do about that, and I started out. When I passed the door of the living room, the Admiral called out, "Is that you, Archer? Come here a minute, eh?"

He was sitting with Alice on a semicircular leather lounge, set into a huge bay window at the front of the room. He got up and moved toward me ponderously, his head down like a charging bull's. His face was a jaundiced yellow, bloodless under the tan.

"You're entirely wrong about the Chardin," he said. "Hilary Todd had nothing to do with stealing it. In fact, it wasn't stolen. I removed it from the gallery myself."

"You denied that this morning."

"I do as I please with my own possessions. I'm accountable to no one, certainly not to you."

"Dr. Silliman might like to know," I said with irony.

"I'll tell him in my own good time."

"Will you tell him why you took it?"

"Certainly. Now, if you've made yourself sufficiently obnoxious, I'll ask you to leave my house."

"Father." Alice came up to him and laid a hand on his arm. "Mr. Archer has only been trying to help."

"And getting nowhere," I said. "I made the mistake of assuming that some of Hugh's friends were honest."

"That's enough!" he roared. "Get out!"

Alice caught up with me on the veranda. "Don't go away mad. Father can be terribly childish, but he means well."

"I don't get it. He lied this morning, or else he's lying now."

"He isn't lying," she said earnestly. "He was simply playing a trick on Dr. Silliman and the trustees. It's what happened to Hugh afterwards that made it seem important."

"Did you know that he took the picture himself?"

"He told me just now, before you came into the house. I made him tell you."

"You'd better let Silliman in on the joke," I said unpleasantly. "He's probably going crazy."

"He is," she said. "I saw him at the gallery this afternoon, and he was tearing his hair. Do you have your car?"

"I came up here in a taxi."

"I'll drive you down."

"Are you sure you feel up to it?"

"It's better when I'm doing something," she said.

An old black sedan was standing in the drive beside the house. We got in, and she backed it into the street and turned downhill towards the center of town.

Watching her face, I said, "Of course you realize I don't believe his story."

"Father's, you mean?" She didn't seem surprised. "I don't know what to believe, myself."

"When did he say he took the Chardin?"

"Last night. Hugh was working on the mezzanine. Father slipped away and took the picture out to the car."

"Didn't Hugh keep the door locked?"

"Apparently not. Father said not."

"But what possible reason could he have for stealing his own picture?"

"To prove a point. Father's been arguing for a long time that it would be easy to steal a picture from the gallery. He's been trying to get the board of trustees to install a burglar alarm. He's really hipped on the subject. He wouldn't lend his Chardin to the gallery until they agreed to insure it."

"For twenty-five thousand dollars," I said, half to myself. Twenty-five thousand dollars was motive enough for a man to steal his own picture. And if Hugh Western witnessed the theft, there was motive for murder. "Your father's made a pretty good story out of it. But where's the picture now?"

"He didn't tell me. It's probably in the house somewhere."

"I doubt it. It's more likely somewhere in Walter Hendryx' house."

She let out a little gasp. "What makes you say that? Do you know Walter Hendryx?"

"I've met him. Do you?"

"He's a horrible man," she said. "I can't imagine why you think he has it."

"It's purely a hunch."

"Where would he get it? Father wouldn't dream of selling it to him."

"Hilary Todd would."

"Hilary? You think Hilary stole it?"

"I'm going to ask him. Let me off at his shop, will you? I'll see you at the gallery later."

The *Closed* sign was still hanging inside the plate glass, and the front door was locked. I went around to the back of the shop by the alley. The door under the stairs was standing partly open. I went in without knocking.

The living room was empty. The smell of alcohol rose from the stain on the wall where Sarah had smashed her glass. I crossed the passage to the door on the other side. It, too, was partly open. I pushed it wider and went in.

Hilary Todd was sprawled face down on the bed, with an open suitcase crushed under the weight of his body. The silver handle of his ice pick stood up between his shoulder blades in the center of a wet, dark stain. The silver glinted coldly in a ray of light which came through the half-closed Venetian blinds.

I felt for his pulse and couldn't find it. His head was twisted sideways, and his empty dark eyes stared unblinking at the wall. A slight breeze from the open window at the foot of the bed ruffled the hair along the side of his head.

I burrowed under the heavy body and went through the

pockets. In the inside breast pocket of the coat I found what I was looking for: a plain white business envelope, unsealed, containing $15,000 in large bills.

I was standing over the bed with the money in my hand when I heard someone in the hallway. A moment later Mary appeared at the door.

"I saw you come in," she said. "I thought—" Then she saw the body.

"Someone killed Hilary."

"Killed Hilary?" She looked at the body on the bed and then at me. I realized that I was holding the money in plain view.

"What are you doing with that?"

I folded the bills and tucked them into my inside pocket. "I'm going to try an experiment. Be a good girl and call the police for me."

"Where did you get that money?"

"From someone it didn't belong to. Don't tell the sheriff about it. Just say that I'll be back in half an hour."

"They'll want to know where you went."

"And if you don't know, you won't be able to tell them. Now do as I say."

She looked into my face, wondering if she could trust me. Her voice was uncertain: "If you're sure you're doing the right thing."

"Nobody ever is."

I went out to my car and drove to Foothill Drive. The sun had dipped low over the sea, and the air was turning colder. By the time I reached the iron gates that cut off Walter Hendryx from ordinary mortals, the valley beyond them was in shadow.

The burly man came out of the gatehouse as if I had pressed a button, and up to the side of the car. "What do you want?" He recognized me then, and pushed his face up to the window. "Beat it, chum. I got orders to keep you away from here."

I restrained an impulse to push the face away, and tried diplomacy. "I came here to do your boss a favor."

"That's not the way he feels. Now blow."

"Look here." I brought the wad of bills out of my pocket, and passed them back and forth under his nose. "There's big money involved."

His eyes followed the moving bills as if they hypnotized him. "I don't take bribes," he said in a hoarse and passionate whisper.

"I'm not offering you one. But you should phone down to

Hendryx, before you do anything rash, and tell him there's money in it."

"Money for him?" There was a wistful note in his voice. "How much?"

"Fifteen thousand, tell him."

"Some bonus." He whistled. "What kind of a house is he building for you, bud, that you should give him an extra fifteen grand?"

I didn't answer. His question gave me too much to think about. He went back into the gatehouse.

Two minutes later he came out and opened the gates. "Mr. Hendryx'll see you. But don't try any funny stuff or you won't come out on your own power."

The maid was waiting at the door. She took me into a big rectangular room with French windows on one side, opening on the terrace. The rest of the walls were lined with books from floor to ceiling—the kind of books that are bought by the set and never read. In front of the fireplace, at the far end, Hendryx was sitting half submerged in an overstuffed armchair, with a blanket over his knees.

He looked up when I entered the room and the firelight danced on his scalp and lit his face with an angry glow. "What's this? Come here and sit down."

The maid left silently. I walked the length of the room and sat down in an armchair facing him. "I always bring bad news, Mr. Hendryx. Murder and such things. This time it's Hilary Todd."

The turtle face didn't change, but his head made a movement of withdrawal into the shawl collar of his robe. "I'm exceedingly sorry to hear it. But my gatekeeper mentioned the matter of money. That interests me more."

"Good." I produced the bills and spread them fanwise on my knee. "Do you recognize this?"

"Should I?"

"For a man that's interested in money, you're acting very coy."

"I'm interested in its source."

"I had an idea that you were the source of this particular money. I have some other ideas. For instance, that Hilary Todd stole the Chardin and sold it to you. One thing I have no idea about is why you would buy a stolen picture and pay for it in cash."

His false teeth glistened coldly in the firelight. Like the man at the gate, he kept his eyes on the money. "The picture wasn't stolen. I bought it legally from its rightful owner."

"I might believe you if you hadn't denied any knowledge of it this afternoon. I think you knew it was stolen."

His voice took on a cutting edge: "It was not." He slipped his blue-veined hand inside his robe and brought out a folded sheet of paper, which he handed me.

It was a bill of sale for the picture, informal but legal, written in longhand on the stationery of the San Marcos Beach Club, signed by Admiral Johnston Turner, and dated that day.

"Now may I ask you where you got hold of that money?"

"I'll be frank with you, Mr. Hendryx. I took it from the body of Hilary Todd, when he had no further use for it."

"That's a criminal act, I believe."

My brain was racing, trying to organize a mass of contradictory facts. "I have a notion that you're not going to talk to anyone about it."

He shrugged his shoulders. "You seem to be full of notions."

"I have another. Whether or not you're grateful to me for bringing you this money, I think you should be."

"Have you any reason for saying that?" He had withdrawn his eyes from the money on my knee and was looking into my face.

"You're in the building business, Mr. Hendryx?"

"Yes." His voice was flat.

"I don't know exactly how you got this money. My guess is that you gouged it out of home-buyers, by demanding a cash side-payment in addition to the appraised value of the houses you've been selling to veterans."

"That's a pretty comprehensive piece of guesswork, isn't it?"

"I don't expect you to admit it. On the other hand, you probably wouldn't want this money traced to you. The fact that you haven't banked it is an indication of that. That's why Todd could count on you to keep this picture deal quiet. And that's why you should be grateful to me."

The turtle eyes stared into mine and admitted nothing. "If I were grateful, what form do you suggest my gratitude should take?"

"I want the picture. I've sort of set my heart on it."

"Keep the money instead."

"This money is no good to me. Dirty money never is."

He threw the blanket off and levered himself out of the chair. "You're somewhat more honest than I'd supposed. You're offering, then, to buy the picture back from me with that money."

"Exactly."

"And if I don't agree?"

"The money goes to the Intelligence Unit of the Internal Revenue Bureau."

There was silence for a while, broken by the fire hissing and sputtering in an irritable undertone.

"Very well," he said at length. "Give me the money."

"Give me the picture."

He waded across the heavy rug, moving his feet a few inches at a time, and pressed a corner of one of the bookcases. It swung open like a door. Behind it was the face of a large wall safe. I waited uncomfortably while he twirled the double dials.

A minute later he shuffled back to me with the picture in his hands. The boy in the blue waistcoat was there in the frame, watching the apple, which looked good enough to eat after more than two hundred years.

Hendryx' withered face had settled into a kind of malevolent resignation. "You realize that this is no better than blackmail."

"On the contrary, I'm saving you from the consequences of your own poor judgment. You shouldn't do business with thieves and murderers."

"You still insist the picture was stolen?"

"I think it was. You probably know it was. Will you answer one question?"

"Perhaps."

"When Hilary Todd approached you about buying this picture, did he claim to represent Admiral Turner?"

"Of course. You have the bill of sale in your hand. It's signed by the Admiral."

"I see that, but I don't know his signature."

"I do. Now, if you have no further questions, may I have my money?"

"One more: Who killed Hugh Western?"

"I don't know," he said heavily and finally.

He held out his brown hand with the palm upward. I gave him the sheaf of bills.

"And the bill of sale, if you please."

"It wasn't part of the bargain."

"It has to be."

"I suppose you're right." I handed it to him.

"Please don't come back a third time," he said as he rang for the maid. "I find your visits tiring and annoying."

"I won't come back," I said. I didn't need to.

I parked in the alley beside the art gallery and got out of the car with the Chardin under my arm. There was talk and laughter and the tiny din of cutlery in the restaurant patio beyond the hedge. On the other side of the alley a light was shining behind the barred window of Silliman's office. I reached up between the bars and tapped on the window. I couldn't see beyond the closed Venetian blinds.

Someone opened the casement. It was Alice, her blond head aureoled against the light. "Who is it?" she said in a frightened whisper.

"Archer." I had a sudden, rather theatrical impulse. I held up the Chardin and passed it to her edgewise between the bars. She took it from my hands and let out a little yelp of surprise.

"It was where I thought it would be," I said.

Silliman appeared at her shoulder, squeaking, "What is it? What is it?"

My brain was doing a double take on the action I'd just performed. I had returned the Chardin to the gallery without using the door. It could have been stolen the same way, by Hilary Todd or anyone else who had access to the building. No human being could pass through the bars, but a picture could.

Silliman's head came out the window like a gray mop being shaken. "Where on earth did you find it?"

I had no story ready, so I said nothing.

A gentle hand touched my arm and stayed, like a bird alighting. I started, but it was only Mary.

"I've been watching for you," she said. "The sheriff's in Hilary's shop, and he's raving mad. He said he's going to put you in jail, as a material witness."

"You didn't tell him about the money?" I said in an undertone.

"No. Did you really get the picture?"

"Come inside and see."

As we turned the corner of the building, a car left the curb in front of it, and started up the street with a roar. It was Admiral Turner's black sedan.

"It looks like Alice driving," Mary said.

"She's gone to tell her father, probably."

I made a sudden decision, and headed back to my car.

"Where are you going?"

"I want to see the Admiral's reaction to the news."

She followed me to the car. "Take me."

"You'd better stay here. I can't tell what might happen."

I tried to shut the door, but she held on to it. "You're always running off and leaving me to make your explanations."

"All right; get in. I don't have time to argue."

I drove straight up the alley and across the parking lot to Rubio Street. There was a uniformed policeman standing at the back door of Hilary's shop, but he didn't try to stop us.

"What did the police have to say about Hilary?" I asked her.

"Not much. The ice pick had been wiped clean of finger-prints, and they had no idea who did it."

I went through a yellow light and left a chorus of indig-nant honkings at the intersection behind me.

"You said you didn't know what would happen when you got there. Do you think the Admiral—" She left the sentence unfinished.

"I don't know. I have a feeling I soon will, though." There were a great many things I could have said. I concentrated on my driving.

"Is this the street?" I asked her finally.

"Yes."

My tires shrieked on the corner, and again in front of the house. She was out of the car before I was.

"Stay back," I told her. "This may be dangerous."

She let me go up the walk ahead of her. The black sedan was in the drive with the headlights burning and the left front door hanging open. The front door of the house was closed but there was a light behind it. I went in without knocking.

Sarah came out of the living room. All day her face had been going to pieces, and now it was old and slack and ugly. Her bright hair was ragged at the edges, and her voice was ragged. "What do you think you're doing?"

"I want to see the Admiral. Where is he?"

"How should I know? I can't keep track of any of my men." She took a step toward me, staggered, and almost fell.

Mary took hold of her and eased her into a chair. Her head leaned limply against the wall, and her mouth hung open. The lipstick on her mouth was like a rim of cracked dry blood.

"They must be here."

The single shot that we heard then was an exclamation point at the end of my sentence. It came from somewhere back of the house, muffled by walls and distance.

I went through into the garden. There were lights in the gardener's cottage, and a man's shadow moved across the window. I ran up the path to the cottage's open door, and froze there.

Admiral Turner was facing me with a gun in his hand. It was a heavy-caliber automatic, the kind the Navy issued. From its round, questioning mouth a wisp of blue smoke trailed. Alice lay face down on the carpeted floor between us.

I looked into the mouth of the gun, into Turner's granite face. "You killed her."

But Alice was the one who answered. "Go away." The words came out in a rush of sobbing that racked her pros-trate body.

"This is a private matter, Archer." The gun stirred slightly in the Admiral's hand. I could feel its pressure across the width of the room. "Do as she says."

"I heard a shot. Murder is a public matter."

"There has been no murder, as you can see."

"You don't remember well."

"I have nothing to do with that," he said. "I was cleaning my gun, and forgot that it was loaded."

"So Alice lay down and cried? You'll have to do better than that, Admiral."

"Her nerves are shaken. But I assure you that mine are not." He took three slow steps towards me, and paused by the girl on the floor. The gun was very steady in his hand. "Now go, or I'll have to use this."

The pressure of the gun was increasing. I put my hands on the doorframe and held myself still. "You seem to be sure it's loaded now," I said.

Between my words I heard the faint, harsh whispering of shifting gravel on the garden path behind me. I spoke up loudly, to drown out the sound.

"You had nothing to do with the murder, you say. Then why did Todd come to the beach club this morning? Why did you change your story about the Chardin?"

He looked down at his daughter as if she could answer the questions. She made no sound, but her shoulders were shaking with inner sobbing.

As I watched the two of them, father and daughter, the pattern of the day came into focus. At its center was the muzzle of the Admiral's gun, the round blue mouth of death.

I said, very carefully, to gain time, "I can guess what Todd said to you this morning. Do you want me to dub in the dialogue?"

He glanced up sharply, and the gun glanced up. There were no more sounds in the garden. If Mary was as quick as I thought, she'd be at a telephone.

"He told you he'd stolen your picture and had a buyer for it. But Hendryx was cautious. Todd needed proof that he had a right to sell it. You gave him the proof. And when Todd completed the transaction, you let him keep the money."

"Nonsense! Bloody nonsense." But he was a poor actor, and a worse liar.

"I've seen the bill of sale, Admiral. The only question left is why you gave it to Todd."

His lips moved as if he was going to speak. No words came out.

"And I'll answer that one, too. Todd knew who killed Hugh Western. So did you. You had to keep him quiet, even if it meant conniving at the theft of your own picture."

"I connived at nothing." His voice was losing its strength. His gun was as potent as ever.

"Alice did," I said. "She helped him to steal it this morning. She passed it out the window to him when Silliman and I were on the mezzanine. Which is one of the things he told you at the beach club, isn't it?"

"Todd has been feeding you lies. Unless you give me your word that you won't repeat those lies, not to anyone, I'm going to have to shoot you."

His hand contracted, squeezing off the automatic's safety. The tiny noise it made seemed very significant in the silence.

"Todd will soon be feeding worms," I said. "He's dead, Admiral."

"Dead?" His voice had sunk to an old man's quaver, rustling in his throat.

"Stabbed with an ice pick in his apartment."

"When?"

"This afternoon. Do you still see any point in trying to shoot me?"

"You're lying."

"No. There's been a second murder."

He looked down at the girl at his feet. His eyes were bewildered. There was danger in his pain and confusion. I was the source of his pain, and he might strike out blindly at me. I watched the gun in his hand, waiting for a chance to move on it. My arms were rigid, braced against the doorframe.

Mary Western ducked under my left arm and stepped into the room in front of me. She had no weapon, except her courage.

"He's telling the truth," she said. "Hilary Todd was stabbed to death today."

"Put down the gun," I said. "There's nothing left to save. You thought you were protecting an unfortunate girl. She's turned out to be a double murderess."

He was watching the girl on the floor. "If this is true, Allie, I wash my hands of you."

No sound came from her. Her face was hidden by her yellow sheaf of hair. The old man groaned. The gun sagged in his hand. I moved, pushing Mary to one side, and took it away from him. He didn't resist me, but my forehead was suddenly streaming with sweat.

"You were probably next on her list," I said.

"No."

The muffled word came from his daughter. She began to get up, rising laboriously from her hands and knees like a hurt fighter. She flung her hair back. Her face had hardly changed. It was as lovely as ever, on the surface, but empty of meaning, like a doll's plastic face.

"I was next on my list," she said dully. "I tried to shoot myself when I realized you knew about me. Father stopped me."

"I didn't know about you until now."

"You did. You must have. When you were talking to Father in the garden, you meant me to hear it all—everything you said about Hilary."

"Did I?"

The Admiral said with a kind of awe: "You killed him, Allie. Why did you want his blood on your hands? Why?" His own hand reached for her, gropingly, and paused in midair. He looked at her as if he had fathered a strange, evil thing.

She bowed her head in silence. I answered for her: "She'd stolen the Chardin for him and met his conditions. But then she saw that he couldn't get away, or if he did he'd be brought back, and questioned. She couldn't be sure he'd keep quiet about Hugh. This afternoon she made sure. The second murder comes easier."

"No!" She shook her blond head violently. "I didn't murder Hugh. I hit him with something, I didn't intend to kill him. He struck me first, he *struck* me, and then I hit him back."

"With a deadly weapon, a metal fist. You hit at him twice with it. The first blow missed and left its mark on the doorframe. The second blow didn't miss."

"But I didn't mean to kill him. Hilary knew I didn't mean to kill him."

"How would he know? Was he there?"

"He was downstairs in his flat. When he heard Hugh fall, he came up. Hugh was still alive. He died in Hilary's car, when we were starting for the hospital. Hilary said he'd help me to cover up. He took that horrible fist and threw it into the sea.

"I hardly knew what I was doing by that time. Hilary did it all. He put the body in Hugh's car and drove it up the mountain. I followed in his car and brought him back. On the way back he told me why he was helping me. He needed money. He knew we had no money, but he had a chance to sell the Chardin. I took it for him this morning. I had to. Everything I did, I did because I had to."

She looked from me to her father. He averted his face from her.

"You didn't have to smash Hugh's skull," I said. "Why did you do that?"

Her doll's eyes rolled in her head, came back to me, glinting with a cold and deathly coquetry. "If I tell you, will you do one thing for me? One favor? Give me father's gun for just a second?"

"And let you kill us all?"

"Only myself," she said. "Just leave one shell in it."

"Don't give it to her," the Admiral said. "She's done enough to disgrace us."

"I have no intention of giving it to her. And I don't have to be told why she killed Hugh. While she was waiting in his studio last night, she found a sketch of his. It was an old sketch, but she didn't know that. She'd never seen it before, for obvious reasons."

"What kind of a sketch?"

"A portrait of a nude woman. She tacked it up on the easel and decorated it with a beard. When Hugh came home he saw what she'd done. He didn't like to have his pictures spoiled, and he probably slapped her face."

"He hit me with his fist," Alice said. "I killed him in self-defense."

"That may be the way you've rationalized it. Actually, you killed him out of jealousy."

She laughed. It was a cruel sound, like vital tissue being ruptured. "Jealousy of *her*?"

"The same jealousy that made you ruin the sketch."

Her eyes widened, but they were blind, looking into herself. "Jealousy? I don't know. I felt so lonely, all alone in the world. I had nobody to love me, since my mother died."

"It isn't true, Alice. You had me." The Admiral's tentative hand came out and paused again in the air, as though there were an invisible wall between them.

"I never had you. I hardly saw you. Then Sarah took you. I had no one, no one until Hugh. I thought at last that I had some one to love me, that I could count on—"

Her voice broke off. The Admiral looked everywhere but at his daughter. The room was like a cubicle in hell where lost souls suffered under the silent treatment. The silence was finally broken by the sound of a distant siren. It rose and expanded until its lamentation filled the night.

Alice was crying, with her face uncovered. Mary Western came forward and put her arm around her. "Don't cry." Her voice was warm. Her face had a grave beauty.

"You hate me, too."

"No. I'm sorry for you, Alice. Sorrier than I am for Hugh."

The Admiral touched my arm. "Who was the woman in the sketch?" he said in a trembling voice.

I looked into his tired old face and decided that he had suffered enough. "I don't know."

But I could see the knowledge in his eyes.

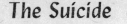

The Suicide

I PICKED HER UP on the Daylight. Or maybe she picked me up. With some of the nicest girls, you never know.

She seemed to be very nice, and very young. She had a flippant nose and wide blue eyes, the kind that men like to call innocent. Her hair bubbled like boiling gold around her small blue hat. When she turned from the window to hear my deathless comments on the landscape and the weather, she wafted spring odors towards me.

She laughed in the right places, a little hectically. But in between, when the conversation lagged, I could see a certain somberness in her eyes, a pinched look around her mouth like the effects of an early frost. When I asked her to join me in the buffet car for a drink, she said:

"Oh, no. Thank you. I couldn't possibly."

"Why not?"

"I'm not quite twenty-one, for one thing. You wouldn't want to contribute to the delinquency of a minor?"

"It sounds like a pleasant enterprise."

She veiled her eyes and turned away. The green hills plunged backward past the train window like giant dolphins against the flat blue background of the sea. The afternoon sun was bright on her hair. I hoped I hadn't offended her.

I hadn't. After a while she leaned towards me and touched my arm with hesitant fingertips.

"Since you're so kind, I'll tell you what I would like." She wrinkled her nose in an anxious way. "A sandwich? Would it cost so very much more than a drink?"

"A sandwich it is."

On the way to the diner, she caught the eye of every man on the train who wasn't asleep. Even some of the sleeping ones stirred, as if her passing had induced a dream. I censored my personal dream. She was too young for me, too innocent. I told myself that my interest was strictly paternal.

She asked me to order her a turkey sandwich, all white meat, and drummed on the tablecloth until it arrived. It disappeared in no time. She was ravenous.

"Have another," I said.

She gave me a look which wasn't exactly calculating, just questioning. "Do you really think I should?"

"Why not? You're pretty hungry."

"Yes, I am. But—" She blushed. "I hate to ask a stranger—you know?"

"No personal obligation. I like to see hungry people eat."

"You're awfully generous. And I am awfully hungry. Are you sure you can afford it?"

"Money is no object. I just collected a thousand-dollar fee in San Francisco. If you can use a full-course dinner, say so."

"Oh, no, I couldn't accept that. But I will confess that I could eat another sandwich."

I signaled to the waiter. The second sandwich went the way of the first while I drank coffee. She ate the olives and slices of pickle, too.

"Feeling better now? You were looking a little peaked."

"Much better, thank you. I'm ashamed to admit it, but I hadn't eaten all day. And I've been on short rations for a week."

I looked her over deliberately. Her dark blue suit was new, and expensively cut. Her bag was fine calfskin. Tiny diamonds winked in the white-gold case of her wristwatch.

"I know what you're thinking," she said. "I could have pawned something. Only I couldn't *bear* to. I spent my last cent on my ticket—I waited till the very last minute, when I had just enough to pay my fare."

"What were you waiting for?"

"To hear from Ethel. But we won't go into that." Her eyes shuttered themselves, and her pretty mouth became less pretty. "It's my worry."

"All right."

"I don't mean to be rude, or ungrateful. I thought I could hold out until I got to Los Angeles. I would have, too, if you hadn't broken me down with kindness."

"Forget about my kindness. I hope there's a job waiting for you in Los Angeles. Or maybe a husband?"

"No." The idea of a husband, or possibly a job, appealed to her sense of humor. She giggled like a schoolgirl. "You have one more guess."

"Okay. You flunked out of school, and couldn't face the family."

"You're half right. But I'm still enrolled at Berkeley, and I have no intention of flunking out. I'm doing very well in my courses."

"What are you taking?"

"Psychology and sociology, mostly. I plan to be a psychiatric social worker."

"You don't look the type."

"I am, though." The signs of early frost showed on her face again. I couldn't keep up with her moods. She was suddenly very serious. "I'm interested in helping people in trouble. I've seen a great deal of trouble. And so many people need help in the modern world."

"You can say that again."

Her clear gaze came up to my face. "You're interested in people, too, aren't you? Are you a doctor, or a lawyer?"

"What gave you that idea?"

"You mentioned a fee you earned, a thousand-dollar fee. It sounded as if you were a professional man."

"I don't know if you'd call my job a profession. I'm a private detective. My name is Archer."

Her reaction was disconcerting. She gripped the edge of the table with her hands, and pushed herself away from it. She said in a whisper as thin and sharp as a razor:

"Did Edward hire you? To spy on me?"

"Of course. Naturally. It's why I mentioned the fact that I'm a detective. I'm very cunning. And who in hell is Edward?"

"Edward Illman." She was breathing fast. "Are you sure he didn't employ you to pick me—to contact me? Cross your heart?"

The colored waiter edged towards our table, drawn by the urgent note in her voice. "Anything the matter, lady?"

"No. It's all right, thank you. The sandwiches were fine."

She managed to give him a strained smile, and he went away with a backward look.

"I'll make a clean breast of everything," I said. "Edward employed me to feed you drugged sandwiches. The kitchen staff is in my pay, and you'll soon begin to feel the effects of the drug. After that comes the abduction, by helicopter."

"Please. You mustn't joke about such things. I wouldn't put it past him, after what he did to Ethel."

"Ethel?"

"My sister, my older sister. Ethel's a darling. But Edward doesn't think so. He hates her—he hates us both. I wouldn't be surprised if he's responsible for all this."

"All what?" I said. "We seem to be getting nowhere. Obviously you're in some sort of a bind. You want to tell me about it, I want to hear about it. Now take a deep breath and start over, from the beginning. Bear in mind that I don't know these people from Adam. I don't even know your name."

"I'm sorry, my name is Clare Larrabee." Dutifully, she inhaled. "I've been talking like a silly fool, haven't I? It's because I'm so anxious about Ethel. I haven't heard from her for several weeks. I have no idea where she is or what's happened to her. Last week, when my allowance didn't come, I began to get really worried. I phoned her house in West Hollywood and got no answer. Since then I've been phoning at least once a day, with never an answer. So finally I swallowed my pride and got in touch with Edward. He said he hasn't seen her since she went to Nevada. Not that I believe him, necessarily. He'd just as soon lie as tell the truth. He perjured himself right and left when they arranged the settlement."

"Let's get Edward straight," I said. "Is he your sister's husband?"

"He was. Ethel divorced him last month. And she's well rid of him, even if he did cheat her out of her fair share of the property. He claimed to be a pauper, practically, but I know better. He's a very successful real estate operator—you must have heard of the Illman Tracts."

"This is the same Illman?"

"Yes. Do you know him?"

"Not personally. I used to see his name in the columns. He's quite a Casanova, isn't be?"

"Edward is a dreadful man. Why Ethel ever married him . . . Of course she wanted security, to be able to send me to college, and everything. But I'd have gone to work, gladly, if I could have stopped the marriage. I could see what kind of a husband he'd make. He even had the nerve to make a—make advances to me at the wedding reception." Her mouth pouted out in girlish indignation.

"And now you're thinking he had something to do with your sister's disappearance?"

"Either that, or she did away with— No, I'm sure it's Edward. He sounded so smug on the long distance telephone yesterday, as if he'd just swallowed the canary. I tell you, that man is capable of anything. If something's happened to Ethel, I know who's responsible."

"Probably nothing has. She could have gone off on a little trip by herself."

"You don't know Ethel. We've always kept in close touch, and she's been so punctual with my allowance. She'd never dream of going away and leaving me stranded at school without any money. I held out as long as I could, expecting to hear from her. When I got down below twenty dollars, I decided to take the train home."

"To Ethel's house in West Hollywood?"

"Yes. It's the only home I have since Daddy passed away. Ethel's the only family I have. I couldn't bear to lose Ethel." Her eyes filmed with tears.

"Do you have taxi fare?"

She shook her head, shamefaced.

"I'll drive you out. I don't live far from there myself. My car's stashed in a garage near Union Station."

"You're being good to me." Her hand crept out across the tablecloth and pressed the back of mine. "Forgive me for saying those silly things, about Edward hiring you."

I told her that would be easy.

We drove out Sunset and up into the hills. Afternoon was changing into evening. The late sunlight flashed like intermittent searchlights from the western windows of the hillside apartment buildings. Clare huddled anxiously in the far corner of the seat. She didn't speak, except to direct me to her sister's house.

It was a flat-roofed building set high on a sloping lot. The walls were redwood and glass, and the redwood had not yet weathered gray. I parked on the slanting blacktop drive and got out. Both stalls of the carport under the house were empty. The draperies were pulled over the picture windows that overlooked the valley.

I knocked on the front door. The noise resounded emptily through the building. I tried it. It was locked. So was the service door at the side.

I turned to the girl at my elbow. She was clutching the handle of her overnight bag with both hands, and looking pinched again. I thought that it was a cold homecoming for her.

"Nobody home," I said.

"It's what I was afraid of. What shall I do now?"

"You share this house with your sister?"

"When I'm home from school."

"And it belongs to her?"

"Since the divorce it does."

"Then you can give me permission to break in."

"All right. But please don't damage anything if you can help it. Ethel is very proud of her house."

The side door had a spring-type lock. I took a rectangle of plastic out of my wallet, and slipped it into the crack between the door and the frame. The lock slid back easily.

"You're quite a burglar," she said in a dismal attempt at humor.

I stepped inside without answering her. The kitchen was bright and clean, but it had a slightly musty, disused odor. The bread in the breadbox was stale. The refrigerator needed defrosting. There was a piece of ham moldering on one shelf, and on another a half-empty bottle of milk which had gone sour.

"She's been gone for some time," I said. "At least a week. We should check her clothes."

"Why?"

"She'd take some along if she left to go on a trip, under her own power."

She led me through the living room, which was simply and expensively furnished in black iron and net, into the master bedroom. The huge square bed was neatly made, and covered with a pink quilted silk spread. Clare avoided looking at it, as though the conjunction of a man and a bed gave her a guilty feeling. While she went through the closet, I searched the vanity and the chest of drawers.

They were barer than they should have been. Cosmetics were conspicuous by their absence. I found one thing of interest in the top drawer of the vanity, hidden under a tangle of stockings: a bankbook issued by the Las Vegas branch of the Bank of Southern California. Ethel Illman had deposited $30,000 on March 14 of this year. On March 17 she had withdrawn $5,000. On March 20 she had withdrawn $6,000. On March 22 she had withdrawn $18,995. There was a balance in her account, after service charges, of $3.65.

Clare said from the closet in a muffled voice:

"A lot of her things are gone. Her mink stole, her good suits and shoes, a lot of her best summer clothes."

"Then she's probably on a vacation." I tried to keep the doubt out of my voice. A woman wandering around with $30,000 in cash was taking a big chance. I decided not to worry Clare with that, and put the little bankbook in my pocket.

"Without telling me? Ethel wouldn't do that." She came out of the closet, pushing her fine light hair back from her forehead. "You don't understand how close we are to each other, closer than sisters usually are. Ever since father died—"

"Does she drive her own car?"

"Of course. It's a last year's Buick convertible, robin's-egg blue."

"If you're badly worried, go to Missing Persons."

"No. Ethel wouldn't like that. She's a very proud person, and shy. Anyway, I have a better idea." She gave me that questioning-calculating look of hers.

"Involving me?"

"Please." Her eyes in the darkening room were like great soft centerless pansies, purple or black. "You're a detective, and evidently a good one. And you're a man. You can stand up to Edward and make him answer questions. He just laughs at me. Of course I can't pay you in advance . . ."

"Forget the money for now. What makes you so certain that Illman is in on this?"

"I just know he is. He threatened her in the lawyer's office the day they made the settlement. She told me so herself. Edward said that he was going to get that money back if he had to take it out of her hide. He wasn't fooling, either. He's beaten her more than once."

"How much was the settlement?"

"Thirty thousand dollars and the house and the car. She could have collected much more, hundreds of thousands, if she'd stayed in California and fought it through the courts. But she was too anxious to get free from him. So she let him cheat her, and got a Nevada divorce instead. And even then he wasn't satisfied."

She looked around the abandoned bedroom, fighting back tears. Her skin was so pale that it seemed to be phosphorescent in the gloom. With a little cry, she flung herself face down on the bed and gave herself over to grief. I said to her shaking back:

"You win. Where do I find him?"

He lived in a cottage hotel on the outskirts of Bel-Air. The gates of the walled pueblo were standing open, and I went in. A few couples were strolling on the gravel paths among the palm-shaded cottages, walking off the effects of the cocktail hour or working up an appetite for dinner. The women were blond, and had money on their backs. The men were noticeably older than the women, except for one, who was noticeably younger. They paid no attention to me.

I passed an oval swimming pool, and found Edward Illman's cottage, number twelve. Light streamed from its open french windows onto a flagstone terrace. A young woman in a narrow-waisted, billowing black gown lay on a chrome chaise at the edge of the light. With her arms hanging loose from her naked shoulders, she looked like an expensive French doll which somebody had accidentally dropped there. Her face was polished and plucked and painted, expressionless as a doll's. But her eyes snapped open at the sound of my footsteps.

"Who goes there?" she said with a slight Martini accent. "Halt and give the password or I'll shoot you dead with my atomic wonder-weapon." She pointed a wavering finger at me and said: "Bing. Am I supposed to know you? I have a terrible memory for faces."

"I have a terrible face for memories. Is Mr. Illman home?"

"Uh-huh. He's in the shower. He's always taking showers. I told him he's got a scour-and-scrub neurosis, his mother was frightened by a washing machine." Her laughter rang like cracked bells. "If it's about business, you can tell me."

"Are you his confidential secretary?"

"I was." She sat up on the chaise, looked pleased with herself. "I'm his fiancée, at the moment."

"Congratulations."

"Uh-huh. He's loaded." Smiling to herself, she got to her feet. "Are you loaded?"

"Not so it gets in my way."

She pointed her finger at me and said bing again and laughed, teetering on her four-inch heels. She started to fall forward on her face. I caught her under the armpits.

"Too bad," she said to my chest. "I don't think you have a terrible face for memories at all. You're much prettier than old Teddy-bear."

"Thanks. I'll treasure the compliment."

I set her down on the chaise, but her arms twined round my neck like smooth white snakes and her body arched against me. She clung to me like a drowning child. I had to use force to detach myself.

"What's the matter?" she said with an up-and-under look. "You a fairy?"

A man appeared in the french windows, blotting out most of the light. In a white terry-cloth bathrobe, he had the shape and bulk of a Kodiak bear. The top of his head was as bald as an ostrich egg. He carried a chip on each shoulder, like epaulets.

"What goes on?"

"Your fiancée swooned, slightly."

"Fiancée hell. I saw what happened." Moving very quickly and lightly for a man of his age and weight, he pounced on the girl on the chaise and began to shake her. "Can't you keep your hands off anything in pants?"

Her head bobbed back and forth. Her teeth clicked like castanets.

I put a rough hand on his shoulder. "Leave her be."

He turned on me. "Who do you think you're talking to?"

"Edward Illman, I presume."

"And who are you?"

"The name in Archer. I'm looking into the matter of your wife's disappearance."

"I'm not married. And I have no intention of getting married. I've been burned once." He looked down sideways at the girl. She peered up at him in silence, hugging her shoulders.

"Your ex-wife, then," I said.

"Has something happened to Ethel?"

"I thought you might be able to tell me."

"Where did you get that idea? Have you been talking to Clare?"

I nodded.

"Don't believe her. She's got a down on me, just like her sister. Because I had the misfortune to marry Ethel, they both think I'm fair game for anything they want to pull. I wouldn't touch either one of them with an insulated pole. They're a couple of hustlers, if you want the truth. They took me for sixty grand, and what did I get out of it but headaches?' '

"I thought it was thirty."

"Sixty," he said, with the money light in his eyes. "Thirty in cash, and the house is worth another thirty, easily."

I looked around the place, which must have cost him fifty dollars a day. Above the palms, the first few stars sparkled like solitaire diamonds.

"You seem to have some left."

"Sure I have. But I work for my money. Ethel was strictly from nothing when I met her. She owned the clothes on her back and what was under them and that was all. So she gives me a bad time for three years and I pay off at the rate of twenty grand a year. I ask you, is that fair?"

"I hear you threatened to get it back from her."

"You have been talking to Clare, eh? All right, so I threatened her. It didn't mean a thing. I talk too much sometimes, and I have a bad temper."

"I'd never have guessed."

The girl said: "You hurt me, Teddy. I need another drink. Get me another drink, Teddy."

"Get it yourself."

She called him several bad names and wandered into the cottage, walking awkwardly like an animated doll.

He grasped my arm. "What's the trouble about Ethel? You said she disappeared. You think something's happened to her?"

I removed his hand. "She's missing. Thirty thousand in cash is also missing. There are creeps in Vegas who would knock her off for one big bill, or less."

"Didn't she bank the money? She wouldn't cash a draft for that amount and carry it around. She's crazy, but not that way."

"She banked it all right, on March fourteenth. Then she drew it all out again in the course of the following week. When did you send her the draft?"

"The twelfth or the thirteenth. That was the agreement. She got her final divorce on March eleventh."

"And you haven't seen her since?"

"I have not. Frieda has, though."

"Frieda?"

"My secretary." He jerked a thumb towards the cottage. "Frieda went over to the house last week to pick up some of my clothes I'd left behind. Ethel was there, and she was all right then. Apparently she's taken up with another man."

"Do you know his name?"

"No, and I couldn't care less."

"Do you have a picture of Ethel?"

"I did have some. I tore them up. She's a well-stacked blonde, natural blonde. She looks very much like Clare, same coloring, but three or four years older. You should be able to get a picture from Clare. And while you're at it, tell her for me she's got a lot of gall setting the police on me. I'm a respectable businessman in this town." He puffed out his chest under the bathrobe. It was thickly matted with brown hair, which was beginning to grizzle.

"No doubt," I said. "Incidentally, I'm not the police. I run a private agency. My name is Archer."

"So that's how it is, eh?" The planes of his broad face gleamed angrily in the light. He cocked a fat red fist. "You come here pumping me. Get out, by God, or I'll throw you out!"

"Calm down. I could break you in half."

His face swelled with blood, and his eyes popped. He swung a roundhouse right at my head. I stepped inside of it and tied him up. "I said calm down, old man. You'll break a vein."

I pushed him off balance and released him. He sat down very suddenly on the chaise. Frieda was watching us from the edge of the terrace. She laughed so heartily that she spilled her drink.

Illman looked old and tired, and he was breathing raucously through his mouth. He didn't try to get up. Frieda came over to me and leaned her weight on my arm. I could feel her small sharp breasts.

"Why didn't you hit him," she whispered, "when you had the chance? He's always hitting other people." Her voice rose. "Teddy-bear thinks he can get away with murder."

"Shut your yap," he said, "or I'll shut it for you."

"Button yours, muscle-man. You'll lay a hand on me once too often."

"You're fired."

"I already quit."

They were a charming couple. I was on the point of tearing myself away when a bellboy popped out of the darkness, like a gnome in uniform.

"A gentleman to see you, Mr. Illman."

The gentleman was a brown-faced young Highway Patrolman, who stepped forward rather diffidently into the light.

"Sorry to trouble you, sir. Our San Diego office asked me to contact you as soon as possible."

Frieda looked from me to him, and began to gravitate in his direction. Illman got up heavily and stepped between them.

"What is it?"

The patrolman unfolded a teletype flimsy and held it up to the light. "Are you the owner of a blue Buick convertible, last year's model?" He read off the license number.

"It was mine," Illman said. "It belongs to my ex-wife now. Did she forget to change the registration?"

"Evidently she did, Mr. Illman. In fact, she seems to've forgotten the car entirely. She left it in a parking space above the public beach in La Jolla. It's been sitting there for the last week, until we hauled it in. Where can I get in touch with Mrs. Illman?"

"I don't know. I haven't seen her for some time."

The patrolman's face lengthened and turned grim. "You mean she's dropped out of sight?"

"Out of my sight, at least. Why?"

"I hate to have to say this, Mr. Illman. There's a considerable quantity of blood on the front seat of the Buick, according to this report. They haven't determined yet if it's human blood, but it raises the suspicion of foul play."

"Good heavens! It's what we've been afraid of, isn't it, Archer?" His voice was as thick as corn syrup with phony emotion. "You and Clare were right after all."

"Right about what, Mr. Illman?" The patrolman looked slightly puzzled.

"About poor Ethel," he said. "I've been discussing her disappearance with Mr. Archer here. Mr. Archer is a private detective, and I was just about to engage his services to make a search for Ethel." He turned to me with a painful smile pulling his mouth to one side. "How much did you say you wanted in advance? Five hundred?"

"Make it two. That will buy my services for four days. It doesn't buy anything else, though."

"I understand that, Mr. Archer. I'm sincerely interested in finding Ethel for a variety of reasons, as you know."

He was a suave old fox. I almost laughed in his face. But I played along with him. I liked the idea of using his money to hang him, if possible.

"Yeah. This is a tragic occurrence for you."

He took a silver money clip shaped like a dollar sign out of his bathrobe pocket. I wondered if he didn't trust his roommate. Two bills changed hands. After a further exchange of information, the patrolman went away.

"Well," Illman said. "It looks like a pretty serious business. If you think I had anything to do with it, you're off your rocker."

"Speaking of rockers, you said your wife was crazy. What kind of crazy?"

"I was her husband, not her analyst. I wouldn't know."

"Did she need an analyst?"

"Sometimes I thought so. One week she'd be flying, full of big plans to make money. Then she'd go into a black mood and talk about killing herself." He shrugged. "It ran in her family."

"This could be an afterthought on your part."

His face reddened.

I turned to Frieda, who looked as if the news had sobered her. "Who was this fellow you saw at Ethel's house last week?"

"I dunno. She called him Owen, I think. Maybe it was his first name, maybe it was his last name. She didn't introduce us." She said it as if she felt cheated.

"Describe him?"

"Sure. A big guy, over six feet, wide in the shoulders, narrow in the beam. A smooth hunk of male. And young," with a malicious glance at Illman. "Black hair, and he had all of it, dreamy dark eyes, a cute little hairline moustache. I tabbed him for a gin-mill cowboy from Vegas, but he could be a movie star if I was a producer."

"Thank God you're not," Illman said.

"What made you think she'd taken up with him?"

"The way he moved around the house, like he owned it. He poured himself a drink while I was there. And he was in his shirtsleeves. A real sharp dresser, though. Custom-made stuff."

"You have a good eye."

"For men, she has," Illman said.

"Lay off me," she said in a hard voice, with no trace of the Martini drawl. "Or I'll really walk out on you, and then where will you be?"

"Right where I am now. Sitting pretty."

"That's what you think."

I interrupted their communion. "Do you know anything about this Owen character, Illman?"

"Not a thing. He's probably some jerk she picked up in Nevada while she was sweating out the divorce."

"Have you been to San Diego recently?"

"Not for months."

"That's true," Frieda said. "I've been keeping close track of Teddy. I have to. Incidently, it's getting late and I'm hungry. Go and put on some clothes, darling. You're prettier with clothes on."

"More than I'd say for you," he leered.

I left them and drove back to West Hollywood. The night-blooming girls and their escorts had begun to appear on the Strip. Gusts of music came from the doors that opened for them. But when I turned off Sunset, the streets were deserted, emptied by the television curfew.

All the lights were on in the redwood house on the hillside. I parked in the driveway and knocked on the front door. The draperies over the window beside it were pulled to one side, then fell back into place. A thin voice drifted out to me.

"Is that you, Mr. Archer?"

I said that it was. Clare opened the door inch by inch. Her face was almost haggard.

"I'm so relieved to see you."

"What's the trouble?"

"A man was watching the house. He was sitting there at the curb in a long black car. It looked like an undertaker's car. And it had a Nevada license."

"Are you sure?"

"Yes. It lighted up when he drove away. I saw it through the window. He only left a couple of minutes ago."

"Did you get a look at his face?"

"I'm afraid not. I didn't dare go out. I was petrified. He shone a searchlight on the window."

"Take it easy. There are plenty of big black cars in town, and quite a few Nevada licenses. He was probably looking for some other address."

"No. I had a—a kind of a fatal feeling when I saw him. I just *know* that he's connected in some way with Ethel's disappearance. I'm scared."

She leaned against the door, breathing quickly. She looked very young and vulnerable. I said:

"What am I going to do with you, kid? I can't leave you here alone."

"Are you going away?"

"I have to. I saw Edward. While I was there, he had a visitor from the HP. They found your sister's car abandoned near San Diego." I didn't mention the blood. She had enough on her mind.

"Edward killed her!" she cried. "I knew it."

"That I doubt. She may not even be dead. I'm going to San Diego to find out."

"Take me along, won't you?"

"It wouldn't be good for your reputation. Besides, you'd be in the way."

"No, I wouldn't. I promise. I have friends in San Diego. Just let me drive down there with you, and I can stay with them."

"You wouldn't be making this up?"

"Honest, I have friends there. Gretchen Falk and her husband, they're good friends of Ethel's and mine. We lived in San Diego for a while, before she married Edward. The Falks will be glad to let me stay with them."

"Hadn't you better phone them first?"

"I can't. The phone's disconnected. I tried it."

"Are you sure these people exist?"

"Of course," she said urgently.

I gave in. I turned out the lights and locked the door and put her bag in my car. Clare stayed very close to me.

As I was backing out, a car pulled in behind me, blocking the entrance to the driveway. I opened the door and got out. It was a black Lincoln with a searchlight mounted over the windshield.

Clare said: "He's come back."

The searchlight flashed on. Its bright beam swiveled towards me. I reached for the gun in my shoulder holster and got a firm grip on nothing. Holster and gun were packed in the suitcase in the trunk of my car. The searchlight blinded me.

A black gun emerged from the dazzle, towing a hand and an arm. They belonged to a quick-stepping cube-shaped man in a double-breasted flannel suit. A snap-brim hat was pulled down over his eyes. His mouth was as full of teeth as a barracuda's. It said:

"Where's Dewar?"

"Never heard of him."

"Owen Dewar. You've heard of him."

The gun dragged him forward another step and collided with my breastbone. His free hand palmed my flanks. All I could see was his unchanging smile, framed in brilliant light. I felt a keen desire to do some orthodontic work on it. But the gun was an inhibiting factor.

"You must be thinking of two other parties," I said.

"No dice. This is the house, and that's the broad. Out of the car, lady."

"I will not," she said in a tiny voice behind me.

"Out, or I'll blow a hole in your boy friend here."

Reluctantly, she clambered out. The teeth looked down at her ankles as if they wanted to chew them. I made a move for the gun. It dived into my solar plexus, doubling me over. Its muzzle flicked the side of my head. It pushed me back against the fender of my car. I felt a worm of blood crawling past my ear.

"You coward! Leave him alone." Clare flung herself at him. He sidestepped neatly, moving on the steady pivot of the gun against my chest. She went to her knees on the blacktop.

"Get up, lady, but keep your voice down. How many boy friends you keep on the string, anyway?"

She got to her feet. "He isn't my boy friend. Who are you? Where is Ethel?"

"That's a hot one." The smile intensified. "You're Ethel. The question is, where's Dewar?"

"I don't know any Dewar."

"Sure you do, Ethel. You know him well enough to marry him. Now tell me where he is, and nobody gets theirselves hurt." The flat voice dropped, and added huskily: "Only I haven't got much time to waste."

"You're wrong," she said. "You're completely mistaken. I'm not Ethel. I'm Clare. Ethel's my older sister."

He stepped back and swung the gun in a quarter-circle, covering us both. "Turn your face to the light. Let's have a good look at you."

She did as she was told, striking a rigid pose. He shifted the gun to his left hand, and brought a photograph out of his inside pocket. Looking from it to her face, he shook his head doubtfully.

"I guess you're leveling at that. You're younger than this one, and thinner." He handed her the photograph. "She your sister?"

"Yes. It's Ethel."

I caught a glimpse of the picture over her shoulder. It was a blown-up candid shot of two people. One was a pretty blonde who looked like Clare five years from now. She was leaning on the arm of a tall dark man with a hairline moustache. They were smirking at each other, and there was a flower-decked altar in the background.

"Who's the man?" I said.

"Dewar. Who else?" said the teeth behind the gun. "They got married in Vegas last month. I got this picture from the Chaparral Chapel. It goes with the twenty-five-dollar wedding." He snatched it out of Clare's hands and put it back in his pocket. "It took me a couple of weeks to run her down. She used her maiden name, see."

"Where did you catch up with her? San Diego?"

"I didn't catch up with her. Would I be here if I did?"

"What do you want her for?"

"I don't want her. I got nothing against the broad, except that she tied up with Dewar. He's the boy I want."

"What for?"

"You wouldn't be inarested. He worked for me at one time." The gun swiveled brightly towards Clare. "You know where your sister is?"

"No, I don't. I wouldn't tell you if I did."

"That's no way to talk now, lady. My motto's cooperation. From other people."

I said: "Her sister's been missing for a week. The HP found her car in San Diego. It had bloodstains on the front seat. Are you sure you didn't catch up with her?"

"I'm asking you the questions, punk." But there was a trace of uncertainty in his voice. "What happened to Dewar if the blonde is missing?"

"I think he ran out with her money."

Clare turned to me. "You didn't tell me all this."

"I'm telling you now."

The teeth said: "She had money?"

"Plenty."

"The bastard. The bastard took us both, eh?"

"Dewar took you for money?"

"You ask too many questions, punk. You'll talk yourself to death one of these days. Now stay where you are for ten minutes, both of you. Don't move, don't yell, don't telephone. I might decide to drive around the block and come back and make sure."

He backed down the brilliant alley of the searchlight beam. The door of his car slammed. All of its lights went off together. It rolled away into darkness, and didn't come back.

It was past midnight when we got to San Diego, but there was still a light in the Falks' house. It was a stucco cottage on a street of identical cottages in Pacific Beach.

"We lived here once," Clare said. "When I was going to high school. That house, second from the corner." Her voice was nostalgic, and she looked around the jerry-built tract as if it represented something precious to her. The pre-Illman era in her young life.

I knocked on the front door. A big henna-head in a housecoat opened it on a chain. But when she saw Clare beside me, she flung the door wide.

"Clare honey, where you been? I've been trying to phone you in Berkeley, and here you are. How are you, honey?"

She opened her arms and the younger woman walked into them.

"Oh, Gretchen," she said with her face on the redhead's breast. "Something's happened to Ethel, something terrible."

"I know it, honey, but it could be worse."

"Worse than murder?"

"She isn't murdered. Put that out of your mind. She's pretty badly hurt, but she isn't murdered."

Clare stood back to look at her face. "You've seen her? Is she here?"

The redhead put a finger to her mouth, which was big and generous-looking, like the rest of her. "Hush, Clare. Jake's asleep, he has to get up early, go to work. Yeah, I've seen her, but she isn't here. She's in a nursing home over on the other side of town."

"You said she's badly hurt?"

"Pretty badly beaten, yeah, poor dear. But the doctor told me she's pulling out of it fine. A little plastic surgery, and she'll be as good as new."

"Plastic surgery?"

"Yeah, I'm afraid she'll need it. I got a look at her face tonight, when they changed the bandages. Now take it easy, honey. It could be worse."

"Who did it to her?"

"That lousy husband of hers."

"Edward?"

"Heck, no. The other one. The one that calls himself Dewar, Owen Dewar."

I said: "Have you seen Dewar?"

"I saw him a week ago, the night he beat her up, the dirty rotten bully." Her deep contralto growled in her throat. "I'd like to get my hands on him just for five minutes."

"So would a lot of people, Mrs. Falk."

She glanced inquiringly at Clare. "Who's your friend? You haven't introduced us."

"I'm sorry. Mr. Archer, Mrs. Falk. Mr. Archer is a detective, Gretchen."

"I was wondering. Ethel didn't want me to call the police. I told her she ought to, but she said no. The poor darling's so ashamed of herself, getting mixed up with that kind of a louse. She didn't even get in touch with *me* until tonight. Then she saw in the paper about her car being picked up, and she thought maybe I could get it back for her without any publicity. Publicity is what she doesn't want most. I guess it's a tragic thing for a beautiful girl like Ethel to lose her looks."

I said: "There won't be any publicity if I can help it. Did you go to see the police about her car?"

"Jake advised me not to. He said it would blow the whole thing wide open. And the doctor told me he was kind of breaking the law by not reporting the beating she took. So I dropped it."

"How did this thing happen?"

"I'll tell you all I know about it. Come on into the living room, kids, let me fix you something to drink."

Clare said: "You're awfully kind, Gretchen, but I must go to Ethel. Where is she?"

"The Mission Rest Home. Only don't you think you better

wait till morning? It's a private hospital, but it's awful late for visitors."

"I've got to see her," Clare said. "I couldn't sleep a wink if I didn't. I've been so worried about her."

Gretchen heaved a sigh. "Whatever you say, honey. We can try, anyway. Give me a second to put on a dress and I'll show you where the place is."

She led us into the darkened living room, turned the television set off and the lights on. A quart of beer, nearly full, stood on a coffee table beside the scuffed davenport. She offered me a glass, which I accepted gratefully. Clare refused. She was so tense she couldn't even sit down.

We stood and looked at each other for a minute. Then Gretchen came back, struggling with a zipper on one massive hip.

"All set, kids. You better drive, Mr. Archer. I had a couple of quarts to settle my nerves. You wouldn't believe it, but I've gained five pounds since Ethel came down here. I always gain weight when I'm anxious."

We went out to my car, and turned towards the banked lights of San Diego. The women rode in the front seat. Gretchen's opulent flesh was warm against me.

"Was Ethel here before it happened?" I said.

"Sure she was, for a day. Ethel turned up here eight or nine days ago, Tuesday of last week it was. I hadn't heard from her for several months, since she wrote me that she was going to Nevada for a divorce. It was early in the morning when she drove up; in fact, she got me out of bed. The minute I saw her, I knew that something was wrong. The poor kid was scared, really scared. She was as cold as a corpse, and her teeth were chattering. So I fed her some coffee and put her in a hot tub, and after that she told me what it was that'd got her down."

"Dewar?"

"You said it, mister. Ethel never was much of a picker. When she was hostessing at the Grant coffee shop back in the old days, she was always falling for the world's worst phonies. Speaking of phonies, this Dewar takes the cake. She met him in Las Vegas when she was waiting for her divorce from Illman. He was a big promoter, to hear him tell it. She fell for the story, and she fell for him. A few days after she got her final decree, she married him. Big romance. Big deal. They were going to be business partners, too. He said he had some money to invest, twenty-five thousand or so, and he knew of a swell little hotel in Acapulco that they could buy at a steal for fifty thousand. The idea was that they should each put up half, and go and live in Mexico in the lap of luxury for the rest of their lives. He didn't show her any of his money, but she believed him. She drew her settlement money out of the bank and came to L. A. with him to close up her house and get set for the Mexican deal."

"He must have hypnotized her," Clare said. "Ethel's a smart business woman."

"Not with something tall, dark, and handsome, honey. I give him that much. He's got the looks. Well, they lived in L.A. for a couple of weeks, on Ethel's money of course, and he kept putting off the Mexican trip. He didn't want to go anywhere, in fact, just sit around the house and drink her liquor and eat her good cooking."

"He was hiding out," I said.

"From what? The police?"

"Worse than that. Some gangster pal from Nevada was gunning for him; still is. Ethel wasn't the only one he fleeced."

"Nice guy, eh? Anyway, Ethel started to get restless. She didn't like sitting around with all that money in the house, waiting for nothing. Last Monday night, a week ago Monday that is, she had a showdown with him. Then it all came out. He didn't have any money or anything else. He wasn't a promoter, he didn't know of any hotel in Acapulco. His whole buildup was as queer as a three-dollar bill. Apparently he made his living gambling, but he was even all washed up with that. Nothing. But she was married to him now, he said, and she was going to sit still and like it or he'd knock her block off.

"He meant it, too, Ethel said. She's got the proof of it now. She waited until he drank himself to sleep that night, then she threw some things in a bag, including her twenty-five thousand, and came down here. She was on her way to get a quickie divorce in Mexico, but Jake and me talked her into staying for a while and thinking it over. Jake said she could probably get an annulment right in California, and that would be more legal."

"He was probably right."

"Yeah? Maybe it wasn't such a bright idea after all. We kept her here just long enough for Dewar to catch her. Apparently she left some letters behind, and he ran down the list of her friends until he found her at our place. He talked her into going for a drive to talk it over. I didn't hear what was said— they were in her room—but he must have used some powerful persuasion. She went out of the house with him as meek as a lamb, and they drove away in her car. That was the last I saw of her, until she got in touch with me tonight. When she didn't come back, I wanted to call the police, but Jake wouldn't let me. He said I had no business coming between a man and his wife, and all that guff. I gave Jake a piece of my mind tonight on that score. I ought to've called the cops as soon as Dewar showed his sneaking face on our front porch."

"What exactly did he do to her?"

"He gave her a bad clobbering, that's obvious. Ethel didn't want to talk about it much tonight. The subject was painful to her in more ways than one."

"Did he take her money?"

"He must have. It's gone. So is he."

We were on the freeway which curved past the hills of Balboa Park. The trees of its man-made jungle were restless against the sky. Below us on the other side, the city sloped like a frozen cascade of lights down to the black concavity of the bay.

The Mission Rest Home was in the eastern suburbs, an old stucco mansion which had been converted into a private hospital. The windows in its thick stucco walls were small and barred, and there were lights in some of them.

I rang the doorbell. Clare was so close to my back I could feel her breath. A woman in a purple flannelette wrapper opened the door. Her hair hung in two gray braids, which were ruler-straight. Her hard black eyes surveyed the three of us, and stayed on Gretchen.

"What is it now, Mrs. Falk?" she said brusquely.

"This is Mrs.— Miss Larrabee's sister Clare."

"Miss Larrabee is probably sleeping. She shouldn't be disturbed."

"I know it's late," Clare said in a tremulous voice. "But I've come all the way from San Francisco to see her."

"She's doing well, I assure you of that. She's completely out of danger."

"Can't I just go in for teensy visit? Ethel will want to see me, and Mr. Archer has some questions to ask her. Mr. Archer is a private detective."

"This is very irregular." Reluctantly, she opened the door. "Wait here, and I'll see if she is awake. Please keep your voices down. We have other patients."

We waited in a dim high-ceilinged room which had once been the reception room of the mansion. The odors of mustiness and medication blended depressingly in the stagnant air.

"I wonder what brought her here," I said.

"She knew old lady Lestina," Gretchen said. "She stayed with her at one time, when Mrs. Lestina was running a boardinghouse."

"Of course," Clare said. "I remember the name. That was when Ethel was going to San Diego State. Then Daddy—got killed, and she had to drop out of school and go to work."

Tears glimmered in her eyes. "Poor Ethel. She's always tried so hard, and been so good to me."

Gretchen patted her shoulder. "You bet she has, honey. Now you have a chance to be good to her."

"Oh, I will. I'll do everything I can."

Mrs. Lestina appeared in the arched doorway. "She's not asleep. I guess you can talk to her for a very few minutes."

We followed her to a room at the end of one wing of the house. A white-uniformed nurse was waiting at the door. "Don't say anything to upset her, will you? She's always fighting sedation as it is."

The room was large but poorly furnished, with a mirrorless bureau, a couple of rickety chairs, a brown-enameled hospital bed. The head on the raised pillow was swathed in bandages through which tufts of blond hair were visible. The woman sat up and spread her arms. The whites of her eyes were red, suffused with blood from broken vessels. Her swollen lips opened and said, "Clare!" in a tone of incredulous joy.

The sisters hugged each other, with tears and laughter. "It's wonderful to see you," the older one said through broken teeth. "How did you get here so fast?"

"I came to stay with Gretchen. Why didn't you call me, Ethel? I've been worried sick about you."

"I'm dreadfully sorry, darling. I should have, shouldn't I? I didn't want you to see me like this. And I've been so ashamed of myself. I've been such a terrible fool. I've lost our money."

The nurse was standing against the door, torn between her duty and her feelings. "Now you promised not to get excited, Miss Larrabee."

"She's right," Clare said. "Don't give it a second thought. I'm going to leave school and get a job and look after you. You need some looking after for a change."

"Nuts. I'll be fine in a couple of weeks." The brave voice issuing from the mask was deep and vibrant. "Don't make any rash decisions, kiddo. The head is bloody but unbowed." The sisters looked at each other in the silence of deep affection.

I stepped forward to the bedside and introduced myself. "How did this happen to you, Miss Larrabee?"

"It's a long story," she lisped, "and a sordid one."

"Mrs. Falk has told me most of it up to the point when Dewar made you drive away with him. Where did he take you?"

"To the beach, I think it was in La Jolla. It was late and there was nobody there and the tide was coming in. And Owen had a gun. I was terrified. I didn't know what more he wanted from me. He already had my twenty-five thousand."

"He had the money?"

"Yes. It was in my room at Gretchen's house. He made me give it to him before we left there. But it didn't satisfy him. He said I hurt his pride by leaving him. He said he had to satisfy his pride." Contempt ran through her voice like a thin steel thread.

"By beating you up?"

"Apparently. He hit me again and again. I think he left me for dead. When I came to, the waves were splashing on me. I managed somehow to get up to the car. It wasn't any good to me, though, because Owen had the keys. It's funny he didn't take it."

"Too easily traced," I said. "What did you do then?"

"I hardly know. I think I sat in the car for a while, wondering what to do. Then a taxi went by and I stopped him and told him to bring me here."

"You weren't very wise not to call the police. They might have got your money back. Now it's a cold trail."

"Did you come here to lecture me?"

"I'm sorry. I didn't mean—"

"I was half crazy with pain," she said. "I hardly knew what I was doing. I couldn't bear to have anybody see me."

Her fingers were active among the folds of the sheets. Clare reached out and stroked her hands into quietness. "Now, now, darling," she crooned. "Nobody's criticizing you. You take things nice and easy for a while, and Clare will look after you."

The masked head rolled on the pillow. The nurse came forward, her face solicitous. "I think Miss Larrabee has had enough, don't you?"

She showed us out. Clare lingered with her sister for a moment, then followed us to the car. She sat between us in brooding silence all the way to Pacific Beach. Before I dropped them off at Gretchen's house, I asked for her permission to go to the police. She wouldn't give it to me, and nothing I could say would change her mind.

I spent the rest of the night in a motor court, trying to crawl over the threshold of sleep. Shortly after dawn I disentangled myself from the twisted sheets and drove out to La Jolla. La Jolla is a semi-detached suburb of San Diego, a small resort town half surrounded by sea. It was a gray morning. The slanting streets were scoured with the sea's cold breath, and the sea itself looked like hammered pewter.

I warmed myself with a short-order breakfast and went the rounds of the hotels and motels. No one resembling Dewar had registered in the past week. I tried the bus and taxi companies, in vain. Dewar had slipped out of town unnoticed. But

I did get a lead on the taxi driver who had taken Ethel to the Mission Rest Home. He had mentioned the injured woman to his dispatcher, and the dispatcher gave me his name and address. Stanley Simpson, 38 Calle Laureles.

Simpson was a paunchy, defeated-looking man who hadn't shaved for a couple of days. He came to the door of his tiny bungalow in his underwear, rubbing sleep out of his eyes. "What's the pitch, bub? If you got me up to try and sell me something, you're in for a disappointment."

I told him who I was and why I was there. "Do you remember the woman?"

"I hope to tell you I do. She was bleeding like a stuck pig, all over the back seat. It took me a couple of hours to clean it off. Somebody pistol-whipped her, if you ask me. I wanted to take her to the hospital, but she said no. Hell, I couldn't argue with her in that condition. Did I do wrong?" His slack mouth twisted sideways in a self-doubting grimace.

"If you did, it doesn't matter. She's being taken good care of. I thought you might have got a glimpse of the man that did it to her."

"Not me, mister. She was all by herself, nobody else in sight. She got out of a parked car and staggered out into the road. I couldn't just leave her there, could I?"

"Of course not. You're a Good Samaritan, Simpson. Exactly where did you pick her up?"

"Down by the Cove. She was sitting in this Buick. I dropped a party off at the beach club and I was on my way back, kind of cruising along—"

"What time?"

"Around ten o'clock, I guess it was. I can check my schedule."

"It isn't important. Incidentally, did she pay you for the ride?"

"Yeah, she had a buck and some change in her purse. She had a hard time making it. No tip," he added gloomily.

"Tough cheese."

His fogged eyes brightened. "You're a friend of hers, aren't you? Wouldn't you say I rate a tip on a run like that? I always say, better late than never."

"Is that what you always say?" I handed him a dollar.

The Cove was a roughly semicircular inlet at the foot of a steep hill surmounted by a couple of hotels. Its narrow curving beach and the street above it were both deserted. An offshore wind had swept away the early morning mist, but the sky was still cloudy, and the sea grim. The long swells slammed the beach like stone walls falling, and broke in foam on the rocks that framed the entrance to the Cove.

I sat in my car and watched them. I was at a dead end. This seaswept place, under this iron sky, was like the world's dead end. Far out at sea, a carrier floated like a chip on the horizon. A Navy jet took off from it and scrawled tremendous nothings on the distance.

Something bright caught my eye. It was in the trough of a wave a couple of hundred yards outside the Cove. Then it was on a crest: the aluminum air-bottle of an Aqua-lung strapped to a naked brown back. Its wearer was prone on a surfboard, kicking with black-finned feet towards the shore. He was kicking hard, and paddling with one arm, but he was making slow progress. His other arm dragged in the opaque water. He seemed to be towing something, something heavy. I wondered if he had speared a shark or a porpoise. His face was inscrutable behind its glass mask.

I left my car and climbed down to the beach. The man on the surfboard came towards me with his tiring one-armed stroke, climbing the walled waves and sliding down them. A final surge picked him up and set him on the sand, almost at my feet. I dragged his board out of the backwash, and helped him to pull in the line that he was holding in one hand. His catch was nothing native to the sea. It was a man.

The end of the line was looped around his body under the armpits. He lay face down like an exhausted runner, a big man, fully clothed in soggy tweeds. I turned him over and saw the aquiline profile, the hairline moustache over the blue mouth, the dark eyes clogged with sand. Owen Dewar had made his escape by water.

The skin-diver took off his mask and sat down heavily, his chest working like a great furred bellows. "I go down for abalone," he said between breaths. "I find this. Caught between two rocks at thirty-forty feet."

"How long has he been in the water?"

"It's hard to tell. I'd say a couple of days, anyway. Look at his color. Poor stiff. But I wish they wouldn't drown themselves in my hunting grounds."

"Do you know him?"

"Nope. Do you?"

"Never saw him before," I said, with truth.

"How about you phoning the police, Mac? I'm pooped. And unless I make a catch, I don't eat today. There's no pay in fishing for corpses."

"In a minute."

I went through the dead man's pockets. There was a set of car keys in his jacket pocket, and an alligator wallet on his hip. It contained no money, but the drivers' license was decipherable: Owen Dewar, Mesa Court, Las Vegas. I put the wallet back, and let go of the body. The head rolled sideways. I saw the small hole in his neck, washed clean by the sea.

"Holy Mother!" the driver said. "He was shot."

I got back to the Falk house around midmorning. The sun had burned off the clouds, and the day was turning hot. By daylight the long, treeless street of identical houses looked cheap and rundown. It was part of the miles of suburban slums that the war had scattered all over Southern California.

Gretchen was sprinkling the brown front lawn with a desultory hose. She looked too big for the pocket-handkerchief yard. The sunsuit that barely covered her various bulges made her look even bigger. She turned off the water when I got out of my car.

"What gives? You've got trouble on your face if I ever saw trouble."

"Dewar is dead. Murdered. A skin-diver found him in the sea off La Jolla."

She took it calmly. "That's not such bad news, is it? He had it coming. Who killed him?"

"I told you a gunman from Nevada was on his trail. Maybe he caught him. Anyway, Dewar was shot and bled to death from a neck wound. Then he was dumped in the ocean. I had to lay the whole thing on the line for the police, since there's murder in it."

"You told them what happened to Ethel?"

"I had to. They're at the rest home talking to her now."

"What about Ethel's money? Was the money on him?"

"Not a trace of it. And he didn't live to spend it. The police pathologist thinks he's been dead for a week. Whoever got Dewar got the money at the same time."

"Will she ever get it back, do you think?"

"If we can catch the murderer, and he still has it with him. That's a big if. Where's Clare, by the way? With her sister?"

"Clare went back to L. A."

"What for?"

"Don't ask me." She shrugged her rosy shoulders. "She got Jake to drive her down to the station before he went to work. I wasn't up. She didn't even tell me she was going." Gretchen seemed peeved.

"Did she get a telegram, or a phone call?"

"Nothing. All I know is what Jake told me. She talked him into lending her ten bucks. I wouldn't mind so much, but it was all the ready cash we had, until payday. Oh well, I guess we'll get it back, if Ethel recovers her money."

"You'll get it back," I said. "Clare seems to be a straight kid."

"That's what I always used to think. When they lived here, before Ethel met Illman and got into the chips, Clare was just about the nicest kid on the block. In spite of all the trouble in her family."

"What trouble was that?"

"Her father shot himself. Didn't you know? They said it was an accident, but the people on the street—we knew different. Mr. Larrabee was never the same after his wife left him. He spent his time brooding, drinking and brooding. Clare reminded me of him, the way she behaved last night after you left. She wouldn't talk to me or look at me. She shut herself up in her room and acted real cold. If you want the honest truth, I don't like her using my home as if it was a motel and Jake was a taxi-service. The least she could of done was say good-bye to me."

"It sounds as if she had something on her mind."

All the way back to Los Angeles, I wondered what it was. It took me a little over two hours to drive from San Diego to West Hollywood. The black Lincoln with the searchlight and the Nevada license plates was standing at the curb below the redwood house. The front door of the house was standing open.

I transferred my automatic from the suitcase to my jacket pocket, making sure that it was ready to fire. I climbed the terraced lawn beside the driveway. My feet made no sound in the grass. When I reached the porch, I heard voices from inside. One was the gunman's hoarse and deathly monotone:

"I'm taking it, sister. It belongs to me."

"You're a liar."

"Sure, but not about this. The money is mine."

"It's my sister's money. What right have you got to it?"

"This. Dewar stole it from me. He ran a poker game for me in Vegas, a high-stakes game in various hotels around town. He was a good dealer, and I trusted him with the house take. I let it pile up for a week, that was my mistake. I should've kept a closer watch on him. He ran out on me with twenty-five grand or more. That's the money you're holding, lady."

"I don't believe it. You can't prove that story. It's fantastic."

"I don't have to prove it. Gelt talks, but iron talks louder. So hand it over, eh?"

"I'll die first."

"Maybe you will at that."

I edged along the wall to the open door. Clare was standing flat against the opposite wall of the hallway. She was clutching a sheaf of bills to her breast. The gunman's broad flannel back was to me, and he was advancing on her.

"Stay away from me, you." Her cry was thin and desperate.

She was trying to merge with the wall, pressed by an orgastic terror.

"I don't like taking candy from a baby," he said in a very reasonable tone. "Only I'm going to have that money back."

"You can't have it. It's Ethel's. It's all she has."

"———— you, lady. You and your sister both."

He raised his armed right hand and slapped the side of her face with the gun barrel, lightly. Fingering the welt it left, she said in a kind of despairing stupor:

"You're the one that hurt Ethel, aren't you? Now you're hurting me. You like hurting people, don't you?"

"Listen to reason, lady. It ain't just the money, it's a matter of business. I let it happen once, it'll happen again. I can't afford to let anybody get away with nothing. I got a reputation to live up to."

I said from the doorway: "Is that why you killed Dewar?"

He let out an animal sound, and whirled in my direction. I shot before he did, twice. The first slug rocked him back on his heels. His bullet went wild, plowed the ceiling. My second slug took him off balance and slammed him against the wall. His blood spattered Clare and the money in her hands. She screamed once, very loudly.

The man from Las Vegas dropped his gun. It clattered on the parquetry. His hands clasped his perforated chest, trying to hold the blood in. He slid down the wall slowly, his face a mask of smiling pain, and sat with a bump on the floor. He blew red bubbles and said:

"You got me wrong. I didn't kill Dewar. I didn't know he was dead. The money belongs to me. You made a big mistake, punk."

"So did you."

He went on smiling, as if in fierce appreciation of the joke. Then his red grin changed to a rictus, and he slumped sideways.

Clare looked from him to me, her eyes wide and dark with the sight of death. "I don't know how to thank you. He was going to kill me."

"I doubt that. He was just combining a little pleasure with business."

"But he shot at you."

"It's just as well he did. It leaves no doubt that it was self-defense."

"Is it true what you said? That Dewar's dead? He killed him?"

"You tell me."

"What do you mean?"

"You've got the money that Dewar took from your sister. Where did you get it?"

"It was here, right in this house. I found it in the kitchen."

"That's kind of hard to swallow, Clare."

"It's true." She looked down at the blood-spattered money in her hands. The outside bill was a hundred. Unconsciously, she tried to wipe it clean on the front of her dress. "He had it hidden here. He must have come back and hid it."

"Show me where."

"You're not being very nice to me. And I'm not feeling well."

"Neither is Dewar. You didn't shoot him yourself, by any chance?"

"How could I? I was in Berkeley when it happened. I wish I was back there now."

"You know when it happened, do you?"

"No." She bit her lip. "I don't mean that. I mean I was in Berkeley all along. You're a witness, you were with me on the train coming down."

"Trains run both ways."

She regarded me with loathing. "You're not nice at all. To think that yesterday I thought you were nice."

"You're wasting time, Clare. I have to call the police. But first I want to see where you found the money. Or where you say you did."

"In the kitchen. You've got to believe me. It took me a long time to get here from the station on the bus. I'd only just found it when he walked in on me."

"I'll believe the physical evidence, if any."

To my surprise, the physical evidence was there. A red-enameled flour canister was standing open on the board beside the kitchen sink. There were fingerprints on the flour, and a floury piece of oilskin wrapping in the sink.

"He hid the money under the flour," Clare said. "I guess he thought it would be safer here than if he carried it around with him."

It wasn't a likely story. On the other hand, the criminal mind is capable of strange things. Whose criminal mind, I wondered: Clare's, or Owen Dewar's, or somebody else's? I said:

"Where did you get the bright idea of coming back here and looking for it?"

"Ethel suggested it last night, just before I left her. She told me this was his favorite hiding place while she was living with him. She discovered it by accident one day."

"Hiding place for what?"

"Some kind of drug he took. He was a drug addict. Do you still think I'm lying?"

"Somebody is. But I suppose I've got to take your word, until I get something better. What are you going to do with the money?"

"Ethel said if I found it, that I was to go down and put it in the bank."

"There's no time for that now. You better let me hold it for you. I have a safe in my office."

"No. You don't trust me. Why should I trust you?"

"Because you can trust me, and you know it. If the cops impound it, you'll have to prove ownership to get it back."

She was too spent to argue. She let me take it out of her hands. I riffled through the bills and got a rough idea of their sum. There was easily twenty-five thousand there. I gave her a receipt for that amount, and put the sheaf of bills in my inside pocket.

It was after dark when the cops got through with me. By that time I was equipped to do a comparative study on the San Diego and Los Angeles P.D.'s. With the help of a friend in the D.A.'s office, Clare's eye-witness account, and the bullet in the ceiling, I got away from them without being booked. The dead man's record also helped. He had been widely suspected of shooting Bugsy Siegel, and had fallen heir to some of Siegel's holdings. His name was Jack Fidelis. R.I.P.

I drove out Sunset to my office. The Strip was lighting up for business again. The stars looked down on its neon conflagration like hard bright knowing eyes. I pulled the Venetian blinds and locked the doors and counted the money: $26,380. I wrapped it up in brown paper, sealed it with wax and tucked it away in the safe. I would have preferred to tear it in little pieces and flush the green confetti down the drain. Two men had died for it. I wasn't eager to become the third.

I had a steak in the restaurant at International Airport, and hopped a shuttle plane to Las Vegas. There I spent a rough night in various gambling joints, watching the suckers blow their vacation money, pinching my own pennies, and talking to some of the guys and girls that raked the money in. The rest of Illman's two hundred dollars bought me the facts I needed.

I flew back to Los Angeles in the morning, picked up my car and headed for San Diego. I was tired enough to sleep standing up, like a horse. But something heavier than sleep or tiredness sat on the back of my neck and pressed the gas pedal down to the floorboards. It was the thought of Clare.

Clare was with her sister in the Mission Rest Home. She

was waiting outside the closed door of Ethel's room when Mrs. Lestina took me down the hall. She looked as if she had passed a rougher night than mine. Her grooming was careless, hair uncombed, mouth unpainted. The welt from Fidelis' gun had turned blue and spread to one puffed eye. And I thought how very little it took to break a young girl down into a tramp, if she was vulnerable, or twist her into something worse than a tramp.

"Did you bring it with you?" she said as soon as Mrs. Lestina was out of earshot. "Ethel's angry with me for turning it over to you."

"I'm not surprised."

"Give it to me. Please." Her hand clawed at my sleeve. "Isn't that what you came for, to give it back to me?"

"It's in the safe in my office in Los Angeles. That is, if you're talking about the money."

"What else would I be talking about? You'll simply have to go back there and get it. Ethel can't leave here without it. She needs it to pay her bill."

"Is Ethel planning to go some place?"

"I persuaded her to come back to Berkeley with me. She'll have better care in the hospital there, and I know of a good plastic surgeon—"

"It'll take more than that to put Ethel together again."

"What do you mean?"

"You should be able to guess. You're not a stupid girl, or are you? Has she got you fooled the way she had me fooled?"

"I don't know what you're talking about. But I don't like it. Every time I see you, you seem to get nastier."

"This is a nasty business. It's rubbing off on all of us, isn't it, kid?"

She looked at me vaguely through a fog of doubt. "Don't you dare call me kid. I thought you were a real friend for a while, but you don't even like me. You've said some dreadful things. You probably think you can scare me into letting you keep our money. Well, you can't."

"That's my problem," I said. "What to do with the money."

"You'll give it back to Ethel and me, that's what you'll do. There are laws to deal with people like you—"

"And people like Ethel. I want to talk to her."

"I won't let you. My sister's suffered enough already."

She spread her arms across the width of the door. I was tempted to go away and send her the money and forget the whole thing. But the need to finish it pushed me, imperative as a gun at my back.

I lifted her by the waist and tried to set her aside. Her

entire body was rigid and jerking galvanically. Her hands slid under my arms and around my neck and held on. Her head rolled on my shoulder and was still. Suddenly, like delayed rain after lightning, her tears came. I stood and held her vibrating body, trying to quench the dangerous heat that was rising in my veins, and wondering what in hell I was going to do.

"Ethel did it for me," she sobbed. "She wanted me to have a good start in life."

"Some start she's giving you. Did she tell you that?"

"She didn't have to. I knew. I tried to pretend to myself, but I knew. When she told me where to look for the money last night—the night before last."

"You knew Ethel took it from Dewar and hid it in her house?"

"Yes. The thought went through my mind, and I couldn't get rid of it. Ethel's always taken terrible chances, and money means so much to her. Not for herself. For me."

"She wasn't thinking of you when she gambled away the money she got from Illman. She went through it in a week."

"Is that what happened to it?"

"That's it. I flew to Las Vegas last night and talked to some of the people that got her money, dealers and stickmen. They remembered her. She had a bad case of gambling fever that week. It didn't leave her until the money was gone. Then maybe she thought of you."

"Poor Ethel. I've seen her before when she had a gambling streak."

"Poor Dewar," I said.

The door beside us creaked open. The muzzle of a blue revolver looked out. Above it, Ethel's eyes glared red from her bandaged face.

"Come in here, both of you."

Clare stretched out her hands towards her sister. "No, Ethel. Darling, you mustn't. Give me that gun."

"I have a use for it. I know what I'm doing."

She backed away, supporting herself on the doorknob.

I said to Clare: "We better do as she says. She won't hurt you."

"Nor you unless you make me. Don't reach for your gun, and don't try anything funny. You know what happened to Dewar."

"Not as well as you do."

"Don't waste any tears on that one. Save them for yourself. Now get in here." The gun wagged peremptorily.

I edged past her with Clare at my back. Ethel shut the door and moved to the bed, her eyes never leaving mine. She sat on its edge, and supported the elbow of her gun arm on her knee, hunched far over like an aged wreck of a woman.

It was strange to see the fine naked legs dangling below her hospital gown, the red polish flaking off her toenails. Her voice was low and resonant.

"I don't like to do this. But how am I going to make you see it my way if I don't? I want Clare to see it, too. It was self-defense, understand. I didn't intend to kill him. I never expected to see him again. Fidelis was after him, and it was only a matter of time until he caught up with Owen. Owen knew that. He told me himself he wouldn't live out the year. He was so sure of it he was paralyzed. He got so he wouldn't even go out of the house.

"Somebody had to make a move, and I decided it might as well be me. Why should I sit and wait for Fidelis to come and take the money back and blow Owen's head off for him? It was really my money, anyway, mine and Clare's."

"Leave me out of this," Clare said.

"But you don't understand, honey," the damaged mouth insisted. "It really was my money. We were legally married, what was his was mine. I talked him into taking it in the first place. He'd never have had the guts to do it alone. He thought Fidelis was God himself. I didn't. But I didn't want to be there when Jack Fidelis found him. So I left him. I took the money out of his pillow when he was asleep and hid it where he'd never look for it. Then I drove down here. I guess you know the rest. He found a letter from Gretchen in the house, and traced me through it. He thought I was carrying the money. When it turned out that I wasn't, he took me out to the beach and beat me up. I wouldn't tell him where it was. He threatened to shoot me then. I fought him for the gun, and it went off. It was a clear case of self-defense."

"Maybe it was. You'll never get a jury to believe it, though. Innocent people don't dump their shooting victims in the drink."

"But I didn't. The tide was coming in. I didn't even touch him after he died. He just lay there, and the water took him."

"While you stood and watched?"

"I couldn't get away. I was so weak I couldn't move for a long time. Then when I finally could, it was too late. He was gone, and he had the keys to the car."

"He drove you out to La Jolla, did he?"

"Yes."

"And held a gun on you at the same time. That's quite a trick."

"He did, though," she said. "That is the way it happened."

"I hear you telling me, Mrs. Dewar."

She winced behind her mask at the sound of her name. "I'm not Mrs. Dewar," she said. "I've taken back my maiden name. I'm Ethel Larrabee."

"We won't argue about the name. You'll be trading it in for a number, anyway."

"I don't think I will. The shooting was self-defense, and once he was dead the money belonged to me. There's no way of proving he stole it, now that Fidelis is gone. I guess I owe you a little thanks for that."

"Put down your gun, then."

"I'm not that grateful," she said.

Clare moved across the room towards her. "Let me look at the gun, Ethel. It's father's revolver, isn't it?"

"Be quiet, you little fool."

"I won't be quiet. These things have to be said. You're way off by yourself, Ethel, I'm not with you. I want no part of this, or the money. You don't understand how strange and dreadful—" Her voice broke. She stood a few feet from her sister, held back by the gun's menace, yet strongly drawn towards it. "That's father's revolver, isn't it? The one he shot himself with?"

"What if it is?"

"I'll tell you, Ethel Larrabee," I said. "Dewar didn't pull a gun on you. You were the one that had the gun. You forced him to drive you out to the beach and shot him in cold blood. But he didn't die right away. He lived long enough to leave his marks on you. Isn't that how it happened?"

The bandaged face was silent. I looked into the terrible eyes for assent. They were lost and wild, like an animal's. "Is that true, Ethel? Did you murder him?" Clare looked down at her sister with pity and terror.

"I did it for you," the masked face said. "I always tried to do what was best for you. Don't you believe me? Don't you know I love you? Ever since father killed himself I've tried—"

Clare turned and walked to the wall and stood with her forehead against it. Ethel put the muzzle of the gun in her mouth. Her broken teeth clenched on it the way a smoker bites on a pipestem. The bone and flesh of her head muffled its roar.

I laid her body out on the bed and pulled a sheet up over it.

Guilt-Edged Blonde

"What happened this morning?"
"Didn't he tell you? You talked to him on the
"He didn't say very much.

Guilt-Edged Blonde

A MAN was waiting for me at the gate at the edge of the runway. He didn't look like the man I expected to meet. He wore a stained tan windbreaker, baggy slacks, a hat as squashed and dubious as his face. He must have been forty years old, to judge by the gray in his hair and the lines around his eyes. His eyes were dark and evasive, moving here and there as if to avoid getting hurt. He had been hurt often and badly, I guessed.

"You Archer?"

I said I was. I offered him my hand. He didn't know what to do with it. He regarded it suspiciously, as if I was planning to try a Judo hold on him. He kept his hands in the pockets of his windbreaker.

"I'm Harry Nemo." His voice was a grudging whine. It cost him an effort to give his name away. "My brother told me to come and pick you up. You ready to go?"

"As soon as I get my luggage."

I collected my overnight bag at the counter in the empty waiting room. The bag was very heavy for its size. It contained, besides a toothbrush and spare linen, two guns and the ammunition for them. A .38 special for sudden work, and a .32 automatic as a spare.

Harry Nemo took me outside to his car. It was a new seven-passenger custom job, as long and black as death. The windshield and side windows were very thick, and they had the yellowish tinge of bullet-proof glass.

"Are you expecting to be shot at?"

"Not me." His smile was dismal. "This is Nick's car."

"Why didn't Nick come himself?"

He looked around the deserted field. The plane I had arrived on was a flashing speck in the sky above the red sun. The only human being in sight was the operator in the control tower. But Nemo leaned towards me in the seat, and spoke in a whisper:

"Nick's a scared pigeon. He's scared to leave the house. Ever since this morning."

128

"What happened this morning?"

"Didn't he tell you? You talked to him on the phone."

"He didn't say very much. He told me he wanted to hire a bodyguard for six days, until his boat sails. He didn't tell me why."

"They're gunning for him, that's why. He went to the beach this morning. He has a private beach along the back of his ranch, and he went down there by himself for his morning dip. Somebody took a shot at him from the top of the bluff. Five or six shots. He was in the water, see, with no gun handy. He told me the slugs were splashing around him like hailstones. He ducked and swam under water out to sea. Lucky for him he's a good swimmer, or he wouldn't've got away. It's no wonder he's scared. It means they caught up with him, see."

"Who are 'they,' or is that a family secret?"

Nemo turned from the wheel to peer into my face. His breath was sour, his look incredulous. "Christ, don't you know who Nick is? Didn't he tell you?"

"He's a lemon-grower, isn't he?"

"He is now."

"What did he used to be?"

The bitter beaten face closed on itself. "I oughtn't to be flapping at the mouth. He can tell you himself if he wants to."

Two hundred horses yanked us away from the curb. I rode with my heavy leather bag on my knees. Nemo drove as if driving was the one thing in life he enjoyed, rapt in silent communion with the engine. It whisked us along the highway, then down a gradual incline between geometrically planted lemon groves. The sunset sea glimmered red at the foot of the slope.

Before we reached it, we turned off the blacktop into a private lane which ran like a straight hair-parting between the dark green trees. Straight for half a mile or more to a low house in a clearing.

The house was flat-roofed, made of concrete and fieldstone, with an attached garage. All of its windows were blinded with heavy draperies. It was surrounded with well-kept shrubbery and lawn, the lawn with a ten-foot wire fence surmounted by barbed wire.

Nemo stopped in front of the closed and padlocked gate, and honked the horn. There was no response. He honked the horn again.

About halfway between the house and the gate, a crawling thing came out of the shrubbery. It was a man, moving very slowly on hands and knees. His head hung down almost to the ground. One side of his head was bright red, as if he had fallen in paint. He left a jagged red trail in the gravel of the driveway.

Harry Nemo said, "Nick!" He scrambled out of the car. "What happened, Nick?"

The crawling man lifted his heavy head and looked at us. Cumbrously, he rose to his feet. He came forward with his legs spraddled and loose, like a huge infant learning to walk. He breathed loudly and horribly, looking at us with a dreadful hopefulness. Then he died on his feet, still walking. I saw the change in his face before it struck the gravel.

Harry Nemo went over the fence like a weary monkey, snagging his slacks on the barbed wire. He knelt beside his brother and turned him over and palmed his chest. He stood up shaking his head.

I had my bag unzipped and my hand on the revolver. I went to the gate, "Open up, Harry."

Harry was saying, "They got him," over and over. He crossed himself several times. "The dirty bastards."

"Open up," I said.

He found a key ring in the dead man's pocket and opened the padlocked gate. Our dragging footsteps crunched the gravel. I looked down at the specks of gravel in Nicky Nemo's eyes, the bullet hole in his temple.

"Who got him, Harry?"

"I dunno. Fats Jordan, or Artie Castola, or Faronese. It must have been one of them."

"The Purple Gang."

"You called it. Nicky was their treasurer back in the thirties. He was the one that didn't get into the papers. He handled the payoff, see. When the heat went on and the gang got busted up, he had some money in a safe deposit box. He was the only one that got away."

"How much money?"

"Nicky never told me. All I know, he come out here before the war and bought a thousand acres of lemon land. It took them fifteen years to catch up with him. He always knew they were gonna, though. He knew it."

"Artie Castola got off the Rock last spring."

"You're telling me. That's when Nicky bought himself the bullet-proof car and put up the fence."

"Are they gunning for you?"

He looked around at the darkening groves and the sky. The sky was streaked with running red, as if the sun had died a violent death.

"I dunno," he answered nervously. "They got no reason to. I'm as clean as soap. I never been in the rackets. Not since I was young, anyway. The wife made me go straight, see?"

I said: "We better get into the house and call the police."

The front door was standing a few inches ajar. I could see at the edge that it was sheathed with quarter-inch steel plate. Harry put my thoughts into words.

"Why in hell would he go outside? He was safe as houses as long as he stayed inside."

"Did he live alone?"

"More or less alone."

"What does that mean?"

He pretended not to hear me, but I got some kind of an answer. Looking through the doorless arch into the living room, I saw a leopardskin coat folded across the back of the chesterfield. There were red-tipped cigarette butts mingled with cigar butts in the ashtrays.

"Nicky was married?"

"Not exactly."

"You know the woman?"

"Naw." But he was lying.

Somewhere behind the thick walls of the house, there was a creak of springs, a crashing bump, the broken roar of a cold engine, grinding of tires in gravel. I got to the door in time to see a cerise convertible hurtling down the driveway. The top was down, and a yellow-haired girl was small and intent at the wheel. She swerved around Nick's body and got through the gate somehow, with her tires screaming. I aimed at the right rear tire, and missed. Harry came up behind me. He pushed my gun-arm down before I could fire again. The convertible disappeared in the direction of the highway.

"Let her go," he said.

"Who is she?"

He thought about it, his slow brain clicking almost audibly. "I dunno. Some pig that Nicky picked up some place. Her name is Flossie or Florrie or something. She didn't shoot him, if that's what you're worried about."

"You know her pretty well, do you?"

"The hell I do. I don't mess with Nicky's dames." He tried to work up a rage to go with the strong words, but he didn't have the makings. The best he could produce was petulance: "Listen, mister, why should you hang around? The guy that hired you is dead."

"I haven't been paid, for one thing."

"I'll fix that."

He trotted across the lawn to the body and came back with an alligator billfold. It was thick with money.

"How much?"

"A hundred will do it."

He handed me a hundred-dollar bill. "Now how about you amscray, bud, before the law gets here?"

"I need transportation."

"Take Nicky's car. He won't be using it. You can park it at the airport and leave the key with the agent."

"I can, eh?"

"Sure. I'm telling you you can."

"Aren't you getting a little free with your brother's property?"

"It's my property now, bud." A bright thought struck him, disorganizing his face. "Incidentally, how would you like to get off of my land?"

"I'm staying, Harry. I like this place. I always say it's people that make a place."

The gun was still in my hand. He looked down at it.

"Get on the telephone, Harry. Call the police."

"Who do you think you are, ordering me around? I took my last order from anybody, see?" He glanced over his shoulder at the dark and shapeless object on the gravel, and spat venomously.

"I'm a citizen, working for Nicky. Not for you."

He changed his tune very suddenly. "How much to go to work for me?"

"Depends on the line of work."

He manipulated the alligator wallet. "Here's another hundred. If you got to hang around, keep the lip buttoned down about the dame, eh? Is it a deal?"

I didn't answer, but I took the money. I put it in a separate pocket by itself. Harry telephoned the county sheriff.

He emptied the ash trays before the sheriff's men arrived, and stuffed the leopardskin coat into the woodbox. I sat and watched him.

We spent the next two hours with loud-mouthed deputies. They were angry with the dead man for having the kind of past that attracted bullets. They were angry with Harry for being his brother. They were secretly angry with themselves for being inexperienced and incompetent. They didn't even uncover the leopardskin coat.

Harry Nemo left the courthouse first. I waited for him to leave, and tailed him home, on foot.

Where a leaning palm tree reared its ragged head above the pavements, there was a court lined with jerry-built frame cottages. Harry turned up the walk between them and entered the first cottage. Light flashed on his face from inside. I heard a woman's voice say something to him. Then light and sound were cut off by the closing door.

An old gabled house with boarded-up windows stood opposite the court. I crossed the street and settled down in the shadows of its veranda to watch Harry Nemo's cottage. Three cigarettes later, a tall woman in a dark hat and a light coat came out of the cottage and walked briskly to the corner and out of sight. Two cigarettes after that, she reappeared at the corner on my side of the street, still walking briskly. I noticed that she had a large straw handbag under her arm. Her face was long and stony under the streetlight.

Leaving the street, she marched up the broken sidewalk to the veranda where I was leaning against the shadowed wall. The stairs groaned under her decisive footsteps. I put my hand on the gun in my pocket, and waited. With the rigid assurance of a WAC corporal marching at the head of her platoon, she crossed the veranda to me, a thin high-shouldered silhouette against the light from the corner. Her hand was in her straw bag, and the end of the bag was pointed at my stomach. Her shadowed face was a gleam of eyes, a glint of teeth.

"I wouldn't try it if I were you," she said. "I have a gun here, and the safety is off, and I know how to shoot it, mister."

"Congratulations."

"I'm not joking." Her deep contralto rose a notch. "Rapid fire used to be my specialty. So you better take your hands out of your pockets."

I showed her my hands, empty. Moving very quickly, she relieved my pocket of the weight of my gun, and frisked me for other weapons.

"Who are you, mister?" she said as she stepped back. "You can't be Arturo Castola, you're not old enough."

"Are you a policewoman?"

"I'll ask the questions. What are you doing here?"

"Waiting for a friend."

"You're a liar. You've been watching my house for an hour and a half. I tabbed you through the window."

"So you went and bought yourself a gun?"

"I did. You followed Harry home. I'm Mrs. Nemo, and I want to know why."

"Harry's the friend I'm waiting for."

"You're a double liar. Harry's afraid of you. You're no friend of his."

"That depends on Harry. I'm a detective."

She snorted. "Very likely. Where's your buzzer?"

"I'm a private detective," I said. "I have identification in my wallet."

"Show me. And don't try any tricks."

I produced my photostat. She held it up to the light from the street, and handed it back to me. "So you're a detective.

You better do something about your tailing technique. It's obvious."

"I didn't know I was dealing with a cop."

"I was a cop," she said. "Not any more."

"Then give me back my .38. It cost me seventy dollars."

"First tell me, what's your interest in my husband? Who hired you?"

"Nick, your brother-in-law. He called me in Los Angeles today, said he needed a bodyguard for a week. Didn't Harry tell you?"

She didn't answer.

"By the time I got to Nick, he didn't need a bodyguard, or anything. But I thought I'd stick around and see what I could find out about his death. He was a client, after all."

"You should pick your clients more carefully."

"What about picking brothers-in-law?"

She shook her head stiffly. The hair that escaped from under her hat was almost white. "I'm not responsible for Nick or anything about him. Harry is my responsibility. I met him in line of duty and I straightened him out, understand? I tore him loose from Detroit and the rackets, and I brought him out here. I couldn't cut him off from his brother entirely. But he hasn't been in trouble since I married him. Not once."

"Until now."

"Harry isn't in trouble now."

"Not yet. Not officially."

"What do you mean?"

"Give me my gun, and put yours down. I can't talk into iron."

She hesitated, a grim and anxious woman under pressure. I wondered what quirk of fate or psychology had married her to a hood, and decided it must have been love. Only love would send a woman across a dark street to face down an unknown gunman. Mrs. Nemo was horsefaced and aging and not pretty, but she had courage.

She handed me my gun. Its butt was soothing to the palm of my hand. I dropped it into my pocket. A gang of Negro boys at loose ends went by in the street, hooting and whistling purposelessly.

She leaned towards me, almost as tall as I was. Her voice was a low sibilance forced between her teeth:

"Harry had nothing to do with his brother's death. You're crazy if you think so."

"What makes you so sure, Mrs. Nemo?"

"Harry couldn't, that's all. I know Harry, I can read him like a book. Even if he had the guts, which he hasn't, he wouldn't dare to think of killing Nick. Nick was his older brother, understand, the successful one in the family." Her voice rasped contemptuously. "In spite of everything I could do or say, Harry worshiped Nick right up to the end."

"Those brotherly feelings sometimes cut two ways. And Harry had a lot to gain."

"Not a cent. Nothing."

"He's Nick's heir, isn't he?"

"Not as long as he stays married to me. I wouldn't let him touch a cent of Nick Nemo's filthy money. Is that clear?"

"It's clear to me. But is it clear to Harry?"

"I made it clear to him, many times. Anyway, this is ridiculous. Harry wouldn't lay a finger on that precious brother of his."

"Maybe he didn't do it himself. He could have had it done for him. I know he's covering for somebody."

"Who?"

"A blond girl left the house after we arrived. She got away in a cherry-colored convertible. Harry recognized her."

"A cherry-colored convertible?"

"Yes. Does that mean something to you?"

"No. Nothing in particular. She must have been one of Nick's girls. He always had girls."

"Why would Harry cover for her?"

"What do you mean, cover for her?"

"She left a leopardskin coat behind. Harry hid it, and paid me not to tell the police."

"Harry did that?"

"Unless I'm having delusions."

"Maybe you are at that. If you think that Harry paid that girl to shoot Nick, or had anything—"

"I know. Don't say it. I'm crazy."

Mrs. Nemo laid a thin hand on my arm. "Anyway, lay off Harry. Please. I have a hard enough time handling him as it is. He's worse than my first husband. The first one was a drunk, believe it or not." She glanced at the lighted cottage across the street, and I saw one half of her bitter smile. "I wonder what makes a woman go for the lame ducks the way I did."

"I wouldn't know, Mrs. Nemo. Okay, I lay off Harry."

But I had no intention of laying off Harry. When she went back to her cottage, I walked around three-quarters of the block and took up a new position in the doorway of a dry-cleaning establishment. This time I didn't smoke. I didn't even move, except to look at my watch from time to time.

Around eleven o'clock, the lights went out behind the blinds in the Nemo cottage. Shortly before midnight the front door opened and Harry slipped out. He looked up and down the street and began to walk. He passed within six feet of my dark doorway, hustling along in a kind of furtive shuffle.

Working very cautiously, at a distance, I tailed him downtown. He disappeared into the lighted cavern of an all night garage. He came out of the garage a few minutes later, driving a prewar Chevrolet.

My money also talked to the attendant. I drew a prewar Buick which would still do seventy-five. I proved that it would, as soon as I hit the highway. I reached the entrance to Nick Nemo's private lane in time to see Harry's lights approaching the dark ranch house.

I cut my lights and parked at the roadside a hundred yards below the entrance to the lane, and facing it. The Chevrolet reappeared in a few minutes. Harry was still alone in the front seat. I followed it blind as far as the highway before I risked my lights. Then down the highway to the edge of town.

In the middle of the motel and drive-in district he turned off onto a side road and in under a neon sign which spelled out TRAILER COURT across the darkness. The trailers stood along the bank of a dry creek. The Chevrolet stopped in front of one of them, which had a light in the window. Harry got out with a spotted bundle under his arm. He knocked on the door of the trailer.

I U-turned at the next corner and put in more waiting time. The Chevrolet rolled out under the neon sign and turned towards the highway. I let it go.

Leaving my car, I walked along the creek bank to the lighted trailer. The windows were curtained. The cerise convertible was parked on its far side. I tapped on the aluminum door.

"Harry?" a girl's voice said. "Is that you, Harry?"

I muttered something indistinguishable. The door opened, and the yellow-haired girl looked out. She was very young, but her round blue eyes were heavy and sick with hangover, or remorse. She had on a nylon slip, nothing else.

"What is this?"

She tried to shut the door. I held it open.

"Get away from here. Leave me alone. I'll scream."

"All right. Scream."

She opened her mouth. No sound came out. She closed her mouth again. It was small and fleshy and defiant. "Who are you? Law?"

"Close enough. I'm coming in."

"Come in then, damn you. I got nothing to hide."

"I can see that."

I brushed in past her. There were dead Martinis on her breath. The little room was a jumble of feminine clothes, silk and cashmere and tweed and gossamer nylon, some of them flung on the floor, others hung up to dry. The leopardskin coat lay on the bunk bed, staring with innumerable bold eyes. She picked it up and covered her shoulders with it. Unconsciously, her nervous hands began to pick the wood-chips out of the fur. I said:

"Harry did you a favor, didn't he?"

"Maybe he did."

"Have you been doing any favors for Harry?"

"Such as?"

"Such as knocking off his brother."

"You're way off the beam, mister. I was very fond of Uncle Nick."

"Why run out on the killing then?"

"I panicked," she said. "It would happen to any girl. I was asleep when he got it, see, passed out if you want the truth. I heard the gun go off. It woke me up, but it took me quite a while to bring myself to and sober up enough to put my clothes on. By the time I made it to the bedroom window, Harry was back, with some guy." She peered into my face. "Were you the guy?"

I nodded.

"I thought so. I thought you were law at the time. I saw Nick lying there in the driveway, all bloody, and I put two and two together and got trouble. Bad trouble for me, unless I got out. So I got out. It wasn't nice to do, after what Nick meant to me, but it was the only sensible thing. I got my career to think of."

"What career is that?"

"Modeling. Acting. Uncle Nick was gonna send me to school."

"Unless you talk, you'll finish your education at Corona. Who shot Nick?"

A thin edge of terror entered her voice. "I don't know, I tell you. I was passed out in the bedroom. I didn't see nothing."

"Why did Harry bring you your coat?"

"He didn't want me to get involved. He's my father, after all."

"Harry Nemo is your father?"

"Yes."

"You'll have to do better than that. What's your name?"

"Jeannine. Jeannine Larue."

"Why isn't your name Nemo if Harry is your father? Why do you call him Harry?"

"He's my stepfather, I mean."

"Sure," I said. "And Nick was really your uncle, and you were having a family reunion with him."

"He wasn't any blood relation to me. I always called him uncle, though."

"If Harry's your father, why don't you live with him?"

"I used to. Honest. This is the truth I'm telling you. I had to get out on account of the old lady. The old lady hates my guts. She's a real creep, a square. She can't stand for a girl to have any fun. Just because my old man was a rummy——"

"What's your idea of fun, Jeannine?"

She shook her feathercut hair at me. It exhaled a heavy perfume which was worth its weight in blood. She bared one pearly shoulder and smiled an artificial hustler's smile. "What's yours? Maybe we can get together."

"You mean the way you got together with Nick?"

"You're prettier than him."

"I'm also smarter, I hope. Is Harry really your stepfather?"

"Ask him if you don't believe me. Ask him. He lives in a place on Tule Street—I don't remember the number."

"I know where he lives."

But Harry wasn't at home. I knocked on the door of the frame cottage and got no answer. I turned the knob, and found that the door was unlocked. There was a light behind it. The other cottages in the court were dark. It was long past midnight, and the street was deserted. I went into the cottage, preceded by my gun.

A ceiling bulb glared down on sparse and threadbare furniture, a time-eaten rug. Besides the living room, the house contained a cubbyhole of a bedroom and a closet kitchenette. Everything in the poverty-stricken place was pathetically clean. There were moral mottoes on the walls, and one picture. It was a photograph of a towheaded girl in a teen-age party dress. Jeannine, before she learned that a pretty face and a sleek body could buy her the things she wanted. The things she thought she wanted.

For some reason, I felt sick. I went outside. Somewhere out of sight, an old car-engine muttered. Its muttering grew on the night. Harry Nemo's rented Chevrolet turned the corner under the streetlight. Its front wheels were weaving. One of the wheels climbed the curb in front of the cottage. The Chevrolet came to a halt at a drunken angle.

I crossed the sidewalk and opened the car door. Harry was at the wheel, clinging to it desperately as if he needed it to hold him up. His chest was bloody. His mouth was bright with blood. He spoke through it thickly:

"She got me."

"Who got you, Harry? Jeannine?"

"No. Not her. She was the reason for it, though. We had it coming."

Those were his final words. I caught his body as it fell sideways out of the seat. Laid it out on the sidewalk and left it for the cop on the beat to find.

I drove across town to the trailer court. Jeannine's trailer still had light in it, filtered through the curtains over the windows. I pushed the door open.

The girl was packing a suitcase on the bunk bed. She looked at me over her shoulder, and froze. Her blond head was cocked like a frightened bird's, hypnotized by my gun.

"Where are you off to, kid?"

"Out of this town. I'm getting out."

"You have some talking to do first."

She straightened up. "I told you all I know. You didn't believe me. What's the matter, didn't you get to see Harry?"

"I saw him. Harry's dead. Your whole family is dying like flies."

She half-turned and sat down limply on the disordered bed. "Dead? You think I did it?"

"I think you know who did. Harry said before he died that you were the reason for it all."

"Me the reason for it?" Her eyes widened in false naïveté, but there was thought behind them, quick and desperate thought. "You mean that Harry got killed on account of me?"

"Harry and Nick both. It was a woman who shot them."

"God," she said. The desperate thought behind her eyes crystallized into knowledge. Which I shared.

The aching silence was broken by a big diesel rolling by on the highway. She said above its roar:

"That crazy old bat. So *she* killed Nick."

"You're talking about your mother. Mrs. Nemo."

"Yeah."

"Did you see her shoot him?"

"No. I was blotto like I told you. But I saw her out there this week, keeping an eye on the house. She's always watched me like a hawk."

"Is that why you were getting out of town? Because you knew she killed Nick?"

"Maybe it was. I don't know. I wouldn't let myself think about it."

Her blue gaze shifted from my face to something behind me. I turned. Mrs. Nemo was in the doorway. She was hugging the straw bag to her thin chest.

Her right hand dove into the bag. I shot her in the right arm. She leaned against the doorframe and held her dangling arm with her left hand. Her face was granite in whose crevices her eyes were like live things caught.

The gun she dropped was a cheap .32 revolver, its nickel

plating worn and corroded. I spun the cylinder. One shot had been fired from it.

"This accounts for Harry," I said. "You didn't shoot Nick with this gun, not at that distance."

"No." She was looking down at her dripping hand. "I used my old police gun on Nick Nemo. After I killed him, I threw the gun into the sea. I didn't know I'd have further use for a gun. I bought that little suicide gun tonight."

"To use on Harry?"

"To use on you. I thought you were on to me. I didn't know until you told me that Harry knew about Nick and Jeannine."

"Jeannine is your daughter by your first husband?"

"My only daughter." She said to the girl: "I did it for you, Jeannine. I've seen too much—the awful things that can happen."

The girl didn't answer. I said:

"I can understand why you shot Nick. But why did Harry have to die?"

"Nick paid him," she said. "Nick paid him for Jeannine. I found Harry in a bar an hour ago, and he admitted it. I hope I killed him."

"You killed him, Mrs. Nemo. What brought you here? Was Jeannine the third on your list?"

"No. No. She's my own girl. I came to tell her what I did for her. I wanted her to know."

She looked at the girl on the bed. Her eyes were terrible with pain and love. The girl said in a stunned voice:

"Mother. You're hurt. I'm sorry."

"Let's go, Mrs. Nemo," I said.

The Sinister Habit

A MAN in a conservative dark gray suit entered my doorway sideways, carrying a dark gray Homburg in his hand. His face was long and pale. He had black eyes and eyebrows and black nostrils. Across the summit of his high forehead, long black ribbons of hair were brushed demurely. Only his tie had color: it lay on his narrow chest like a slumbering purple passion.

His sharp black glance darted around my office, then back into the corridor. His hairy nostrils sniffed the air as if he suspected escaping gas.

"Is somebody following you?" I said.

"I have no reason to think so."

I had my coat off and my shirt unbuttoned. It was a hot afternoon at the start of the smog season. My visitor looked at me in a certain way that reminded me of schoolteachers. "Might you be Archer?"

"It's a reasonable conclusion. Name's on the door."

"I can read, thank you."

"Congratulations, but this is no talent agency."

He stiffened, clutching his blue chin with a seal-ringed hand, and gave me a long, sad, hostile stare. Then he shrugged awkwardly, as though there was no help for it.

"Come in if you like," I said. "Close it behind you. Don't mind me, I get snappy in the heat."

He shut the door violently, almost hard enough to crack the expensive one-way glass panel. He jumped at the noise it made, and apologized:

"I'm sorry. I've been under quite a strain."

"You're in trouble?"

"Not I. My sister . . ." He gave me one of his long looks. I assumed an air of bored discretion garnished with a sprig of innocence.

"Your sister," I reminded him after a while. "Did she do something, or get something done to her?"

"Both, I'm afraid." His teeth showed in a tortured little smile which drew down the corners of his mouth. "She and I maintain a school for girls in—in the vicinity of Chicago.

141

I can't emphasize too much the importance of keeping this matter profoundly secret."

"You're doing your part. Sit down, Mr.—"

He took a pinseal wallet out of his inside breast pocket, handling it with a kind of reverence, and produced a card. He hesitated with the card in his hand.

"Let me guess," I said. "Don't tell me. Does your name begin with a consonant or a vowel?"

He sat down with great caution, after inspecting the chair for concealed electrodes, and made me the gift of his card. It was engraved: "J. Reginald Harlan, M.A. The Harlan School."

I read it out loud. He winced.

"All right, Mr. Harlan. Your sister's in some kind of a jam. You run a girls' school—"

"She's headmistress. I'm registrar and bursar."

"—which makes you vulnerable to scandal. Is it sexual trouble she's in?"

He crossed his legs, and clasped his sharp knee with both hands. "Now how could you possibly know that?"

"Some of my best friends are sisters. I take it she's younger than you."

"A few years my junior, yes, but Maude's no youngster. She's a mature woman, at least I'd always supposed that she was mature. It's her age, her age and position, that make this whole affair so incredible. For a woman of Maude's social and professional standing, with a hundred virginal minds in her charge, suddenly to go mad over a man! Can you understand such behavior?"

"Yes. I've seen enough of it."

"I can't." But a faint, attractive doubt softened his eyes for a moment. Perhaps he was wondering when some long overdue lightning might blast and illuminate him. "I'd always supposed that the teens were the dangerous age. Perhaps after all it's the thirties." One hand crawled up his chest like a pallid crab and fondled the purple tie.

"It depends on the person," I said, "and the circumstances."

"I suppose so." He inverted the hat in his lap and gazed down into it. "Now that I come to think of it, Mother's breakdown occurred when she was in her thirties. I wonder, could Maude be simply reverting to type, impelled by something unstable in her genes?"

"Did Mother have blue genes?"

Harlan smiled his tortured smile. "Indeed she did. You put it very aptly. But we won't go into the case of Mother. It's my sister I'm concerned with."

"What did she do? Elope?"

"Yes, in the most scandalous and disrupting way, with a man she scarcely knew, a dreadful sort of man."

"Tell me about him."

He looked down into his hat again, as if its invisible contents fascinated and horrified him. "There's very little to tell. I don't even know his name. I saw him only once, last Friday—a week ago tomorrow. He drove up to the school in a battered old car, right in the midst of our Commencement exercises. Maude didn't even introduce him to me. She introduced him to no one, and if you saw him you would understand why. He was an obvious roughneck, a big hairy brute of a fellow with a red beard, in filthy old slacks and a beret and a turtleneck sweater. She walked up to him in front of all the parents and took his arm and strolled away with him under the elms, completely hypnotized."

"You mean she never came back?"

"Oh, she came back that night for a time, long enough to pack. I was out myself—I had a number of social duties to perform, Commencement night. When I got in, she was gone. She left me a brief note, and that was all."

"You have it with you?"

His hand went into his breast pocket and tossed a sheet of folded stationery onto the desk. Its copybook handwriting said:

"Dear Reginald:

"I am going to be married. My total despair of making you understand forces me to leave as I am leaving. Do not worry about me, and above all do not try to interfere. If this seems cruel, bear in mind that I am fighting for life itself. My husband-to-be is a great and warm personality who has suffered in his time as I have suffered. He is waiting outside for me now.

"Be assured, dear Reginald, that a part of my affection will remain with you and the school. But I shall never return to either.

"Your sister."

I pushed the note across the desk to Harlan. "Were you and your sister on good terms?"

"I'd always thought so. We had our little differences over the years, in carrying on Father's work and interpreting the tradition of the School. But there was a deep mutual respect between Maude and me. You can see it in the note."

"Yes." I could see other things there, too. "What's the suffering she refers to?"

"I have no idea." He gave a cruel yank to the purple tie.

"We've had a good life together, Maude and I, a rich full life of service to girlhood and young womanhood. We've been prosperous and happy. To have her turn on me like this—out of a clear sky! Suddenly, after eleven years of devotion, the School meant nothing to her. *I* meant nothing to her. Father's memory meant nothing. I tell you, that brute has bewitched her. Her entire system of values has been subverted."

"Maybe she's just fallen in love. The older they are when it happens, the harder it hits them. Hell, maybe he's even lovable."

Harlan sniffed. "He's a lewd rascal. I know a lewd rascal when I see one. He's a womanizer and a drinker and probably worse."

I glanced at my liquor cabinet. It was closed and innocent-looking. "Aren't you a little prejudiced?"

"I know whereof I speak. The man's a ruffian. Maude is a woman of sensibility who requires the gentlest conditions of life. He'll pulverize her spirit, brutalize her body, waste her money. It's Mother's situation all over again, only worse, much worse. Maude is infinitely more vulnerable than Mother ever was."

"What happened to your mother?"

"She divorced Father and ran away with a man, an art teacher at the School. He led her a merry life, I assure you, until he died of drink." This seemed to give Harlan a certain satisfaction. "Mother is living in Los Angeles now. I haven't seen her for nearly thirty years, but Maude came out to visit her during the Easter recess. Against my expressed wishes, I may add."

"And Maude came back to Los Angeles with her husband?"

"Yes. She wired me yesterday from here. I caught the first possible plane."

"Let me see the telegram."

"I don't have it. It was read to me on the telephone." He added waspishly: "She might have used a less public means of communicating her disgrace."

"What did she say?"

"That she was very happy. Turning the knife in the wound, of course." His face darkened, and through his eyes I caught a glimpse of the red fires banked inside him. "She warned me not to try and follow her, and apologized for taking the money."

"What money?"

"She wrote a check last Friday before she left, which nearly exhausted our joint checking account. A check for a thousand dollars."

"But it belonged to her?"

"In the legal sense, not morally. It's always been understood that I disburse the money." A doleful whine entered his voice. "The man is clearly after our money, and the deuce of it is, there's nothing to prevent Maude from drawing on our capital. She might even sell the School!"

"She owns it?"

"I'm afraid she does, legally. Father left her the School. I—my administrative ability was a little slow in developing—a gradual growth, you know. Poor Father didn't live to see me mature." He coughed, choking on his own unction. "The buildings alone are worth nearly two hundred thousand. The added value of our prestige is incalculable."

He paused in a listening attitude, as though he could hear the unholy gurgle of money going down the drain. I put on my coat.

"You want them traced, is that it? To see that the marriage is regular, and make sure that he isn't a confidence man?"

"I want to see my sister. If I could just *talk* to her—well, something might be saved. She may have lost her mind. I can't permit her to wreck her life, and mine, as Mother wrecked Father's and her own."

"Where does your mother live in Los Angeles?"

"She has a house in a place called Westwood, I believe. I've never been there."

"I think we ought to visit her. You haven't been in touch with her?"

"Certainly not. And I have no wish to see her now."

"I think you should. If Maude was out here with her at Easter, your mother may know the man. It doesn't sound as though your sister eloped on the spur of the moment."

"You may be right," he said slowly. "It hadn't occurred to me that she may have met him out here. And then he followed her to Chicago, eh? Of course. It's the logical hypothesis."

We had a short talk about money. Harlan endorsed a fifty-dollar traveler's check to me, and we went downstairs to my car.

It wasn't far to Westwood, as distances go in Los Angeles. We joined the early evening traffic rushing like lemmings towards the sea and the suburbs. Shielding his eyes with his hand against the sun's horizontal rays, Harlan told me a little about his mother. Enough for me to know what to expect.

She lived in a frame cottage on a hillside overlooking the distant campus. The front yard was choked with a dozen varieties of cactus, some of which speared as high as the roof.

The house needed paint and it hung on the slope a little off balance, like its tenant.

She opened the screen door, blinking against the sun. Her face was gouged and eroded by years and trouble. Black hair, shot with gray, hung in straight limp bangs over her forehead. Large tarnished metal rings depended from her earlobes. Several gold chains hung around her withered neck, and tinkled when she moved. She was dressed in sandals and a brown homespun robe which looked like sacking, cinched in by a rope at the waist.

Her eyes were dusty black and very remote. She didn't seem to know Harlan. He said in a new voice, a husky questioning whisper:

"Mother?"

She peered at him, and her face organized itself in wrinkles around her brightening eyes. She smiled. Her teeth were to-bacco-colored, but her smile was generous. It turned to laughter. Red-stained by the sun, she looked like an old gypsy on a *vino* jag.

"My God in heaven! You're Reginald."

"Yes." He took off his hat. "I fail to see what you're laughing about, however."

"It's just," she gasped, "you look so much like your father."

"Is that so comical? I hope I do. I've patterned my life on Father's, tried to live up to his code. I only wish I could say as much for Maude."

Her laughter died. "You've no right to criticize Maude. She's worth two of you, and you know it. Maude's a fine woman."

"A fine fool!" he said hotly. "Throwing herself away, embezzling money—"

"Watch your language. Maude is my daughter." The old woman had a certain dignity.

"She's very much your daughter, apparently. Is she here with you?"

"No, she's not. I know why you've come, of course. I warned Maude you'd try and drag her back to the salt mines."

"Then you've seen her. Where is she?"

"I have no intention of telling you. Maude is well and happy —happy for the first time in her life."

"You're going to tell me," he said between clenched teeth.

He grabbed her pipestem wrist. She batted her eyes in fear-ful defiance, her seamed lips shrinking back from her long teeth. I took him by the shoulder and the arm and jerked him back on his heels, breaking his grip.

"Take it easy, Harlan. You can't force information out of people."

He gave me a look of dull hatred, then transferred it to his mother. She returned it.

"The same old Reginald," she said, "who used to love pinning beetles to a board. Who is this gentleman, by the way?"

"Mr. Archer." He added heavily: "A private detective."

She flung up her hands and grimaced. "Ah, Reggie. You're outdoing yourself. You haven't changed a bit."

"Neither have you, Mother. But you and I are not the point at issue. Please don't try to divert me. I want to know where Maude and her—her consort are."

"You won't find out from me. Aren't you satisfied with thirty years of Maude's life? Do you have to have it all?"

"I know what's best for Maude. I doubt that you do, after the frightful hash you've made of your own life." He looked with contempt at the peeling walls, the patched screen door, the discarded old woman who had taken refuge behind it. "If you're responsible for this brainstorm of hers—"

He ran out of words. Fury had strung him as taut as a wire. I could practically hear him hum. And I kept my shoulder between him and the door.

"It's no brainstorm," she said. "Maude found a man who suited her at last, and she had the good sense to forsake everything for him. Just as I did." Memory smoothed her face; a surge of romantic feeling sang like a warped record through her voice: "I'm proud of my part in this."

"You admit it, then?"

"Why shouldn't I? I brought her and Leonard Lister together last spring, when she was here with me. Leonard's a splendid man, and they took to each other at once. Maude needed a powerful male personality to break through to her, after all those spinster years—"

"What did you say his name was?"

"Leonard Lister," I said.

The old woman's hand had gone to her mouth. She said between yellow fingers: "I didn't mean to tell you. Now that you've got it out of me—you must have heard of Leonard. He's a brilliant creative artist in the theatre."

"Have you ever heard of him, Archer?"

"No."

"Leonard Lister?" the old woman said. "Surely you know his name, if you live in Los Angeles. He's a well-known director in the experimental theatre. He's even taught at the University. Leonard has wonderful plans for making poetic film, like Cocteau's in France."

"No doubt his plans include Maude's money," Harlan said.

"You *would* think of such a thing. But it's not true. He loves her for herself."

"I see. I see. And you're the honest broker who procured your own daughter for a fortune-hunter. How much is this brilliant fellow going to pay you for your services?"

The sunset had faded out. Deprived of its borrowed color, the old woman's face behind the screen was drawn and bloodless.

"You know it's not true, and you mustn't say such things. Maude has been kind to you. You owe her some tolerance. Why don't you give up gracefully and go home?"

"Because my sister has been misled. She's in the hands of fools and knaves. Which are you, Mother?"

"Neither. And Maude is better off than she's ever been in her life." But her assurance was failing under his one-track pressure.

"*This* I desire to see for myself. Where are they?"

"You shan't find out from me." She looked at me with an obscure appeal in her eyes.

"Then I'll find out for myself."

It wasn't hard to do. Leonard Lister was in the telephone book. He had an apartment address in Santa Monica, on one of the grid of streets above Lincoln Boulevard. I tried to talk Harlan, an obvious troublemaker, into letting me take it from here. But he was as hot as a cocker with bird scent in his nostrils. I had to let him come, or drop the case. And he'd probably make more trouble by himself.

It was almost dark when we found the place, an old two-story stucco house set back from the street behind a brown patch of lawn. Lister's apartment was a small studio built over an attached garage. A flight of concrete steps slanted up the outside wall of the garage. There were lights in the house, and behind the blinded windows of the apartment. Under the late twilight stillness, our feet rustled in the dry grass.

"Imagine Maude being reduced to this," Harlan said. "A woman of exquisite refinement, come to live in a slum with a—a gigolo."

"Uh-huh. You better let me do the talking. You could get hurt, tossing that language around."

"No ruffian can intimidate me."

But he let me go ahead of him up the flight of steps. It was lit by an insect-repellent yellow bulb over the door at the top. I knocked on the door. There was no answer. I knocked again. Harlan reached past me and turned the knob. The door was locked.

"Pick the lock," he said in an urgent whisper. "They're in there lying low, I'm sure of it. You must have skeleton keys?"

"I also have a license to lose."

He hammered the door till it vibrated in its frame. His

seal-ringed knuckle made little dents in the paint. Soft footsteps approached from the other side. I thrust Harlan back with my arm. He almost lost his balance on the narrow landing.

The door opened. "What goes on?"

The man in the doorway wore a striped cotton bathrobe, and nothing else. His shoulders and bare chest were Herculean, a little bowed and softened by his age. He was in his late forties, perhaps. His red hair was shaggy and streaked with gray. His thick mouth gleamed like a bivalve in the red nest of his beard. His eyes were deepset and dreamy, the kind of eyes that watch the past or the future but seldom look directly at the present.

Over the shoulders which nearly filled the doorframe, I could see into the lighted room. It was cramped and meanly furnished with a studio bed, a few chairs. Books spilled from homemade shelves constructed out of red bricks and unfinished boards. In the cubbyhole kitchenette on the far side, a woman was working. I could see her dark head, her slim back with apron strings tied at the waist, and hear dishes rattling.

I told Lister who I was, but he was looking at the man behind me.

"Mr. Harlan, isn't it? This is quite a surprise. I can't say it's a pleasant one." His voice had the ease that great size gives a man. "Now what do you want, Mr. Harlan?"

"You know perfectly well. My sister."

Lister stepped out, closing the door behind him. It became very cozy with the three of us on the yard-square landing, like the components of fission coming together. Lister's bare feet were silent on the concrete. His voice was soft:

"Maude is busy. I'm pretty busy myself. I was just going to take a shower. So my advice to you is, go away. And don't bother coming back. We're going to be indefinitely busy."

"Busy spending her money?" Harlan said.

Lister's teeth flashed in his beard. His voice took on an edge.

"It's easy to see why Maude won't speak to you. Now take your detective friend and remove yourself from my doorstep."

"So the old hag got in touch with you? How much of a percentage are you paying her?"

Lister moved quickly around me. He took Harlan by the front of his coat, lifted him, shook him once, and set him back on his feet.

"Speak of your mother with some respect, you little schnook."

Harlan leaned on the railing, gripping it firmly like a child daring adults to dislodge him. His face in the yellow light looked sick with humiliation. He said in stubborn malice:

"I want to see my sister. I want to see what you've done to her, you bully."

I said: "Let's go," and laid a hand on his arm.

"Are you on his side, too?" He was almost crying.

"A man's home is his castle, after all. He doesn't like you, Reginald. Neither does she, apparently."

"You can say that again," Lister said. "The little leech has sucked her blood for too long. Now get out of here before you make me mad for real."

"Come on, Reginald. We're getting nowhere."

I detached him from the railing. Below and behind me, a man's voice was raised. "Trouble up there, Lister?" The voice sounded as if its owner hoped so.

He was a gray-haired man in a Hawaiian print shirt, standing spraddle-legged in the splash of light at the foot of the stairs. It colored his spongy face and made his eyes look colorless.

"No trouble, Dolph. These gentlemen are just leaving."

Lister stood with his back against the door, a seedy hero in a dirty bathrobe defending his two-bit castle, and watched us go down the stairs. The door closed sharply, and the yellow light went out. Harlan muttered under his breath.

The gray-headed man was waiting for us at the bottom. He whispered through an alcoholic haze:

"Cops?"

I didn't answer. He jerked at my coatsleeve, naggingly:

"What's lover-man been up to now?"

"You wouldn't be interested."

"That's what you think. You got another think coming. He's got a woman with him, hasn't he?"

"None of your business."

I pulled my coatsleeve free. But he was hard to shake off. He thrust his pudgy face forward into mine.

"What Lister does is my business. I got a right to know if my tenants are living in sin."

I started to walk away from him and his breath. He followed me across the driveway, bracing his wavering stride with one outstretched hand against the closed garage door. His voice trailed huskily after me:

"What's the beef about? I got a right to know. I'm a respectable man, see. I don't run any callhouse for brokendown four-flushers."

"Wait a minute," Harlan said. "Are you Lister's landlord?"

"Sure thing. I never liked the s. o. b., it was the little woman that rented him the apartment. *She* thought he was class. I saw through him at a glance. Another movie has-been. A never-was."

He sagged against the stucco wall. Harlan leaned over him like a prosecutor, his face a leaden silhouette in the dim light from a blinded window.

"What else do you know about Lister, my man?"

"I'm going to throw him out on his ear if he don't watch himself."

"You mentioned his dealings with women. What about that?"

"I don't know what goes on up there. But I'm going to find out."

"Why don't you go up now? You have the right to, you know, you own the place."

"By God, I will."

I went back to Harlan and took his arm. "Let's get out of here, Reginald. You've made enough trouble for one night."

"I make trouble? Nonsense. My sister's married to a criminal, a whoremonger."

The man against the wall wagged his gray head solemnly. "You couldn't be righter. Is the woman with him your sister?"

"Yes."

"And she's married to him?"

"I believe so. But I can't let her stay with him. I'm going to take her home—"

"Not tonight, Reginald." I tightened my grip on his arm.

"I have to do something. I have to act."

He tried to break away from me. His hat fell off, and his meager hair fell down over his ears. He almost screeched:

"How dare you? Take your hands off me."

A woman's full-breasted shadow fell on the blind. Her voice issued sharply from the window:

"Jack! Are you still out there?"

The gray-headed man straightened up as if he'd been touched by live current. "Yeah. I'm here."

"Come inside. You're drunk, and you've been talking nonsense."

"Who's going to make me?" He said it under his breath.

She heard him. "I said come in. You're making a laughing stock of yourself. And tell your friends to go home."

He turned his back on us and walked uncertainly to the front door. Harlan tried to follow him. I held Harlan. The door slammed. A bolt clicked home.

"Now see what you've done," Harlan said, "with your mishandling and your interference! I was just about to learn something."

"You never will."

I released him and went to the car, not caring whether he came along or not. He caught up with me at the curb, wiping his hat with a handkerchief and breathing audibly.

"The least you can do for the money I paid you is drop me at my hotel. The cab fares are scandalous here."

"All right. Where is it."

"The Oceano Hotel, in Santa Monica."

"This is Santa Monica."

"Really?" He added a moment later: "I'm not surprised. Something guided me to Santa Monica. Maude and I have had a sort of telepathic communication, going back virtually to infancy. Especially when she's in trouble."

"I wonder if she is in trouble."

"With that brute?" He laughed harshly. "Did you observe his conduct to me?"

"It seemed fairly normal under the circumstances."

"Normal for this Godforsaken place, perhaps. But I'm not going to put up with it. And incidentally, if you intend to do nothing further, I expect a rebate of at least fifty per cent."

I wanted to ask him who had stolen his rattle when he was a baby. Instead I said: "You'll get paid in services. I'll spend tomorrow on Lister. If he's a wrong number, I'll find out. If he isn't—"

"It's clear that he is. You heard his landlord's remarks."

"The guy was drunk. And I wouldn't go around calling people names without some proof. You almost got your head knocked off."

"I don't care what happens to me. It's Maude I'm anxious about. I have only one sister."

"You have only one head."

He sulked the rest of the way. I let him out at the white curb without a word. In the neon kaleidescope of the ocean front, against the pink backdrop of the hotel, he looked like a displaced shadow from a dark dream. Not my dream, I congratulated myself.

Prematurely.

In the morning I called a friend in the District Attorney's office. Lister had a record: two drunken driving convictions, a battery complaint reduced to disorderly conduct, nothing worse. He had been a small-time producer before television. His last recorded place of employment was the University.

I made another telephone call, and paid a visit to the University. The spring semester had ended, and Summer School not yet begun, so the campus was bare of students. But most of the faculty were on the job. The acting head of the Speech Department, a man named Schilling, was in his office.

Schilling wasn't a typical professor. Under the flesh which covered his face with a middle-aging mask, he had the profile of a juvenile lead. He was dressed like an actor in a very sharp gabardine suit and an open-throated sports shirt. The wavy brown hair which undulated back from his widow's peak was very carefully arranged. I wondered if it was dyed. I said:

"It's nice of you to give me your time, doctor."

"Not at all. Sit down, Mr. Archer." He sat at his desk by the window, where the light could make the most of his features. "When I spoke to you on the telephone, you expressed an interest in one of the members—one of the ex-members of our faculty family." He enunciated his words with great distinctness, listening to the rich tones of his voice. They seemed to please him.

"Leonard Lister." I sat down in a straight chair at the end of the paper-strewn desk.

"Exactly what kind of information do you wish? And what use would you put it to? We have our little professional secrets, too, you know, even in this sheltered world of ours."

"I want to know if he's honest. That's the main thing. He seems to have married into a fairly wealthy family. They don't know much about him." Which was putting it mildly.

"And they've employed you to investigate him?"

"That's the idea. Certain members of the family think he may be crooked."

"Oh no, I wouldn't say that."

"Why did you fire him?"

"We didn't fire him, exactly. Leonard didn't have tenure, he was only a Special Lecturer in the Department. And we simply failed to renew his contract at the end of the fall semester."

"You had a reason, though, and it wasn't incompetence?"

"Certainly not incompetence. Leonard knows the theatre. He's been in it for twenty years, in New York and on the Continent as well as here. And he was quite a figure in the movies at one time. He made a mint while it lasted, and he had a country house and a yacht and even an actress wife, I believe. Then he lost it. This was years ago. I don't know all that happened to him in the interim, but he was glad to accept my offer of a teaching job."

"What did he teach?"

"We used him mostly for Extension work, directing plays for various groups and lecturing on the drama. He was well liked by his students."

"Then what was the matter with him?"

He hesitated. "I suppose I should say the matter was ethical. He's quite a fellow in his way—I've always liked him personally—but he simply didn't subscribe to the code of the teaching profession. Leonard spent some time in France, you know, in the old expatriate days, and a good deal of the Left Bank rubbed off on him. He drank too much, he liked women too much, he couldn't face up to the realities of his position. He's an enormous man—I don't know whether you know him—"

"I know him."

"—but he's not really very grownup. Out of touch, you might say, almost manic at times."

"Could you be more specific, doctor?"

He looked away from me, out the window, and ran his hand carefully over his hair. "I hate to blacken another man's reputation. And after all, the name of the University is involved. It's a very delicate matter."

"I realize that. I'll keep it confidential. All this is simply for my own information."

"Well." He turned back to me. All he'd needed was a little coaxing. "Leonard had a habit of messing with his women students, with one of them in particular. Rumors got around, as they always do, and I cautioned Leonard. I gave him fair warning. He failed to profit by it, so I kept a close eye on him. This Department is precarious enough without a major scandal on top of everything else. Fortunately, I caught him personally, and kept it quiet."

Schilling was lighting up with a theatrical glow. Apparently he was reenacting his big moment. "Along towards the end of the fall semester, on an afternoon in December, I saw them go into his office together—it's just down the hall from mine. You should have seen the look on her face, the cowlike adoration. Well, I secured a master key from the maintenance department and after a suitable interval, I went in. There they were, *in flagrante*, if you understand me."

"Was she a young girl?"

"No. It could have been worse. As a matter of fact, she was a married woman. Quite a few of our students are young married women with—ah—theatrical ambitions. But even as it was, the situation was too bad to be allowed to continue. I put an end to it, and Leonard left us. I haven't seen him since."

"What happened to the woman?"

"She dropped out of her course. She showed no promise, anyway, and I for one was happy to see her go. You should have heard the names she called me that afternoon, when after all I was only doing my duty. I *told* Leonard he was playing with dynamite. Why, the woman was a hellcat." With the forefinger of his left hand, he traced his profile from hairline to chin, and smiled to himself. "I'm afraid that's all the information I have."

"One more thing. You said he was honest."

"Except in that little matter of women, yes."

"Honest in money matters?"

"So far as I know. Leonard never cared for money. He cares so little for it, in fact, that he's financially irresponsible. Well, now that he's married into wealth, I suppose he'll be settling down. I hope for his sake he can. And I very much hope I haven't said anything that will damage his standing with the family."

"Not if he's dropped the other woman. What was her name, by the way?"

"Dolphine. Stella Dolphine. Quite an unusual name." He spelled it for me.

I looked it up in Shilling's telephone directory. There was only one Dolphine listed: a Jack Dolphine who lived at the same address as Leonard Lister.

In full daylight, the stucco house in Santa Monica had an abandoned look. The blinds were drawn on all the windows, upstairs and down. The dying lawn, the unkempt flowerbeds strangling in crab grass, seemed to reflect the lives of people bound and paralyzed by their unhappiness. I noticed, though, that the lawn had recently been hosed, and a few drying puddles lay on the uneven concrete of the driveway.

I climbed the outside stairs to Lister's apartment. Nobody answered my knock. I turned the knob. The door was locked. I went down and lifted the overhead door of the garage. It was empty.

I pressed the bellpush beside the front door and waited. Shuffling footsteps dragged through the house. The gray-haired man in the Hawaiian shirt opened the door and peered out into the sun. He had had a bad night. His eyes were blurred by alcohol and grief, his mouth was raw and defenseless. The slack flesh of his face hung like melting plasticine on the bones. So did his body. He was a soft-boiled egg without a shell.

He didn't seem to recognize me.

"Mr. Dolphine?"

"Yeah." He recognized my voice. "Say, what's the pitch? You were here last night; you said you were a cop."

"It was your idea. I'm a private cop. Name's Archer."

"Whaddaya know, I was a private cop myself—plant guard at Douglas. But I retired when my investments started to pay off. I own six houses and an apartment court. Maybe you wouldn't think it to look at me."

"Good for you. What happened to the tenants in your apartment?"

"Lister, you mean? You tell me. He moved out."

"For keeps?"

"Damn right for keeps." He floundered across the doorstep, preceded by his breath, and laid one hand on my shoulder, confidentially. It also helped to hold him up. "I was all set to give him his walking papers, only he saved me the trouble. Packed up his stuff, what there was of it, and left."

"And the woman went with him? His wife?"

"Yeah, she went along."

"In his car?"

"That's correct."

He gave me a description of the car, a blue Buick sedan, prewar, on its second or third hundred thousand. Dolphine didn't know the license number. The Listers had left no forwarding address.

"Could I speak to Mrs. Dolphine?"

"What you want with her?" His hand grew heavier on my shoulder. His eyes were narrow and empty between puffed lids.

"She might know where Lister went."

"You think so?"

"Yes." I shrugged, dislodging his hand. "I hear she's a friend of his."

"You do, eh?"

He fell against me, his upturned face transfigured by sudden rage, and reached for my throat. He was strong, but his reactions were clumsy. I knocked his hands up and away. He staggered back against the doorpost, his arms outstretched in the attitude of crucifixion.

"That was a silly thing to do, Dolphine."

"I'm sorry." He was shuddering, as if he had given himself a terrible scare. "I'm not a well man. This excitement—" His hands came together, clutching at the hula girls on his chest. An asthmatic wheeze twanged like a loose guitar string in the back passages of his head. His face was blotched white.

"What excitement?"

"Stella's left me. She took me for all she could, then dropped me like a hotcake. I'll give you a piece of advice. Don't ever marry a younger woman—"

"When did this happen?"

"Last night. She took off with Lister."

"Both of the women went with him?"

"Yessir. Stella and the other one. Both of them." A drunken whimsy pulled his face lopsided. "I guess the big red bull thinks he can look after two. He's welcome. I've had enough."

"Did you see them leave?"

"Not me. I was in bed."

"How do you know your wife took off with Lister?"

"She told me she was gonna." He lifted the heavy burden of his shoulders, and dropped it. "What could I do?"

"You must have some idea where they went."

"Nah, I don't know and I don't want to. Let them go. She was no good to me anyway." The asthma wheezed behind his words, like an unspoken grief. "So I say let her go, it's a good riddance for me."

He sat down on the step and covered his face with his hands. His hair was wild and torn, like a handful of gray feathers. I left him.

I drove to the Oceano Hotel and called Harlan on the intra-mural telephone. He answered immediately, his voice high and nagging.

"Where on earth have you been? I've been trying to get you."

"Checking on Lister," I said. "He's decamped with your sister—"

"I know. He telephoned me. My worst forebodings were justified. It's money he wants, and he's coming here to try and collect."

"When?"

"At twelve noon. I'm to meet him in the lobby."

I looked at the electric clock on the wall of the desk clerk's alcove: twenty minutes past eleven.

"I'm in the lobby now. Shall I come up?"

"I'll come down." He hesitated. "I have a visitor."

I sat on a red plastic settee near the elevator door. The metal arrow above it turned from one to three and back to one. The door slid open. Harlan's mother emerged, tinkling and casting vague glances around the lobby. She wore a greenish black cape over her sackcloth dress, which made her look like an old bird of ill omen.

She saw me and came forward, taking long skinny-legged strides in her flat sandals.

"Good morning, Mrs. Harlan."

"My name is not Harlan," she said severely. But she neglected to tell me what it was. "Are you following me, young man? I warn you—"

"You don't have to. I came to see your son. I guess you did, too."

"Yes, my son." A black mood clawed her face downward. From its furrows her eyes glittered like wet black stones. "You look like a decent man. I know something of spiritual auras.

It's my study, my life work. And I'll tell you, Mr. Whatsis, since you're involved with Reginald, my son has an evil aura. He was a cold-hearted boy and he's grown into a cold-hearted man. He won't even help his own sister in her extremity."

"Extremity?"

"Yes, she's in very serious trouble. She wouldn't tell me what it was. But I know my daughter—"

"When did you see her?"

"I haven't seen her. She telephoned me last night, and she was desperate for money. Of course she knows I have none, I've been living off her bounty for ten years. She wanted me to intercede with Reginald. As I have done." Her mouth closed like a pouch with a drawstring.

"He won't open the family coffers?"

She shook her head, dislodging tears from the corners of her eyes. The arrow over the elevator door had turned to three and back again to one. Harlan stepped out. His mother gave him a sidelong glance and started away. She flapped across the lobby and out into the street, a bird of ill omen who had seen a more ominous bird.

Harlan came up to me with a tentative smile and an outstretched hand. His handshake was dead.

"I didn't mean to be unpleasant last night. We Harlans are rather emotional."

"Forget it, I'm not proud."

He glanced at the sunlit door through which his mother had vanished. "Has she been filling you with fantasies? I ought to warn you, she's not entirely sane."

"Uh-huh. She told me that Maude needs money."

"Lister does, at any rate."

"How much money?"

"Five thousand dollars. He says he's bringing Maude's check for that amount. I'm to expedite payment by telephoning our bank in Chicago. It amounts to his asking *me* to cash the check."

"Did you talk to your sister at all?"

"No. It's one of the things that alarm me. Just *one* of them. He had a long involved explanation, to the effect that she's not well enough to leave the house, and there's no telephone where they're staying."

"He didn't say where that was?"

"Absolutely not. He was most evasive. I tell you he means her no good, if she's still alive—"

"Don't jump to conclusions. The most important thing is to find out where she is. So handle him carefully. Accept what he says."

"You don't mean I should cash the check?" He spoke with great feeling, five thousand dollars' worth of it.

"It's your sister's money, isn't it? Maybe she does need it. She told your mother she did."

"So Mother claims. But the old fool would lie for her. I suspect they're in cahoots."

"That I doubt."

Harlan paid no attention. "How could Maude need the money? She took a thousand dollars with her last week."

"Maybe they stopped off at Vegas."

"Nonsense. Maude detests the very idea of gambling. She's quite a frugal person, like myself. She couldn't spend a thousand dollars in a week, unless the man is bleeding her."

"Sure she could, on her honeymoon. This whole thing may not be as bad as you think. I've made some inquiries, and Lister has a fair reputation." I decided that was stretching it, and added: "At least he isn't totally bad."

"Neither was Landru," Harlan said darkly.

"We'll see." It was ten to twelve by the electric clock. "Don't accuse him of anything. But tell him he'll have to come back for the cash. I'll wait outside and tail him when he comes out. You sit tight. I'll get in touch with you when I find out where they're holed up."

He nodded several times.

"And for God's sake, take it easy with him, Harlan. I don't believe that he's a commercial killer. But he could turn out to be a passional one."

Lister had the virtue of punctuality, at least. At one minute to twelve, an old Buick sedan appeared from the direction of downtown Santa Monica. It pulled up at the curb a hundred feet short of the hotel entrance. Lister got out and locked his car. His beret and dark glasses gave him the look of a decadent Viking.

I was parked across the wide boulevard, facing in the wrong direction. As soon as Lister had entered the hotel, I U-turned and found a parking space a few cars behind the Buick. I got out for a closer look at it.

Its blue paint was faded and almost hidden by road grime. The fenders were crumpled. I peered through the dusty glass at the luggage on the back seat: a woman's airplane set with the monogram MH, a man's scuffed leather bag covered with European hotel labels and steamship stickers, a canvas haversack stuffed with oblong shapes which were probably books. A long object wrapped in brown paper leaned across the luggage. It had the shape of a spade.

I looked around. There were too many people on the street for me to do a windwing job.

Back in my own car, I made a note of the license number and waited. The blue glare from the sea, relayed by the chrome of passing cars, bothered my eyes. I put on a pair of sunglasses. A few minutes later, Lister appeared on the sidewalk, swaggering towards me. He had taken off his dark glasses, and his blue eyes seemed to be popping from white lids. He looked elated. I remembered what Schilling had said about his manic side, and wished I could see the lower part of his face, where danger often shows. Perhaps the beard had a purpose.

Lister got into the Buick and headed north. I trailed him through heavy noon traffic at a variable distance. He drove with artistic abandon, burning rubber at the Sunset stoplight. Six or eight miles north of it he turned off the highway, tires screeching again. I braked hard and took the turn onto gravel slowly.

The gravel road slanted steeply up a hillside. The Buick disappeared over the rim. I ate my way through its dust to the top and saw it a quarter-mile ahead, going fast. The road wound down into a small closed valley where a few ranch houses stood in cultivated fields. A tractor clung like a slow orange beetle to the far hillside. The air between was so still that the Buick's dust hung like a colloid over the road. I ate another couple of miles of it, by way of lunch.

Beyond the third and last ranch house, a County sign announced: *This is not a through road*. A rusty mailbox sagged on a post beside it. I caught a glimpse of the faded stenciling on the mailbox. "Leonard Lister," I thought it said.

The Buick was far ahead by now, spinning into the defile between two bluffs at the inner end of the valley. It spun out of sight. The road got worse, became a single dirt track rutted and eroded by the rains of many springs. At its narrowest point an old landslide almost blocked it.

I was so taken up with the road that I almost passed the house before I noticed it. It stood far back, at the end of a eucalyptus-shadowed lane. I saw the Buick, standing empty, through the trees; and I kept on going. When I was out of sight of the house I turned my car and left it with the doors locked.

I climbed through yellow mustard and purple lupine to a point from which I could look down on the house. It was a ruin. Its cracked stucco walls leaned crazily. Part of the tile roof had caved in. I guessed that it had been abandoned when water undermined its foundations. Rank geraniums rioted in the front yard, and wild oats stood fender-high around the Buick.

In the back yard, close against the wall of the house, a

broad-backed man was digging a hole. The bright iron of his spade flashed now and then in the sun. I moved down the slope towards him. The hole was about six feet long by two feet wide. Lister's head, when he paused to rest, cast a jut-jawed shadow at the foot of the stucco wall.

I sat down with the yellow mustard up to my eyes, and watched him work. After a while he took his shirt off. His heavy white shoulders were peppered with reddish freckles. The metal of his spade was losing its brightness. In an hour the hole was approximately four feet deep. Lister's red hair was dark with sweat, and his arms were running with it. He stuck the spade into the pile of adobe he had dug, and went into the house.

I started down the hillside. A hen pheasant whirred up from under my feet. In the glazed stillness, its wings made a noise like a jato take-off. I watched the house but there was no response, no face at the broken windows. I stepped over the sagging wire fence and crossed the back yard.

The door hung open on what had been a back kitchen. Its floor was littered with broken plaster which crunched under my feet. Through the bare ribs of the ceiling daylight gleamed. The silence was finely stitched with a tiny tumult of insects. I thought I could hear the murmur of voices somewhere; then the sound of heavy footsteps moved towards me through the house.

I had my revolver ready. Lister came through the inner doorway, carrying a burlap bundle upright in his arms. His head was craned awkwardly sideways, watching his feet, and he failed to see me until I spoke.

"Hold it, gravedigger."

His head came up, eyes wide and blue in the red sweat-streaked face. His reaction was incredibly quick and strong. Without losing a step he came forward, thrusting his bundle out at arm's length into my face. I fired as I went down backwards with the burlap thing on top of me. I pushed it off. It was heavy and stiff, like refrigerated meat. One of Lister's heels stamped down on my gun hand, the other came into my face. The daylight in the ceiling glimmered redly and died.

When my eyes blinked open, sunlight stabbed into them from the open door. One of my arms was numb, pinned under the thing in the burlap shroud. I disengaged myself from its embrace and sat up against the wall. The rumor of insects sounded in my head like small-arms fire between the heavy artillery of my pulse. I sat poised for a while between consciousness and unconsciousness. Then my vision cleared. I dabbed at my swollen face with my usable hand.

My revolver lay on the floor. I picked it up and spun the

cylinder: its chambers had been emptied. Still sitting, I dragged the burlap bundle towards me and untied the twine that held its wrapping in place. Peeling the burlap down with a shaky hand, I saw a lock of black wavy hair stiff with blood.

I got up and unwrapped the body completely. It was the body of a woman who had been beautiful. Its beauty was marred by a depressed contusion which cut slantwise like a groove across the left temple. Bending close, I could also see a pair of purplish ovals on the front of the throat. Thumbprints.

Her skin shone like ivory in the light from the doorway. I covered her with the burlap. Then I noticed that my wallet was lying open on the floor. Nothing seemed to be missing from it, but the photostat of my license was halfway out of its holder.

I went through the house. It was a strange place for a honeymoon, even for a honeymoon that ended in murder. There were no lights, and no furniture, with the exception of some patio furniture—canvas chairs and a redwood chaise with a ruptured pad—in what had been the living room. This room had a fairly weatherproof ceiling, and was clearly the one that Lister and his wife had occupied. There were traces of a recent fire in the fireplace: burned fragments of eucalyptus bark and a few scraps of scorched cloth. The ashes were not quite cold.

I crossed the room to the wooden chaise, noticing the marks of a woman's heels in the dust on the floor. In the dust beside the chaise someone had written three words in long sloping script: *Ora pro nobis*. The meaning of the phrase came back to me across twenty years or more. *Ora pro nobis*. Pray for us. Now and in the hour of our death. . . .

For a minute I felt as insubstantial as a ghost. The dead woman and the living words were realer than I was. The actual world was a house with its roof falling in, dissolved so thin you could see the sunlight through it.

When I heard the car noise outside, I didn't believe my ears. I went to the front door, which stood open. A new tan Studebaker was toiling up the overgrown lane under the eucalyptus trees. It stopped where the Buick had been, and Harlan got out.

I stood back behind the door and watched him through the crack. He approached cautiously, his black glance shifting from one side to the other. When his foot was on the lintel, I showed myself and the empty gun in my hand. He froze in midstride, with a rigor that matched the dead woman's.

"For heaven's sake, put that gun down. You gave me a dreadful start."

"Before I put it down, I want to know how you got here. Have you been talking to Lister?"

"I saw him at noon, you know that. He told me about this

place he used to own. I didn't get out on the street in time to intercept you. Now put the gun away, there's a good fellow. What on earth happened to your face?"

"That can wait. I don't understand yet why you're here."

"Wasn't that the plan, that I should join you here? I rented a car and got here as soon as I could. It took me a long time to find this place. And no wonder. Are they inside?"

"One of them is."

"My sister?" His hand grasped my arm. The long white fingers were stronger than they looked, and they were hard to shake off.

"You tell me."

I took him through the house to the back kitchen. Pulling back the burlap that covered the damaged head, I watched Harlan's face. It didn't change. Not a muscle moved. Either Harlan was as cold as the cadaver, or deliberately suppressing his emotion.

"I've never seen this woman before."

"She's not your sister? Take a good long look." I uncovered the body.

Harlan averted his eyes, his cheeks flushing purple. But his look came creeping sideways back to the body.

"This is your sister, isn't it, Mr. Harlan?"

I had to repeat the question to make him hear. He shook his head. "I never saw her before."

"I don't believe you."

"You don't seriously think I'd refuse to identify my own flesh and blood?"

"If there was money in it."

He didn't hear me. He was fascinated by the uncovered body. I replaced the burlap and told him what had happened, cutting it short when I saw he wasn't interested.

I took him to the front room and showed him the writing in the dust.

"Is that your sister's handwriting?"

"I couldn't possibly tell." -

"Look closely."

Harlan squatted, leaning one arm on the chaise. "It's not her writing."

"Did she know Latin?"

"Of course. She taught it. I'm surprised that you do."

"I don't, but my mother was Catholic."

"I see." Rising awkwardly, he stumbled forward on one knee, obliterating the writing.

"Damn you, Harlan!" I said. "You're acting as if you murdered her yourself."

"Don't be absurd." He smiled his thin white-edged smile.

"You're morally certain that's Maude in the back room, aren't you?"

"I'm morally certain you were lying. You were too careful not to recognize her."

"Well." He dusted his knee with his hands. "I suppose I had better tell you the truth, since you know it anyway. You're perfectly right, it's my sister. She wasn't murdered, however."

The sense of unreality returned to the room. I sat down on the chaise, which complained like an animal under my weight.

"It's a tragic story," Harlan said slowly. "I was rather hoping not to have to tell it. Maude died last night by accident. After I left the studio, she quarreled with Lister over his refusal to admit me. She became quite irrational, in fact. Lister tried to quiet her, but she got away from him and flung herself bodily down those outside steps. The fall killed her."

"Is that Lister's version?"

"It's the simple truth. He came to my hotel room a short while ago, and told me what had happened. The man was in terrible earnest. I know genuine anguish when I see it, and I can tell when a man is telling the truth."

"You're better than I am, then. I think he's playing you for a sucker."

"What?"

"I caught him practically red-handed, trying to bury the body. Now he's lying out of it the best way he can. It strikes me as very peculiar that you swallowed it."

Harlan's black eyes probed my face. "I assure you his story is the truth. He told me about everything, you see, including the matter of—burial. Put yourself in his place. When Maude killed herself—was killed—last night, Lister saw immediately that suspicion would fall on him, especially my suspicion. He's had some trouble with the police, he told me. Inevitably in his panic he acted like a guilty man. He thought of this deserted place, and brought the body here to dispose of it. His action was rash and even illegal, but I think understandable under the circumstances."

"You're very tolerant all of a sudden. What about the five grand he's been trying to con you for?"

"I beg your pardon."

"The check for five thousand, has it slipped your mind?"

"We'll forget about it," he said impassively. "It's my affair, strictly between him and me."

I was beginning to get hold of the situation, if not the motives behind it. Somehow or other Lister had persuaded Harlan to cover for him. I said with all the irony I could muster:

"So we'll bury the body and forget about it."

"Precisely my idea. Not we, however. You. I can't afford to become involved in any illegality whatsoever."

"What makes you think I can?"

He brought a leatherette folder out of his coat pocket and opened it to show me the travelers' checks inside. There were ten hundreds. "One thousand dollars," he said, "seems to me an adequate sexton's fee. Enough to assure forgetfulness as well."

His look was very knowing, but his passion for money was making him idiotic. He was like a tone-deaf man who couldn't believe that other people heard music and even liked it. But I didn't argue. I let him sign the checks and listened to his instructions. Bury her and forget her.

"I sincerely hate to do this to Maude," he said before he left. "It goes against my grain to leave my sister in an unmarked grave, but I have to consider the greatest good of the greatest number. It would ruin the School if this matter got into the newspapers. I can't let mere fraternal piety interfere with the welfare of the School."

Naturally I didn't bury the body. I left it where it lay and followed Harlan back to Santa Monica. I caught the Studebaker before it reached the city, but I let it stay ahead of me.

He parked on Wilshire Boulevard and went into an air travel agency. Before I could find a parking space, he was out again and climbing into his car. I made a note of the agency's name, and followed the Studebaker back to the Oceano Hotel. Harlan left it at the white curb for the garageman. There were shells in my dashboard compartment, and I reloaded my revolver.

The lobby of the hotel was deserted except for the desk clerk and a pair of old ladies playing canasta. I found a telephone booth at the rear, and called the travel agency. A carefully preserved British accent said:

"Sanders' travel agency, Mr. Sanders speaking."

"This is J. Reginald Harlan," I said fussily. "Does that mean anything to you?"

"Indeed it does, Mr. Harlan. I trust your reservations are satisfactory?"

"I'm not entirely sure about that. You see, I'm eager to get there as soon as I can."

"I absolutely assure you, Mr. Harlan, I've put you on the earliest available flight. Ten o'clock from International Airport." A trace of impatience threaded through the genteel tones.

"When do I get there?"

"I thought I'd made that clear. It's written on your envelope."

"I seem to have misplaced the envelope."

"You're scheduled to arrive tomorrow morning at eight o'clock, Chicago time. All right?"

"Thank you."

"Not at all."

I called the hotel switchboard and asked for Harlan.

"Who is speaking, please?" the operator yodeled.

"Lister. Leonard Lister."

"One moment, Mr. Lister, I'll ring Mr. Harlan's room. He's expecting you."

"Don't bother. I'll just go up. What was the number again?"

"Three-fourteen, sir."

I took the elevator to the third floor. The elevator boy noticed my face, opened his mouth to comment, caught my eye, and shut his mouth without speaking. Harlan's room was at the front of the hotel, in a good location. I knocked.

"Is that you, Leonard?"

"Uh-huh."

Harlan opened the door, and I crowded through. He raised his fists together in front of his chest, like a woman. Looking at me as if he hated me, he said:

"Come in, Mr. Archer."

"I'm in."

"Sit down then. I'm afraid I wasn't expecting to see you again. So soon," he added. "There hasn't been any trouble?"

"No trouble. Just the same routine murder."

"But it was an accident—"

"Maybe the fall downstairs was an accident. I don't think that fall killed her. There are thumbprints on her throat."

"But this is all news to me. Do sit down, Mr. Archer, won't you?"

"I'll stand. In the second place, your sister wrote a prayer in the dust in that house. She was alive when Lister took her there. In the third place, you just bought tickets to Chicago, and you're expecting another visit from Lister. Aren't you getting pretty cozy with him?"

"He's my brother-in-law, after all." His voice was bland.

"And you're very fond of him, eh?"

"Leonard has his points."

He sat down in an armchair by the window. Past his narrow cormorant skull I could see the sky and the sea, wide and candid, flecked with the white purity of sails. I spent too much of my time trying to question liars in rented rooms.

"I think he's your partner in crime. You both stand to gain by your sister's death. From what I've seen of the two of you, you're capable of murdering for gain."

"You've changed your mind about Lister, eh?"

"Not as much as you have."

Harlan made his hands flop in the air. "My dear good fellow, you couldn't possibly be further wrong. Even apart from the money I've paid you, I do earnestly hope for your sake that you won't act on your ridiculous theory. In the first place," he mimicked me, "if I were in league with Lister, I wouldn't have sought your help yesterday, would I?"

"You must have had a reason. I don't see it, though."

"I came to you in all sincerity. But now I know more about the situation. I tell you in all sincerity that if Lister had killed my sister I'd hunt him down to the ends of the earth. You don't know me."

"What about the plane tickets?"

"You've made a mistake. I bought no tickets, and if I had it's no concern of yours. Look here." He showed me the return half of a round-trip ticket between Los Angeles and Chicago. "You see, I'm flying home to Chicago tomorrow, by myself."

"Mission accomplished?"

"Deuce take you!" They were the strongest words I'd heard him use. He rose and came towards me. "Get out of my room now. I'm sick of the sight of you."

"I'm staying."

"I'll call the house detective."

"Hell, call the police."

He went to the room telephone and lifted the receiver. I stood and watched his bluff fade into nothing. He put the receiver down. I sat in the armchair he had vacated, and he went into the bathroom. I heard him in there retching. He had meant it literally when he said I made him sick.

The phone rang after a while, and I answered it. A woman's voice said: "Reggie? I'm calling from a drugstore. May we come to your room? Leonard thinks it would be safer."

"Naturally," I said in a higher voice than my own.

"Did you get the tickets?"

"Absolutely."

The bathroom door had opened. Harlan flung himself on my back. I hung up carefully before I turned on him. He fought with his nails and his teeth. I had to quiet him the hard way, with my left fist. I dragged him into the bathroom and shut the door on him.

Then I sat on the bed and looked at the telephone. Lister had a woman with him, and she knew Harlan. She knew Harlan well enough to call him Reggie, and Reggie had bought plane tickets for her and Lister. With a wrench that shook me down to my heels, the entire case turned over in my head and lodged at a crazy angle. Over its tilted edge, I saw Dolphine's moon-dead face, and the faceless face of the woman who had left him.

I found his name again in the directory. His telephone rang six times, and then his voice came dimly over the wires:

"Jack Dolphine speaking."

I said bluntly, to keep him from hanging up: "Mrs. Dolphine has left you, I understand."

"What's that? Who is this?"

"The private cop you talked to this morning, about the Lister case. It's turned into a murder case."

"Murder? How does Stella come into it?"

"That's the question, Mr. Dolphine. Is she there?"

There was a long silence, ending in a "No," that was almost as soft as silence.

"When did she leave?"

"I told you. Last night. Anyway she was gone when I got up this morning." Self-pity or some other emotion rose audibly in his throat. "This murder, you don't mean Stella?" The emotion choked him.

"Pull yourself together. Did your wife really leave with Lister?"

"Far as I know. Did he kill her? Is that what you're trying to tell me?"

"I'm not trying to tell you anything. I have a corpse on my hands. You should be able to identify it."

"You put the arm on Lister?" He sounded very eager.

"Not yet. I'm going to shortly."

"Don't let him go, whatever you do. He's a dangerous man. He killed her, I know he killed her."

He was choking up again. I said sharply:

"How do you know?"

"He threatened to. I heard them talking before he went east, a couple of weeks ago. They were quarreling back and forth in his studio, yelling at each other like wild animals. She wanted to marry him, divorce me and go off with him. He said he was going to marry another woman, a woman he really loved. She said she wouldn't let him. And he told her if she interfered, he'd strangle her with his hands."

"Will you swear to that?"

"I'll swear to it. It's the truth." His voice dropped. *"Did he strangle her?"*

"A woman's dead. I don't know who she is, until I get her identified. I'm in Santa Monica, at the Oceano Hotel. Can you come here now?"

"I guess so. I know where it is. Is *Stella* there?"

There was a flurry of footsteps in the hall.

"Maybe she soon will be. Make it as quick as you can, and come right up. I'm in room three-fourteen."

Somebody knocked on the hall door. I hung up, took my revolver out, and carried it to the door, which I swung wide. Lister was surprised to see me. His eyes bulged in their white rings. His right hand started a movement, which the woman beside him interrupted. She wrapped both arms around his arm, and hung her weight on him:

"Please, Leonard, no more violence. I couldn't bear any more violence."

But there had been violence, and she had borne it. Its marks were on her face. One of her eyes had been blackened, one cheek was ridged diagonally with deep scratches. Otherwise she was a handsome woman of thirty or so, tall and slender-hipped in a tailored suit. A new-looking hat sat smartly on her dark head. But her single usable eye was glaring in desperation:

"Are you a policeman?"

Lister's free hand covered her mouth. "Be quiet now. Don't say a word. I'll do the talking."

They stumbled into the room in a kind of lockstep. I shut the door with my heel. The woman sat on the bed. The marks on her face were vivid against her pallor. Lister stood in front of her.

"Where's Harlan?"

"I'll ask the questions. You'll answer them."

"Who do you think you are?"

He took a threatening step. I leveled my revolver at his stomach.

"The one with the gun. It's loaded. I'll use it if I have to."

The woman spoke behind him. "Listen to me, Leonard. It isn't any use. Violence only breeds further violence. Haven't you learned that yet?"

"Don't worry, there won't be any trouble. I know how to deal with these Hollywood dollar-chasers." He turned to me, a white sneer flashing in his beard. "It *is* money you're after, isn't it?"

"That's what Harlan thought. He paid me a thousand dollars to bury a dead woman and forget her. I'm turning his checks over to the police."

"I hear you telling me."

"You'll see me do it, Lister. I'm turning you over to them at the same time."

"Unless I pay you, eh? How much?"

The woman sighed. "Dearest. These shifts and strategems—can't you see how squalid, how squalid and miserable they are? We've tried your way and it's failed, wretchedly. It's time to try my way."

"We can't, Maude. And we haven't failed." He sat on the bed and put one arm around her narrow shoulders. "Just let me talk to him, I've dealt with his kind before. He's only a private detective. Your brother hired him yesterday."

"Where is my brother now?" she asked me. "Is he all right?"

"In there. He's a little battered."

I indicated the bathroom door with my gun. For some reason it was embarrassing to hold a naked weapon in front of her. I pushed it down into my waistband, leaving my jacket open in case I needed it quickly.

"You're Maude Harlan."

"I was. I am Mrs. Leonard Lister. This is my husband." She looked up into my face. I caught a glimpse of the thing between them. It flared like sudden lightning in blue darkness.

"The dead one is Stella Dolphine."

"Is that her first name? It's strange to have killed a woman without even knowing her name."

"No." The word was torn painfully from Lister's throat. "My wife doesn't know what she's saying, she's had a bad time."

"It's over now, Leonard. I'm afraid I'm not very adequate in the role of criminal." She gave him a bright smile, distorted by her wounds, and me the sad vestige of it. "Leonard wasn't there. He was taking a shower when the woman—when Mrs. Dolphine came to our door. I killed her."

"Why?"

"It was my fault," Lister said, "all of it, from the beginning. I had no right to marry Maude, to drag her down into the life I live. I was crazy to bring her back to that apartment."

"Why did you?"

His white-ringed eyes rolled around, straining for a look at himself. "I don't know, really. Stella thought she owned me. I had to prove that she didn't." His eyes steadied. "I'm a disastrous fool."

"Be still." Her fingers touched his hairy mouth. The back of her hand was scratched. "It was an ill fate. I scarcely know how it happened. It simply happened. She asked me who I was, and I told her I was Leonard's wife. She said that *she* was his wife in the eyes of heaven. She tried to force her way into the apartment. I asked her to leave. She told me that I was the one who ought to leave, that I should go home with my brother. When I refused, she attacked me. She pulled me by the hair onto the outside landing. I must have pushed her away somehow. She fell backwards down the steps, all the way to the bottom. I heard her skull strike the concrete." Her small hand went to her own mouth, as if to hold it still. "I think I fainted then."

"Yes," Lister said. "Maude was unconscious on the landing when I came out of the shower. I carried her inside. It took me some time to bring her to and find out what had happened. I put her to bed and went down to see to Stella. She was dead, at the foot of the steps. "Dead." His voice cracked.

"You were in love with her, Leonard," his wife said.

"Not after I met you."

"She was beautiful." There was a questioning sadness in her voice.

"She isn't any more," I said. "She's dead, and you've been carrying her body around the countryside. What sense was there in that?"

"No sense." Behind his hairy mask, Lister had the shame-faced look of a delinquent boy. "I panicked. Maude wanted to call the police right away. But I've had one or two little scrapes with them, in the past. And I knew what Dolphine would do if he found Stella dead at my door. He hates me." The naive blue eyes were bewildered by the beginnings of insight. "I don't blame him."

"What would he do?"

"Cry murder, and pin it on me."

"I don't see how. The way your wife described it, it's a clear case of manslaughter, probably justifiable."

"Is it? I wouldn't know. I felt so guilty about Stella, I wasn't thinking too well. I simply wanted to hide her and get Maude out of the country, away from the mess I'd made."

"That's what the five thousand was for?"

"Yes."

"You were going by way of Chicago?"

"The plan was changed. Maude's brother advised me to take her back to Chicago instead. After you tracked us down, I came here to him and made a clean breast of everything. He said leaving the country was an admission of guilt, in case the matter ever came to trial."

"It will."

"Does it really need to?" He leaned towards me, the bed squealing under his shifting weight. "If you have any human-ity, you'll let us go to Chicago. My wife is a gentlewoman. I don't know if that means anything to you."

"Does it to you?"

He dropped his eyes. "Yes. She can't go through a Los Angeles trial, with the dirt they'll dig up about me and throw in her face."

I said: "I have some humanity, not enough to go round. Right now Stella Dolphine is using most of it."

"You said yourself it was justifiable manslaughter."

"The way your wife tells it, it is."

"Don't you believe me?" She sounded astonished.

"As far as your story goes, I believe you. But you don't know all the facts. There are thumbprints on Stella Dolphine's throat. I've seen prints like them on the throats of other women who were strangled."

"No," she whispered. "I swear it. I only pushed her."

I looked at the delicate hands that were twisting in her lap. "You couldn't have made those marks. You pushed her down the stairs and knocked her out and set her up for somebody else. Somebody else found her unconscious and throttled her. Lister?"

His head sank like an exhausted bull's. He didn't look at his wife.

"Stella Dolphine made trouble for you, and she was in a position to make more trouble. You decided to put an end to it by finishing her off. Is that the way it happened?"

"The sinister habit," he said. "The sinister habit of asking questions, as Cocteau calls it. You've got a bad case of it, Archer."

"Liars bring it out in me."

"All right," he said to the floor. "If I admit it, and take the blame, will you let Maude go free, back to Chicago with her brother?"

She pressed her face against his bowed shoulder and said: "No. You didn't do it, Leonard. You're only trying to protect me."

"Did *you?*"

She shook her head slowly against his body. He turned and held her. I looked past them out the window to the darkening sea. They were fairly decent people, as people go, harried by the future and the past but holding together on the sharp ridge of the instant. And I was tormenting them. The case turned over behind my eyes again, a many-headed monster struggling to be born out of my mind.

Harlan opened the bathroom door and came out shakily. His nose was bleeding. He looked at me with hatred, at the lovers with desolation. Unnoticed by them, he stood like a wallflower against the doorframe.

"I should never have come here," he said bitterly.

I turned to them. "This has gone far enough."

They were blind and deaf, alone together on the sharp ridge, held flesh to flesh. A door creaked. I thought it was Harlan closing the bathroom door, and I looked in the wrong direction. Dolphine was in the room before I saw him. A heavy service revolver wavered in his hand. He advanced on Lister and his wife.

"You killed her, you devils."

Lister tried to get up from the bed. The woman held him. Her back was to the gun.

The gun spoke once, very loudly, its echoes rumbling like delayed thunder. Harlan had crossed to the center of the room, perhaps with some idea of defending his sister. He took the slug in the body. It stopped him like a wall. He fell. I fired across him.

Dolphine dropped his revolver. He spread his hands across his stomach and backed against the wall, where he sat down. He was wheezing. Water ran from his eyes and nose. His face worked, trying to realize his grief and failing. Blood began to run between his fingers. I stood over him.

"How do you know they killed her?"

"I saw them. I saw it all."

"You were in bed."

"No, I was in the garage. They threw her down the steps, and came down after and choked her. Lister did. I saw him."

"You didn't call the police."

"No. I—" His mouth groped for words. "I'm a sick man. I was too sick to call them. Upset. I couldn't talk."

"You're sicker now, but you're going to have to talk. It wasn't Lister, was it? It was you."

He choked, and began to cough blood. Great pumping sobs forced red words out of his mouth.

"She got what she deserved. I thought when I told her he'd married the other one, that she would come back to my bed. But she wouldn't look at me. All she could think about was getting him back. When I was the one that loved her."

"I can see that."

"I did. I loved her."

He lifted his red-laced hands in front of his eyes and began to scream. He rolled sideways with his face to the wall, screaming. He died that night.

Harlan was dead already. He should never have come there.

Wild Goose Chase

THE PLANE turned in towards the shoreline and began to lose altitude. Mountains detached themselves from the blue distance. Then there was a city between the sea and the mountains, a little city made of sugar cubes. The cubes increased in size. Cars crawled like colored beetles between the buildings, and matchstick figures hustled jerkily along the white morning pavements. A few minutes later I was one of them.

The woman who had telephoned me was waiting at the airport, as she had promised. She climbed out of her Cadillac when I appeared at the entrance to the waiting room, and took a few tentative steps towards me. In spite of her height and her blondeness, the dark harlequin glasses she wore gave her an oddly Oriental look.

"You must be Mr. Archer."

I said I was, and waited for her to complete the exchange of names—she hadn't given me her name on the telephone. All she had given me, in fact, was an urgent request to catch the first plane north, and assurances that I would be paid for my time.

She sensed what I was waiting for. "I'm sorry to be so mysterious. I really can't afford to tell you my name. I'm taking quite a risk in coming here at all."

I looked her over carefully, trying to decide whether this was another wild goose chase. Although she was well-groomed in a sharkskin suit, her hair and face were slightly disarranged, as if a storm had struck her a glancing blow. She took off her glasses to wipe them. I could see that the storm was inside of her, roiling the blue-green color of her eyes.

"What's the problem?" I said.

She stood wavering between me and her car, beaten by surges of sound from the airfield where my plane was about to take off again. Behind her, in the Cadillac's front seat, a little girl with the coloring of a Dresden doll was sitting as still as one. The woman glanced at the child and moved farther away from the car:

"I don't want Janie to hear. She's only three and a half but she understands a great deal." She took a deep gasping breath,

174

like a swimmer about to dive. "There's a man on trial for murder here. They claim he murdered his wife."

"Glenway Cave?"

Her whole body moved with surprise. "You know him?"

"No, I've been following the trial in the papers."

"Then you know he's testifying today. He's probably on the witness stand right now." Her voice was somber, as if she could see the courtroom in her mind's eye.

"Is Mr. Cave a friend of yours?"

She bit her lip. "Let's say that I'm an interested observer."

"And you don't believe he's guilty."

"Did I say that?"

"By implication. You said they *claim* he murdered his wife."

"You have an alert ear, haven't you? Anyway, what I believe doesn't matter. It's what the jury believes. Do you think they'll acquit him?"

"It's hard to form an opinion without attending the trial. But the average jury has a prejudice against the idea of blowing off your wife's head with a twelve-gauge shotgun. I'd say he stands a good chance of going to the gas chamber."

"The gas chamber." Her nostrils dilated, and she paled, as if she had caught a whiff of the fatal stuff. "Do you seriously think there's any danger of that?"

"They've built a powerful case against him. Motive. Opportunity. Weapon."

"What motive?"

"His wife was wealthy, wasn't she? I understand Cave isn't. They were alone in the house; the housekeeping couple were away for the weekend. The shotgun belonged to Cave, and according to the chemical test his driving gloves were used to fire it."

"You *have* been following the trial."

"As well as I could from Los Angeles. Of course you get distortions in the newspapers. It makes a better story if he looks guilty."

"He isn't guilty," she said in a quiet voice.

"Do you know that, or merely hope it?"

She pressed one hand across her mouth. The fingernails were bitten down to the quick. "We won't go into that."

"Do you know who murdered Ruth Cave?"

"No. Of course not."

"Am I supposed to try and find out who did?"

"Wouldn't that be very difficult, since it happened so long ago? Anyway, it doesn't really matter to me. I barely knew the woman." Her thoughts veered back to Cave. "Won't a great deal depend on the impression he makes on the witness stand?"

"It usually does in a murder trial."

"You've seen a lot of them, haven't you?"

"Too many. I take it I'm going to see another."

"Yes." She spoke sharply and definitely, leaning forward. "I don't dare go myself. I want you to observe the jurors, see how Glen—how Mr. Cave's testimony affects them. And tell me if you think he's going to get off."

"What if I can't tell?"

"You'll have to give me a yes or no." Her breast nudged my arm. She was too intent on what she was saying to notice. "I've made up my mind to go by your decision."

"Go where?" I said.

"To hell if necessary—if his life is really in danger."

"I'll do my best. Where shall I get in touch with you?"

"I'll get in touch with you. I've made a reservaiton for you at the Rubio Inn. Right now I'll drop you at the courthouse. Oh, yes—the money." She opened her leather handbag, and I caught the gleam of a blue revolver at the bottom of the bag. "How much?"

"A hundred dollars will do."

A few bills changed hands, and we went to the car. She indicated the right rear door. I went around to the left so that I could read the white slip on the steering column. But the leatherette holder was empty.

The little girl stood up in the front seat and leaned over the back of it to look at me. "Hello. Are you my daddy?" Her eyes were as blue and candid as the sky.

Before I could answer, her mother said: "Now Janie, you know he isn't your daddy. This is Mr. Archer."

"Where is my daddy?"

"In Pasadena, darling. You know that. Sit down, Janie, and be still."

The little girl slid down out of my sight. The engine roared in anger.

It was ten minutes past eleven by the clock on the courthouse tower. Superior Court was on the second floor. I slid into one of the vacant seats in the back row of the spectators' section. Several old ladies turned to glare at me, as though I had interrupted a church service.

The trial was more like an ancient tribal ceremony in a grotto. Red draperies were drawn over the lofty windows. The air was dim with human exhalations. Black iron fixtures suspended from the ceiling shed a wan light on the judge's gray head, and on the man on the witness stand.

I recognized Glenway Cave from his newspaper pictures. He was a big handsome man in his early thirties who had once been bigger and handsomer. Four months in jail waiting for trial had pared him down to the bone. His eyes were pressed deep into hollow sockets. His double-breasted gabardine suit hung loosely on his shoulders. He looked like a suitable victim for the ceremony.

A broad-backed man with a straw-colored crewcut was bent over the stenograph, talking in an inaudible voice to the court reporter. Harvey, chief attorney for the defense. I had met Rod Harvey several times in the course of my work, which was one reason why I had followed the trial so closely.

The judge chopped the air with his hatchet face: "Proceed with your examination, Mr. Harvey."

Harvey raised his clipped blond head and addressed the witness: "Mr. Cave, we were attempting to establish the reason behind your—ah—misunderstanding with your wife. Did you and Mrs. Cave have words on the evening of May nineteenth?"

"We did. I've already told you that." Cave's voice was shallow, with high-pitched overtones.

"What was the nature of the conversation?"

"It was more of an argument than a conversation."

"But a purely verbal argument?" Harvey sounded as if his own witness had taken him by surprise.

A sharp-faced man spoke up from the prosecution end of the attorneys' table. "Objection. The question is leading—not to say *mis*leading."

"Sustained. The question will be stricken."

Harvey shrugged his heavy tweed shoulders. "Tell us just what was said then, Mr. Cave. Beginning at the beginning."

Cave moved uncomfortably, passing the palm of one hand over his eyes. "I can't recall it *verbatim*. It was quite an emotional scene—"

Harvey cut him off. "Tell us in your own words what you and Mrs. Cave were talking about."

"The future," Cave said. "Our future. Ruth was planning to leave me for another man."

An insect-buzzing rose from the spectators. I looked along the row where I was sitting. A couple of seats to my right, a young woman with artificial violets at her waist was leaning forward, her bright dark eyes intent on Cave's face. She seemed out of place among the frowsy old furies who surrounded her. Her head was striking, small and boyishly chic, its fine bony structure emphasized by a short haircut. She turned, and her brown eyes met mine. They were tragic and opaque.

The D.A.'s voice rose above the buzzing. "I object to this testimony. The witness is deliberately blackening the dead woman's reputation, without corroborative evidence of any kind, in a cowardly attempt to save his own neck."

He glanced sideways at the jury. Their faces were stony. Cave's was as white as marble. Harvey's was mottled red. He said, "This is an essential part of the case for the defense. A great deal has been made of Mr. Cave's sudden departure from home on the day of his wife's death. I am establishing the reason for it."

"We know the reason," the D.A. said in a carrying undertone.

Harvey looked up mutely at the judge, whose frown fitted the lines in his face like an old glove.

"Objection overruled. The prosecution will refrain from making unworthy comments. In any case, the jury will disregard them."

But the D.A. looked pleased with himself. He had made his point, and the jury would remember. Their twenty-four eyes, half of them female, and predominantly old, were fixed on Cave in uniform disapproval.

Harvey spoke in a voice thickened by emotion. "Did your wife say who the man was that she planned to leave you for?"

"No. She didn't."

"Do you know who it was?"

"No. The whole thing was a bolt from the blue to me. I don't believe Ruth intended to tell me what she had on her mind. It just slipped out, after we started fighting." He caught himself up short. "Verbally fighting, I mean."

"What started this verbal argument?"

"Nothing important. Money trouble. I wanted to buy a Ferrari, and Ruth couldn't see any sense in it."

"A Ferarri motor car?"

"A racing car, yes. I asked her for the money. She said that she was tired of giving me money. I said that I was equally tired of taking it from her. Then it came out that she was going to leave me for somebody else." One side of Cave's mouth lifted in a sardonic smile. "Somebody who would love her for herself."

"When did she plan to leave you?"

"As soon as she could get ready to go to Nevada. I told her to go ahead, that she was free to go whenever and wherever she wanted to go, with anybody that suited her."

"And what did you do then?"

"I packed a few clothes and drove away in my car."

"What time did you leave the house?"

"I don't know exactly."

"Was it dark when you went?"

"It was getting dark, but I didn't have to use my headlights right away. It couldn't have been later than eight o'clock."

"And Mrs. Cave was alive and well when you left?"

"Certainly she was."

"Was your parting friendly?"

"Friendly enough. She said good-bye and offered me some money. Which I didn't take, incidentally. I didn't take much of anything, except for bare esentials. I even left most of my clothes behind."

"Why did you do that?"

"Because she bought them for me. They belonged to her. I thought perhaps her new man might have a use for them."

"I see."

Harvey's voice was hoarse and unsteady. He turned away from Cave, and I could see that his face was flushed, either with anger or impatience. He said without looking at the prisoner, "Did the things you left behind include a gun?"

"Yes. A twelve-gauge double-barreled shotgun. I used it for shooting rabbits, mostly, in the hills behind the house."

"Was it loaded?"

"I believe so. I usually kept it loaded."

"Where did you leave your shotgun?"

"In the garage. I kept it there. Ruth didn't like to have a gun in the house. She had a phobia—"

Harvey cut in quickly. "Did you also leave a pair of driving gloves, the gloves on the table here marked by the prosecution as Exhibit J?"

"I did. They were in the garage, too."

"And the garage door—was it open or closed?"

"I left it open, I think. In any case, we never kept it locked."

"Mr. Cave," Harvey said in a deep voice, "did you kill your wife with the shotgun before you drove away?"

"I did not." In contrast with Harvey's, Cave's voice was high and thin and unconvincing.

"After you left around eight o'clock, did you return to the house again that night?"

"I did not. I haven't been back since, as a matter of fact, I was arrested in Los Angeles the following day."

"Where did you spend the night—that is, after eight o'clock?"

"With a friend."

The courtroom began to buzz again.

"What friend?" Harvey barked. He suddenly sounded like a prosecutor cross-examining a hostile witness.

Cave moved his mouth to speak, and hesitated. He licked his dry lips. "I prefer not to say."

"Why do you prefer not to say?"

"Because it was a woman. I don't want to involve her in this mess."

Harvey swung away from the witness abruptly and looked up at the judge. The judge admonished the jury not to discuss the case with anyone, and adjourned the trial until two o'clock.

I watched the jurors file out. Not one of them looked at Glenway Cave. They had seen enough of him.

Harvey was the last man to leave the well of the courtroom. I waited for him at the little swinging gate which divided it from the spectators' section. He finished packing his brief-case and came towards me, carrying the case as if it was weighted.

"Mr. Harvey, can you give me a minute?"

He started to brush me off with a weary gesture, then recognized my face. "Lew Archer? What brings you here?"

"It's what I want to talk to you about."

"This case?"

I nodded. "Are you going to get him off?"

"Naturally I am. He's innocent." But his voice echoed hollowly in the empty room and he regarded me doubtfully. "You wouldn't be snooping around for the prosecution?"

"Not this time. The person who hired me believes that Cave is innocent. Just as you do."

"A woman?"

"You're jumping to conclusions, aren't you?"

"When the sex isn't indicated, it's usually a woman. Who is she, Archer?"

"I wish I knew."

"Come on now." His square pink hand rested on my arm. "You don't accept anonymous clients any more than I do."

"This one is an exception. All I know about her is that she's anxious to see Cave get off."

"So are we all." His bland smile tightened. "Look, we can't talk here. Walk over to the office with me. I'll have a couple of sandwiches sent up."

He shifted his hand to my elbow and propelled me towards the door. The dark-eyed woman with the artificial violets at her waist was waiting in the corridor. Her opaque gaze passed over me and rested possessively on Harvey.

"Surprise." Her voice was low and throaty to match her boyish look. "You're taking me to lunch."

"I'm pretty busy, Rhea. And I thought you were going to stay home today."

"I tried to. Honestly. But my mind kept wandering off to the courthouse, so I finally up and followed it." She moved towards him with a queer awkwardness, as if she was embarrassingly conscious of her body, and his. "Aren't you glad to see me, darling?"

"Of course I'm glad to see you," he said, his tone denying the words.

"Then take me to lunch." Her white-gloved hand stroked his lapel. "I made a reservation at the club. It will do you good to get out in the air."

"I told you I'm busy, Rhea. Mr. Archer and I have something to discuss."

"Bring Mr. Archer along. I won't get in the way. I promise." She turned to me with a flashing white smile. "Since my husband seems to have forgotten his manners, I'm Rhea Harvey."

She offered me her hand, and Harvey told her who I was. Shrugging his shoulders resignedly, he led the way outside to his bronze convertible. We turned towards the sea, which glimmered at the foot of the town like a fallen piece of sky.

"How do you think it's going, Rod?" she said.

"I suppose it could have been worse. He could have got up in front of the judge and jury and confessed."

"Did it strike you as that bad?"

"I'm afraid it was pretty bad." Harvey leaned forward over the wheel in order to look around his wife at me. "Were you in on the debacle, Archer?"

"Part of it. He's either very honest or very stupid."

Harvey snorted. "Glen's not stupid. The trouble is, he simply doesn't care. He pays no attention to my advice. I had to stand there and ask the questions, and I didn't know what crazy answers he was going to come up with. He seems to take a masochistic pleasure in wrecking his own chances."

"It could be his conscience working on him," I said.

His steely blue glance raked my face and returned to the road. "It could be, but it isn't. And I'm not speaking simply as his attorney. I've known Glen Cave for a long time. We were roommates in college. Hell, I introduced him to his wife."

"That doesn't make him incapable of murder."

"Sure, any man is capable of murder. That's not my point. My point is that Glen is a sharp customer. If he had decided to kill Ruth for her money, he wouldn't do it that way. He wouldn't use his own gun. In fact, I doubt very much that he'd use a gun at all. Glen isn't that obvious."

"Unless it was a passional crime. Jealousy can make a man lose his sophistication."

"Not Glen. He wasn't in love with Ruth—never has been. He's got about as much sexual passion as a flea." His voice was edged with contempt. "Anyway, this tale of his about another man is probably malarkey."

"Are you sure, Rod?"

He turned on his wife almost savagely. "No, I'm not sure. I'm not sure about anything. Glen isn't confiding in me, and

I don't see how I can defend him if he goes on this way. I wish to God he hadn't forced me into this. He knows as well as I do that trial work isn't my forte. I advised him to get an attorney experienced in this sort of thing, and he wouldn't listen. He said if I wouldn't take on his case that he'd defend himself. And he flunked out of law school in his second year. What could I do?"

He stamped the accelerator, cutting in and out of the noon traffic on the ocean boulevard. Palm trees fled by like thin old wild-haired madmen racing along the edge of the quicksilver sea.

The beach club stood at the end of the boulevard, a white U-shaped building whose glass doors opened "For Members and Guests Only." Its inner court contained a swimming pool and an alfresco dining space dotted with umbrella tables. Breeze-swept and sluiced with sunlight, it was the antithesis of the dim courtroom where Cave's fate would be decided. But the shadow of the courtroom fell across our luncheon and leeched the color and flavor from the food.

Harvey pushed away his salmon salad, which he had barely disturbed, and gulped a second Martini. He called the waiter to order a third. His wife inhibited him with a barely perceptible shake of her head. The waiter slid away.

"This woman," I said, "the woman he spent the night with. Who is she?"

"Glen told me hardly anything more than he told the court." Harvey paused, half gagged by a lawyer's instinctive reluctance to give away information, then forced himself to go on. "It seems he went straight from home to her house on the night of the shooting. He spent the night with her, from about eight-thirty until the following morning. Or so he claims."

"Haven't you checked his story?"

"How? He refused to say anything that might enable me to find her or identify her. It's just another example of the obstacles he's put in my way, trying to defend him."

"Is this woman so important to his defense?"

"Crucial. Ruth was shot sometime around midnight. The p.m. established that through the stomach contents. And at that time, if he's telling the truth, Glen was with a witness. Yet he won't let me try to locate her, or have her subpoenaed. It took me hours of hammering at him to get him to testify about her at all, and I'm not sure that wasn't a mistake. That miserable jury—" His voice trailed off. He was back in court fighting his uphill battle against the prejudices of a small elderly city.

And I was back on the pavement in front of the airport, listening to a woman's urgent whisper: *You'll have to give me a yes or no. I've made up my mind to go by your decision.*

Harvey was looking away across the captive water, fish-netted under elastic strands of light. Under the clear September sun I could see the spikes of gray in his hair, the deep small scars of strain around his mouth.

"If I could only lay my hands on the woman." He seemed to be speaking to himself, until he looked at me from the corners of his eyes. "Who do *you* suppose she is?"

"How would I know?"

He leaned across the table confidentially. "Why be so cagey, Archer? I've let down my hair."

"This particular hair doesn't belong to me."

I regretted the words before I had finished speaking them. Harvey said, "When will you see her?"

"You're jumping to conclusions again."

"If I'm wrong, I'm sorry. If I'm right, give her a message for me. Tell her that Glen—I hate to have to say this, but he's in jeopardy. If she likes him well enough to—"

"Please, Rod." Rhea Harvey seemed genuinely offended. "There's no need to be coarse."

I said, "I'd like to talk to Cave before I do anything. I don't know that it's the same woman. Even if it is, he may have reasons of his own for keeping her under wraps."

"You can probably have a few minutes with him in the courtroom." He looked at his wristwatch and pushed his chair back violently. "We better get going. It's twenty to two now."

We went along the side of the pool, back toward the entrance. As we entered the vestibule, a woman was just coming in from the boulevard. She held the heavy plate-glass door for the little flaxen-haired girl who was trailing after her.

Then she glanced up and saw me. Her dark harlequin glasses flashed in the light reflected from the pool. Her face became disorganized behind the glasses. She turned on her heel and started out, but not before the child had smiled at me and said: "Hello. Are you coming for a ride?" Then she trotted out after her mother.

Harvey looked quizzically at his wife. "What's the matter with the Kilpatrick woman?"

"She must be drunk. She didn't even recognize us."

"You know her, Mrs. Harvey?"

"As well as I care to." Her eyes took on a set, glazed expression—the look of congealed virtue faced with its opposite. "I haven't seen Janet Kilpatrick for months. She hasn't been showing herself in public much since her divorce."

Harvey edged closer and gripped my arm. "Would Mrs. Kilpatrick be the woman we were talking about?"

"Hardly."

"They seemed to know you."

I improvised. "I met them on the Daylight one day last month, coming down from Frisco. She got plastered, and I guess she didn't want to recall the occasion."

That seemed to satisfy him. But when I excused myself, on the grounds that I thought I'd stay for a swim in the pool, his blue ironic glance informed me that he wasn't taken in.

The receptionist had inch-long scarlet fingernails and an air of contemptuous formality. Yes, Mrs. Kilpatrick was a member of the club. No, she wasn't allowed to give out members' addresses. She admitted grudgingly that there was a pay telephone in the bar.

The barroom was deserted except for the bartender, a slim white-coated man with emotional Mediterranean eyes. I found Mrs. Janet Kilpatrick in the telephone directory: her address was 1201 Coast Highway. I called a taxi, and ordered a beer from the bartender.

He was more communicative than the receptionist. Sure, he knew Glenway Cave. Every bartender in town knew Glenway Cave. The guy was sitting at this very bar the afternoon of the same day he murdered his wife.

"You think he murdered her?"

"Everybody else thinks so. They don't spend all that money on a trial unless they got the goods on them. Anyway, look at the motive he had."

"You mean the man she was running around with?"

"I mean two million bucks." He had a delayed reaction. "What man is that?"

"Cave said in court this morning that his wife was going to divorce him and marry somebody else."

"He did, eh? You a newspaperman by any chance?"

"A kind of one." I subscribed to several newspapers.

"Well, you can tell the world that that's a lot of baloney. I've seen quite a bit of Mrs. Cave around the club. She had her own little circle, see, and you can take it from me she never even looked at other guys. *He* was always the one with the roving eye. What can you expect, when a young fellow marries a lady that much older than him?" His faint accent lent flavor to the question. "The very day of the murder he was making a fast play for another dame, right here in front of me."

"Who was she?"

"I wouldn't want to name names. She was pretty far gone that afternoon, hardly knew what she was doing. And the poor lady's got enough trouble as it is. Take it from me."

I didn't press him. A minute later a horn tooted in the street.

A few miles south of the city limits a blacktop lane led down from the highway to Mrs. Kilpatrick's house. It was a big old-fashioned redwood cottage set among trees and flowers above a bone-white beach. The Cadillac was parked beside the vine-grown verandah, like something in a four-color advertisement. I asked my driver to wait, and knocked on the front door.

A small rectangular window was set into the door. It slid open, and a green eye gleamed like a flawed emerald through the aperture.

"You," she said in a low voice. "You shouldn't have come here."

"I have some questions for you, Mrs. Kilpatrick. And maybe a couple of answers. May I come in?"

She sighed audibly. "If you must." She unlocked the door and stood back to let me enter. "You will be quiet, won't you? I've just put Janie to bed for her afternoon nap."

There was a white silk scarf draped over her right hand, and under the silk a shape which contrasted oddly with her motherly concern—the shape of a small hand gun.

"You'd better put that thing away. You don't need it, do you?"

Her hand moved jerkily. The scarf fell from the gun and drifted to the floor. It was a small blue revolver. She looked at it as if it had somehow forced its way into her fist, and put it down on the telephone table.

"I'm sorry. I didn't know who was at the door. I've been so worried and frightened—"

"Who did you think it was?"

"Frank, perhaps, or one of his men. He's been trying to take Janie away from me. He claims I'm not a fit mother. And maybe I'm not," she added in the neutral tones of despair. "But Frank is worse."

"Frank is your husband?"

"My ex-husband. I got a divorce last year and the court gave me custody of Janie. Frank has been fighting the custody order ever since. Janie's grandmother left her a trust fund, you see. That's all Frank cares about. But I'm her mother."

"I think I see what it's all about," I said. "Correct me if I'm wrong. Cave spent the night with you—the night he was supposed to have shot his wife. But you don't want to testify at his trial. It would give your ex-husband legal ammunition to use in the custody fight for Janie."

"You're not wrong." She lowered her eyes, not so much in shame as in submission to the facts. "We got talking in the bar at the club that afternoon. I hardly knew him, but I—well, I was attracted to him. He asked if he could come and see me that night. I was feeling lonely, very low and lonely. I'd had a good deal to drink. I let him come."

"What time did he arrive?"

"Shortly after eight."

"And he stayed all night?"

"Yes. He couldn't have killed Ruth Cave. He was with me. You can understand why I've been quietly going crazy since they arrested him— sitting at home and biting on my nails and wondering what under heaven I should do." Her eyes came up like green searchlights under her fair brow. "What *shall* I do, Mr. Archer?"

"Sit tight for a while yet. The trial will last a few more days. And he may be acquitted."

"But you don't think he will be, do you?"

"It's hard to say. He didn't do too well on the stand this morning. On the other hand, the averages are with him, as he seems to realize. Very few innocent men are convicted of murder."

"He didn't mention me on the stand?"

"He said he was with a woman, no names mentioned. Are you two in love with each other, Mrs. Kilpatrick?"

"No, nothing like that. I was simply feeling sorry for myself that night. I needed some attention from a man. He was a pieces of flotsam and I was a piece of jetsam and we were washed together in the dark. He did get rather—en.otional at one point, and said that he would like to marry me. I reminded him that he had a wife."

"What did he say to that?"

"He said his wife wouldn't live forever. But I didn't take him seriously. I haven't even seen him since that night. No, I'm not in love with him. If I let him die, though, for something I know he didn't do—I couldn't go on living with myself." She added, with a bitter grimace, "It's hard enough as it is."

"But you do want to go on living."

"Not particularly. I have to because Janie needs me."

"Then stay at home and keep your doors locked. It wasn't smart to go to the club today."

"I know. I needed a drink badly. I'm out of liquor, and it was the nearest place. Then I saw you and I panicked."

"Stay panicked. Remember if Cave didn't commit that murder, somebody else did—and framed him for it. Somebody who is still at large. What do you drink, by the way?"

"Anything. Scotch, mostly."

"Can you hold out for a couple of hours?"

"If I have to." She smiled, and her smile was charming. "You're very thoughtful."

When I got back to the courtroom, the trial was temporarily stalled. The jury had been sent out, and Harvey and the D.A. were arguing in front of the judge's bench. Cave was sitting by himself at the far end of the long attorneys' table. A sheriff's deputy with a gun on his thigh stood a few feet behind him, between the red-draped windows.

Assuming a self-important legal look, I marched through the swinging gate into the well of the courtroom and took the empty chair beside Cave. He looked up from the typed transcript he was reading. In spite of his prison pallor he was a good-looking man. He had a boyish look about him and the kind of curly brown hair that women are supposed to love to run their fingers through. But his mouth was tight, his eyes dark and piercing.

Before I could introduce myself, he said, "You the detective Rod told me about?"

"Yes. Name is Archer."

"You're wasting your time, Mr. Archer, there's nothing you can do for me." His voice was a dull monotone, as if the cross-examination had rolled over his emotions and left them flat.

"It can't be that bad, Cave."

"I didn't say it was bad. I'm doing perfectly well, and I know what I'm doing."

I held my tongue. It wouldn't do to tell him that his own lawyer had lost confidence in his case. Harvey's voice rose sharp and strained above the courtroom mutter, maintaining that certain questions were irrelevant and immaterial.

Cave leaned towards me and his voice sank lower. "You've been in touch with her?"

"She brought me into the case."

"That was a rash thing for her to do, under the circumstances. Or don't you know the circumstances?"

"I understand that if she testifies she risks losing her child."

"Exactly. Why do you think I haven't had her called? Go back and tell her that I'm grateful for her concern but I don't need her help. They can't convict an innocent man. I didn't shoot my wife, and I don't need an alibi to prove it."

I looked at him, admiring his composure. The armpits of his gabardine suit were dark with sweat. A fine tremor was running through him.

"Do you know who did shoot her, Cave?"

"I have an opinion. We won't go into it."

"Her new man?"

"We won't go into it," he repeated, and buried his aquiline nose in the transcript.

The judge ordered the bailiff to bring in the jury. Harvey sat down beside me, looking disgruntled, and Cave returned to the witness stand.

What followed was moral slaughter. The D.A. forced Cave

to admit that he hadn't had gainful employment since his release from the army, that his sole occupations were amateur tennis and amateur acting, and that he had no means of his own. He had been completely dependent on his wife's money since their marriage in 1946, and had used some of it to take extended trips in the company of other women.

The prosecutor turned his back on Cave in histrionic disgust. "And you're the man who dares to impugn the morals of your dead wife, the woman who gave you everything."

Harvey objected. The judge instructed the D.A. to rephrase his "question."

The D.A. nodded, and turned on Cave. "Did you say this morning that there was another man in Mrs. Cave's life?"

"I said it. It was true."

"Do you have anything to confirm that story?"

"No."

"Who is this unknown vague figure of a man?"

"I don't know. All I know is what Ruth told me."

"She isn't here to deny it, is she? Tell us frankly now, Mr. Cave, didn't you invent this man? Didn't you make him up?"

Cave's forehead was shining with sweat. He took a handkerchief out of his breast pocket and wiped his forehead, then his mouth. Above the white fabric masking his lower face, he looked past the D.A. and across the well of the courtroom. There was silence for a long moment.

Then Cave said mildly, "No, I didn't invent him."

"Does this man exist outside your fertile brain?"

"He does."

"Where? In what guise? Who is he?"

"I don't know," Cave said on a rising note. "If you want to know, why don't you try and find him? You have plenty of detectives at your disposal."

"Detectives can't find a man who doesn't exist. Or a woman either, Mr. Cave."

The D.A. caught the angry eye of the judge, who adjourned the trial until the following morning. I bought a fifth of scotch at a downtown liquor store, caught a taxi at the railroad station, and rode south out of town to Mrs. Kilpatrick's house.

When I knocked on the door of the redwood cottage, someone fumbled the inside knob. I pushed the door open. The flaxen-haired child looked up at me, her face streaked with half-dried tears.

"Mummy won't wake up."

I saw the red smudge on her knee, and ran in past her. Janet Kilpatrick was prone on the floor of the hallway, her bright hair dragging in a pool of blood. I lifted her head and saw the hole in her temple. It had stopped bleeding.

Her little blue revolver lay on the floor near her lax hand. One shot had been fired from the cylinder.

The child touched my back. "Is Mummy sick?"

"Yes, Janie. She's sick."

"Get the doctor," she said with pathetic wisdom. "Wasn't he here?"

"I don't know. I was taking my nap."

"Was anybody here, Janie?"

"Somebody was here. Mummy was talking to somebody. Then there was a big bang and I came downstairs and Mummy wouldn't wake up."

"Was it a man?"

She shook her head.

"A woman, Janie?"

The same mute shake of her head. I took her by the hand and led her outside to the cab. The dazzling postcard scene outside made death seem unreal. I asked the driver to tell the child a story, any story so long as it was cheerful. Then I went back into the grim hallway and used the telephone.

I called the sheriff's office first. My second call was to Frank Kilpatrick in Pasadena. A manservant summoned him to the telephone. I told him who I was and where I was and who was lying dead on the floor behind me.

"How dreadful!" He had an Ivy League accent, somewhat withered by the coastal sun. "Do you suppose that Janet took her own life? She's often threatened to."

"No," I said, "I don't suppose she took her own life. Your wife was murdered."

"What a tragic thing!"

"Why take it so hard, Kilpatrick? You've got the two things you wanted—your daughter, and you're rid of your wife."

It was a cruel thing to say, but I was feeling cruel. I made my third call in person, after the sheriff's men had finished with me.

The sun had fallen into the sea by then. The western side of the sky was scrawled with a childish finger-painting of colored cirrus clouds. Twilight flowed like iron-stained water between the downtown buildings. There were lights on the second floor of the California-Spanish building where Harvey had his offices.

Harvey answered my knock. He was in shirtsleeves and his tie was awry. He had a sheaf of papers in his hand. His breath was sour in my nostrils.

"What is it, Archer?"

"You tell me, lover-boy."

"And what is that supposed to mean?"

"You were the one Ruth Cave wanted to marry. You were going to divorce your respective mates and build a new life together—with her money."

He stepped backward into the office, a big disordered man who looked queerly out of place among the white-leather and black-iron furniture, against the limed-oak paneling. I followed him in. An automatic door closer shushed behind me.

"What in hell is this? Ruth and I were good friends and I handled her business for her—that's all there was to it."

"Don't try to kid me, Harvey. I'm not your wife, and I'm not your judge . . . I went to see Janet Kilpatrick a couple of hours ago."

"Whatever she said, it's a lie."

"She didn't say a word, Harvey. I found her dead."

His eyes grew small and metallic, like nailheads in the putty of his face. "Dead? What happened to her?"

"She was shot with her own gun. By somebody she let into the house, somebody she wasn't afraid of."

"Why? It makes no sense."

"She was Cave's alibi, and she was on the verge of volunteering as a witness. You know that, Harvey—you were the only one who did know, outside of Cave and me."

"I didn't shoot her. I had no reason to. Why would I want to see my client convicted?"

"No, you didn't shoot her. You were in court at the time that she was shot—the world's best alibi."

"Then why are you harassing me?"

"I want the truth about you and Mrs. Cave."

Harvey looked down at the papers in his hand, as if they might suggest a line to take, an evasion, a way out. Suddenly his hands came together and crushed the papers into a misshapen ball.

"All right, I'll tell you. Ruth was in love with me. I was—fond of her. Neither of us was happily married. We were going to go away together and start over. After we got divorces, of course."

"Uh-huh. All very legal."

"You don't have to take that tone. A man has a right to his own life."

"Not when he's already committed his life."

"We won't discuss it. Haven't I suffered enough? How do you think I felt when Ruth was killed?"

"Pretty bad, I guess. There went two million dollars."

He looked at me between narrowed lids, in a fierce extremity of hatred. But all that came out of his mouth was a weak denial. "At any rate, you can see I didn't kill her. I didn't kill either of them."

"Who did?"

"I have no idea. If I did, I'd have had Glen out of jail long ago."

"Does Glen know?"

"Not to my knowledge."

"But he knew that you and his wife had plans?"

"I suppose he did—I've suspected it all along."

"Didn't it strike you as odd that he asked you to defend him, under the circumstances?"

"Odd, yes. It's been terrible for me, the most terrible ordeal."

Maybe that was Cave's intention, I thought, to punish Harvey for stealing his wife. I said, "Did anybody besides you know that Janet Kilpatrick was the woman? Did you discuss it with anybody?"

He looked at the thick pale carpeting between his feet. I could hear an electric clock somewhere in the silent offices, whirring like the thoughts in Harvey's head. Finally he said, "Of course not," in a voice that was like a crow cawing.

He walked with an old man's gait into his private office. I followed and saw him open a desk drawer. A heavy automatic appeared in his hand. But he didn't point it at me. He pushed it down inside the front of his trousers and put on his suit jacket.

"Give it to me, Harvey. Two dead women are enough."

"You know then?"

"You just told me. Give me that gun."

He gave it to me. His face was remarkably smooth and blank. He turned his face away from me and covered it with his hands. His entire body hiccuped with dry grief. He was like an overgrown child who had lived on fairy tales for a long time and now couldn't stomach reality.

The telephone on the desk chirred. Harvey pulled himself together and answered it.

"Sorry, I've been busy, preparing for re-direct . . . Yes, I'm finished now . . . Of course I'm all right. I'm coming home right away."

He hung up and said, "That was my wife."

She was waiting for him at the front door of his house. The posture of waiting became her narrow, sexless body, and I wondered how many years she had been waiting.

"You're so thoughtless, Rod," she chided him. "Why didn't you tell me you were bringing a guest for dinner?" She turned to me in awkward graciousness. "Not that you're not welcome, Mr. Archer."

Then our silence bore in on her. It pushed her back into the high white Colonial hallway. She took up another pose and lit a cigarette with a little golden lighter shaped like a lipstick. Her hands were steady, but I could see the sharp edges of fear behind the careful expression on her face.

"You both look so solemn. Is something wrong?"

"Everything is wrong, Rhea."

"Why, didn't the trial go well this afternoon?"

"The trial is going fine. Tomorrow I'm going to ask for a directed acquittal. What's more, I'm going to get it. I have new evidence."

"Isn't that grand?" she said in a bright and interested tone. "Where on earth did you dig up the new evidence?"

"In my own backyard. All these months I've been so preoccupied trying to cover up my own sordid little secret that it never occurred to me that you might have secrets, too."

"What do you mean?"

"You weren't at the trial this afternoon. Where were you? What were you doing?"

"Errands—I had some errands. I'm sorry, I didn't realize you—wanted me to be there."

Harvey moved towards her, a threat of violence in the set of his shoulders. She backed against a closed white door. I stepped between them and said harshly, "We know exactly where you were, Mrs. Harvey. You went to see Janet Kilpatrick. You talked your way into her house, picked up a gun from the table in the hall, and shot her with it. Didn't you?"

The flesh of her face was no more than a stretched membrane.

"I swear, I had no intention—All I intended to do was talk to her. But when I saw that she realized, that she *knew*—"

"Knew what, Mrs. Harvey?"

"That I was the one who killed Ruth. I must have given myself away, by what I said to her. She looked at me, and I saw that she knew. I saw it in her eyes."

"So you shot her?"

"Yes. I'm sorry." She didn't seem to be fearful or ashamed. The face she turned on her husband looked starved, and her mouth moved over her words as if they were giving her bitter nourishment. "But I'm not sorry for the other one, for Ruth. You shouldn't have done it to me, Rod. I warned you, remember? I warned you when I caught you with Anne that if you ever did it to me again—I would kill the woman. You should have taken me seriously."

"Yes," he said drearily. "I guess I should have."

"I warned Ruth, too, when I learned about the two of you."

"How did you find out about it, Mrs. Harvey?"

"The usual way—an anonymous telephone call. Some friend of mine, I suppose."

"Or your worst enemy. Do you know who it was?"

"No. I didn't recognize the voice. I was still in bed, and the telephone call woke me up. He said—it was a man—he said that Rod was going to divorce me, and he told me why. I went to Ruth that very morning—Rod was out of town—and I asked her if it was true. She admitted it was. I told her flatly I'd kill her unless she gave you up, Rod. She laughed at me. She called me a crazy woman."

"She was right."

"Was she? If I'm insane, I know what's driven me to it. I could bear the thought of the other ones. But not her! What made you take up with *her*, Rod—what made you want to marry that gray-haired old woman? She wasn't even attractive, she wasn't nearly as attractive as I am."

"She was well-heeled," I said.

Harvey said nothing.

Rhea Harvey dictated and signed a full confession that night. Her husband wasn't in court the following morning. The D.A. himself moved for a directed acquittal, and Cave was free by noon. He took a taxi directly from the courthouse to the home of his late wife. I followed him in a second taxi. I still wasn't satisfied.

The lawns around the big country house had grown knee-high and had withered in the summer sun. The gardens were overgrown with rank flowers and ranker weeds. Cave stood in the drive for a while after he dismissed his taxi, looking around the estate he had inherited. Finally he mounted the front steps.

I called him from the gate. "Wait a minute, Cave."

He descended the steps reluctantly and waited for me, a black scowl twisting his eyebrows and disfiguring his mouth. But they were smooth and straight before I reached him.

"What do you want?"

"I was just wondering how it feels."

He smiled with boyish charm. "To be a free man? It feels wonderful. I guess I owe you my gratitude, at that. As a matter of fact, I was planning to send you a check."

"Save yourself the trouble. I'd send it back."

"Whatever you say, old man." He spread his hands disarmingly. "Is there something else I can do for you?"

"Yes. You can satisfy my curiosity. All I want from you is a yes or no." The words set up an echo in my head, an echo of Janet Kilpatrick's voice. "Two women have died and a third is on her way to prison or the state hospital. I want to hear you admit your responsibility."

"Responsibility? I don't understand."

"I'll spell it out for you. The quarrel you had with your wife didn't occur on the nineteenth, the night she was murdered. It came earlier, maybe the night before. And she told you who the man was."

"She didn't have to tell me. I've known Rod Harvey for years, and all about him."

"Then you must have known that Rhea Harvey was insanely jealous of her husband. You thought of a way to put her jealousy to work for you. It was you who telephoned her that morning. You disguised your voice, and told her what her husband and your wife were planning to do. She came to this house and threatened your wife. No doubt you overheard the conversation. Seeing that your plan was working, you left your loaded shotgun where Rhea Harvey could easily find it and went down to the beach club to establish an alibi. You had a long wait at the club, and later at Janet Kilpatrick's house, but you finally got what you were waiting for."

"They also serve who only stand and wait."

"Does it seem so funny to you, Cave? You're guilty of conspiracy to commit murder."

"I'm not guilty of anything, old man. Even if I were, there's nothing you could possibly do about it. You heard the court acquit me this morning, and there's a little rule of law involving double jeopardy."

"You were taking quite a risk, weren't you?"

"Not so much of a risk. Rhea's a very unstable woman, and she had to break down eventually, one way or the other."

"Is that why you asked Harvey to defend you, to keep the pressure on Rhea?"

"That was part of it." A sudden fury of hatred went through him, transfiguring his face. "Mostly I wanted to see him suffer."

"What are you going to do now, Cave?"

"Nothing. I plan to take it easy. I've earned a rest. Why?"

"A pretty good woman was killed yesterday on account of you. For all I know you planned that killing the same way you planned the other. In any case, you could have prevented it."

He saw the mayhem in my eyes and backed away. "Take it easy, Archer. Janet was no great loss to the world, after all."

My fist smashed his nervous smile and drove the words down his throat. He crawled away from me, scrambled to his feet and ran, jumping over flowerbeds and disappearing around the corner of the house. I let him go.

A short time later I heard that Cave had been killed in a highway accident near Palm Springs. He was driving a new Ferrari at the time.

THE END